continued. . .

"An exciting new addition to the modern fabulist genre."
—Emily Temple, Flavorwire.com

"These stories are wrought with forceful clarity, Borgesian inventiveness, and enchanting, devious wit—an unforgettable debut from a uniquely gifted writer."
—Wells Tower, author of *Everything Ravaged, Everything Burned*

"These are beautiful, strange truths—mad, weird, funny, and unforgettable. Manuel Gonzales possesses a brand-new American literary voice. This is vital work from an exciting new writer."
—Ben Marcus, author of *The Flame Alphabet*

"This book has everything you could ask for in a collection, and even things you hadn't thought to ask for, but secretly wanted: unicorns, mobsters, swamp monsters, and werewolves. Manuel Gonzales weaves the supernatural into the lives of everyday citizens, from anthropologists to airline passengers, and the result is pure magic mixed with humor and deep humanity."
—Hannah Tinti, author of *The Good Thief*

"You know that feeling you get when you pick up a book and realize you are hearing a voice you have never heard before but will be hearing for a long time? I had that feeling on page five. Please pick up this book—you will have that feeling. Dark, smart, and strange in a way that initially had me grasping for comparison but that ultimately revealed itself to be something new."
—Charles Yu, author of *How to Live Safely in a Science Fictional Universe*

"Manuel Gonzales's [*The Miniature Wife*] is a marvel—a beautiful, hilarious, and moving reinvention of the gothic, a testimony to the sublime powers of the imagination and language. This a book of extraordinary joy, compassion, horror, and grace all rolled into one."
—Dinaw Mengestu, author of *How to Read the Air* and *The Beautiful Things That Heaven Bears*

The Miniature Wife
and Other Stories

MANUEL GONZALES

RIVERHEAD BOOKS
New York

RIVERHEAD BOOKS
Published by the Penguin Group
Penguin Group (USA) LLC
375 Hudson Street, New York, New York 10014, USA

USA • Canada • UK • Ireland • Australia • New Zealand • India • South Africa • China

penguin.com

A Penguin Random House Company

Acknowledgment is made to the publications in which these stories first appeared:
"Juan Refugio Rocha: A Meritorious Life" in *McSweeney's*; "Keith, Stebbins, Hoardwood
& Niles: An Illustrated History of Meritorious Lives" in *The American Journal of Print*;
"Cash to a Killing" on esquire.com; "The Disappearance of the Sebali Tribe" in *Open
City*; "Pilot, Co-Pilot, Writer" in *One Story Magazine* and anthologized in *Flight Patterns:
A Century of Stories About Flying* (edited by Dorothy Spears. New York: Open City Books,
2009); "The Artist's Voice: Hearing Is Believing" in *Fence* and anthologized in *A Best of
Fence: The First 9 Years*, Volume 2, Fiction & Nonfiction (edited by Rebecca Wolff.
Albany: Fence Books, 2009); "William Corbin: A Meritorious Life" in *The Lifted Brow*.

The Library of Congress has catalogued the Riverhead hardcover edition as follows:

Gonzales, Manuel, date.
The miniature wife and other stories / Manuel Gonzales.
p.   cm.
ISBN 978-1-59448-604-3
I. Title.
PS3607.O56227M56   2013   2012026167
813'.6—dc23

First Riverhead hardcover edition: January 2013
First Riverhead trade paperback edition: February 2014
Riverhead trade paperback ISBN: 978-1-59463-227-3

Cover design by Janet Hansen
Book design by Amanda Dewey

For Sharon

CONTENTS

Pilot, Copilot, Writer   1

The Miniature Wife   25

William Corbin: A Meritorious Life   47

The Sounds of Early Morning   53

The Artist's Voice   63

Henry Richard Niles: A Meritorious Life   93

Cash to a Killing   97

Harold Withy Keith: A Meritorious Life   103

The Animal House   109

All of Me   135

Life on Capra II   159

Juan Refugio Rocha: A Meritorious Life   181

The Disappearance of the Sebali Tribe   185

One-Horned & Wild-Eyed   213

"Wolf!"   241

Farewell, Africa   257

Juan Manuel Gonzales: A Meritorious Life   273

Escape from the Mall   277

"Things fall apart."

—W. B. YEATS

Pilot, Copilot, Writer

I.

We have been circling the city now at an altitude of between seven thousand and ten thousand feet for, according to our best estimates, around twenty years.

⚙

I once asked the Pilot—this was early into the hijacking, maybe a week—how we were doing in terms of gasoline and how he planned to refuel, but he did not tell me. He laughed and patted me on the shoulder as if we were good friends together on a road trip and I had just asked him how we were going to get there without a map. Back in the cabin, I asked a man who was an engineer if he knew how we had managed to stay aloft for so long, and he gave me a complex explanation, most of which I did not understand, centered around a rumored "perpetual oil."

"Is there such a thing?" I asked him. "Perpetual oil?"

"Well," he said. "I'm not sure that there isn't."

⊛

The Pilot called my name over the intercom a number of times before I realized it was me he was calling for. By the time I figured it out, the other passengers were leaning into the aisle and stretching over their seats to see who it was being summoned. I stood up and a low murmuring passed through the cabin. I suppose everyone assumed I was being called to be executed, since the hijacking had just happened a day or two before and we hadn't been told anything else by the hijacker since. There had been speculation about demands, about actions, about executions, but nobody knew, really, what was going to happen. I didn't blame the others for thinking that I had been called in to be the first casualty, as I had assumed the same. But why me instead of the man in front of me or the woman across the aisle or any-one else on board, one of the flight attendants maybe? A woman grabbed my arm as I walked toward the front of the plane and shook her head, entreating me with her eyes not to go, to sit back down, but I didn't want to make the Pilot mad, so I pulled myself free and made my way.

When I knocked on the Pilot's door, I heard his voice say in a singsong way, "Come in." He turned to look at me as I entered his cabin. "Sit, sit," he said, gesturing to the seat next to him, the copilot's seat.

I sat and he smiled and, without looking at me, said, "So you are the writer."

Unsure of what else to say, I said, "Yes. That's me."

"My name is Josiah," he said. "Josiah Jackson." He handed me a pad of paper and a pen. "Write that down," he said.

I wrote on the top of the sheet of paper *Josiah*. And then, for good measure, underneath that, I wrote *Josiah Jackson*. I tore the sheet off the pad and gave it to him for his inspection.

He laughed as if I had made a very good joke, and then he said, "You are no less than what I had expected you to be."

We sat next to each other in silence for a moment, then two moments, until finally he said, "Okay. You can go now."

Feeling a certain amount of relief knowing that I wasn't to be executed and feeling confident in having made him, for whatever reason, laugh, I asked him why he had hijacked the plane and why we were still circling Dallas. At this he gave me a stern and serious look. "I do not usually answer questions, but since it is you: We are circling because I only know how to fly to the left." He looked at me and then laughed again, and said, "No, no. I'm only kidding." Then he turned back to look at the sky, which was now growing dark, and said no more.

◈

The plane was full. The overhead compartments were full, too. The woman next to me had somehow managed to board the plane with more carry-on items than are normally allowed, but as she and I had been the last passengers to board, she was forced to cram as much as possible under the seat, and then, noticing that I had not carried much with me onto the plane, she asked if she could place just one or two items under the seat in front of me.

"Just this small bag and this other small bag," she said. "You can just kick them out of the way, if you want. They're nothing but dirty clothes."

I told her I didn't mind, but in fact I minded a little, and after we had taken off and the seat-belt light was turned off and she left for the restroom, I did kick one of the bags, but it wasn't filled with clothes and I heard, or felt, something break. I was waiting, after she came back to her seat, for the right time to tell her that I had accidentally broken whatever it was that had been in her bag, but then the hijack happened and nobody thought about anything like their bags or their connecting flights for a long time, and then, as she was an older woman who became even older as the years passed by, she eventually forgot about almost everything else and passed away in her sleep before I was ever able to apologize.

◈

For a while, we all fought over the window seats because no one believed me when I said that we weren't going anywhere, that we were merely circling and circling over the same city. I was pulled out of my seat and pushed aside, and even though I didn't care to look out the window anymore, knowing that it would be the same view again and again, I didn't like being jerked away like that, and I grabbed the guy who had pushed me by his collar and pulled him roughly back, but he was lighter than I expected him to be and the both of us fell into a pregnant woman, who pushed into another passenger, and then we all started fighting. After a while, we were pulled apart by the Pilot, who said, "I have to fly the plane, and I can't keep coming out here like this to babysit you. So sit down and shut up."

Afterward, no one cared to look out of the windows but me and a few others, and as the days and weeks and months passed, these people, too, stopped looking, pulled down their window shades, turned their heads to look anywhere else but outside at the Dallas skyline, because, they said, their necks hurt and the sight of Reunion Tower only made them depressed.

◈

"Nobody move" is what he yelled. "This is a holdup!" Then he began to laugh at what he thought was a clever and tension-breaking joke. Since he was dressed as a pilot and had a soft Southern accent, we laughed, too. But then, it did turn out to be a holdup of sorts.

◈

We weren't sure for a long time what had happened to the other pilots, the real pilots. Had they been abducted on their way through the airport? Were they now bound and gagged and locked in a broom closet, or possibly murdered? It wasn't difficult, despite his laughter and his slight paunch, to picture our Pilot engaging in such activities. But how had our Pilot managed to maneuver through security? How did he fool the flight attendants, who surely should have known he wasn't a real pilot?

Only later did we find out, from one of the flight attendants, that he was the real pilot. That he had been flying for ten years. That she had flown with him a number of times. But that no one knew what had happened to the copilot.

At one point, looking out the window at the city below—the streets and the highways and the trees and buildings—I saw a long freight train moving slowly along the tracks that run parallel to Highway 635, and I was reminded of a story I had written in which a man had tried to build a scale model of nineteenth-century America and the trains that crossed it. He lived underground, as did a number of other people in this story, and so had no concept of how large exactly the continent was. Looking out the window at this height made me realize that such a model was now laid out before me, and I understood that I, too, had no concept of how large exactly the continent was. That the scope of my imagination was shown to be so much smaller in scale and weight than the continent that I had been trying to imagine through the eyes of a man who had never seen it before depressed me, and so I closed my window shade for the first time and leaned my head back against the seat and tried to sleep.

⊙

Sometimes I will go for weeks, months, even, without looking at myself in the bathroom mirror. I know the bathroom well enough to be able to perform whatever human functions I need to perform with my eyes closed. Then, after a long enough time has passed, I will suddenly open my eyes and stare directly into my own face in the mirror, hoping the sight of age will shock me into feeling some kind of emotion, sadness or anger or humility, but I have decided that anything besides boredom and thirst and a dull, physical ache is beyond the reach of airplane passengers.

⊙

I have tried to write other things besides this since the plane was hijacked. The Pilot gave me pen and paper, and I at first expected that he expected me to chronicle the hijacking. I wrote a few pages—descriptions, mainly: the color of the woman's hair next to me, the stale, cold air of the cabin, etc., etc.—and showed them to him, but then he didn't want them, said he didn't have time to read them. "Don't you know I'm busy?" he said, laughing, but also, or so it seemed, peeved that I had bothered him. I've never been comfortable with rejection of this sort, and, for the first year or so, his words kept me from writing anything down at all. Then, slowly, I began to take notes for a story and then notes for a novel and then notes for another novel and another story, but all they have been are notes.

◈

We were given permission to use our cell phones. The Pilot said he didn't care about signals or about whom we called. Everything he said, he said with a laugh, though none of us could ever tell what he thought was so funny. We called our loved ones. I called my wife. I told her we had been hijacked. She knew, she said, because it was all over the evening news. We said those things we were supposed to say, but I felt that her heart wasn't in it, that maybe she was distracted by the news story on the television. Maybe my heart wasn't in it, either. A baby had been crying for some time in the row or two rows behind me. We, my wife and I, didn't have kids and she wasn't pregnant and we had only been married for a short while, so I had a hard time feeling as bad for myself as for the old man who was missing his wife's birthday, who then missed—as time went on—their fortieth anniversary, and then her funeral; or the man whose pregnant wife was on board with us (the one I pushed down by accident), whose unborn child he might never see. But then, they (the old man, the pregnant wife) never appeared to feel too sad about it all, either. Mostly, once I hung up with my wife, I felt worn out by the need to shout so much over the poor reception, and twice our phones hung up by mistake—lost signal, etc.—and each time involved a series of callbacks and messages until we were finally able to reconnect. Looking around the cabin at the other passengers as they also hung up with their loved ones, I had the feeling that they had been worn out, too. No one much used their cell phones after those first few days, and eventually all of the batteries died out, anyway.

My eyes adjusted so completely to looking at the city from high up that when I imagined myself on the ground, walking through the downtown area, or driving from north Dallas to Plano or Grapevine, I could not figure out how I would navigate from such a narrow perspective. How would I know my way around? How would I avoid being run over by a car or hit by a trailer truck?

As the years passed, I learned to pick out details, as if I were a hawk or an owl. I got to where I could see my parents' house, my wife's mother's house, the church where my wife remarried; not just see the general area where they should have been, but see them, in detail. Sometimes I will see a little boy or girl whose ball has bounced into the street run out after it unaware of the teenager speeding around the corner, or some situation like this, and the first couple of times I saw this, I yelled at the child (or dog or blind old man) to watch out, but I soon realized how foolish I sounded, how I startled the other passengers with my yelling, and so I stopped.

◇

A young man in first class—a business executive or some such, I suppose—began a regimen of walking and stretching and worked very hard to convince everyone else on the plane to follow suit.

"This poor excuse for food," he complained, "will only make us sick and flabby."

He said, about our muscles, "Use them or lose them, people."

He would walk down the aisle and pat random bellies, or he would jog down the aisle, bouncing on his toes, his arms up around his face as if he were preparing for a boxing match. A few of the passengers joined him. Calisthenics, jumping jacks, yoga stretches. Most of us, though, sat in our seats and watched him bounce up and down, his face sickly and pale and sweaty. It turned out that he wasn't eating the food at all, and it was really no surprise, in hindsight, that he was the first to go. After that, the exercise regimens came to an end.

◇

The phone in front of my seat rang once. It was my mother. I do not know how she knew how to contact me on the plane. Other phones rang at other seats, too, and I suppose it is possible that the airline gave these callers our numbers. She sounded the same on the phone as she had when I had last spoken with her, some seven or eight years before, but I knew that she must have looked much older than I remembered, and as we spoke, I closed my eyes and tried to add wrinkles and creases to her face, gray hairs to her scalp, liver spots to the back of the hand that held the phone.

She told me about my father, his heart attack. She told me that she had gone to my wife's second wedding, and that it was a nice, small affair. She asked me about what we had been eating, and, so she wouldn't worry, I did not mention the weight I had lost, or the flavorless liquid the Pilot had us drink. She asked if I had met anyone on the plane, a nice woman, perhaps, someone, anyone to keep me from feeling lonely. So she wouldn't worry, I told her about the pregnant woman, who had not been pregnant now for quite some time, but I was embarrassed talking about it on the phone since I knew that she could hear me saying these things to my mother even though both of us knew nothing had ever happened between the two of us except for one night, during a heavy storm, when the cabin lights blew out and she grabbed my hand out of fright. I tried talking to her once or twice after that night, but her son, who had grown into a rather big boy at seven years old, locked me in the bathroom when his mother wasn't looking and threatened to keep me locked in there unless I promised to leave his mother alone.

After a while, a second woman's voice came on the line and informed my mother and me that the call would end soon and that the phones would be disconnected and shut off once we hung up. We said our good-byes. I told her to tell my wife hello. Then we hung up.

◈

Early on, I figured that what I would miss most from my former life, assuming that we would not make it through the tragedy alive, would be my wife: the presence of her, the sound of her voice, the feel of her pressed next to me at night in our bed, her small soft hand enveloped by my own. But I have found that, not being dead, not even being seriously injured, not being lost or, technically, alone, but instead finding myself in this plane, what I miss most are those basic qualities of life—standing up, walking around, sleeping lying flat, sex—and what I miss above all is food.

We ran out of the ham and cheese sandwiches within six weeks, despite the rationing, and the pretzels were eaten within the next month after that. At first, we were disappointed that we had no more food, until it dawned on us that, unless the Pilot wanted to starve himself or, even if he had been hoarding his own supplies in the cockpit, unless he wanted to circle Dallas with a plane full of the starved and emaciated and, eventually, dead, he would have to finally land.

A full two days passed after the last bag of pretzels had been emptied before the Pilot finally came out of his cockpit. Expecting him to admit defeat, or to inform us of his plans to land in some remote island in the Pacific or simply to crash us into the earth (by then, anything would have been preferable to the constant sight of the city below us), we waited patiently for him to speak. He frowned and looked down at his feet. "As you are probably all now aware, we have run out of food, which means we must now draw straws to see who of us will be the first to be eaten." He paused as we each looked at our neighbor, and perhaps if he had actually made us try to eat one another, we would have then risen up, wrested control of the plane from him, found a way to land, ended the ordeal. But before we could do or say anything, he smiled broadly at us and laughed, saying, "No, no, no. I'm just joking." He then proceeded to walk down the aisle, pulling out a bag he'd hidden behind his back, and began to hand out small vials of a clear liquid to each passenger as he passed. With each vial handed out, he would repeat, "Two drops should do. No more than two drops. Don't want to overdo it. Two drops should do just fine." Once he was finished, he walked to the front of the plane again, turned to us, and said, "Bon appétit," and then stepped back into his cockpit, the door closing solidly behind him.

As we ran low on drops, the Pilot would bring us new vials.

I'm not sure how they work or what sustenance they provide. While I am still hungry after my two drops, while I still have an insatiable appetite and the desire for some unnameable flavor in my mouth (the drops at first had a mild grassy taste to them, but are now as good as flavorless, as I can't taste anything at all, or else I seem to have forgotten almost entirely what anything might taste like) and I have lost weight and will probably continue to lose weight, I have not starved. As far as I know, no one who has taken the drops has.

◇

The Pilot would come out of his cabin two or three times a day. As he grew older and as his blond hair turned, in places, white, I began to wonder how he felt in the mornings when he woke up, if he felt as old and tired as I sometimes felt.

I assumed he slept. He locked the cabin door at night, so none of us knew for sure. I asked him once if he slept and he didn't answer me, and then I asked him, if he did sleep, who flew the plane. He laughed and patted his belly and said, "My copilot." When I asked him, recently, if his copilot would also be the one to fly the plane once he has died, he did not respond, pretending not to have heard my question.

◇

It is surprising to me how quickly news of the hijacking spread. I called my wife within the hour of being told we had been hijacked, and she already knew. The people of Dallas organized a vigil that very night. We could see the huddled bunch of them with their candles standing on the tarmac of the Dallas/Fort Worth Airport. Someone—a gentleman from the rear of the plane—said, "Them standing there, we couldn't land even if we wanted to." In the morning, the same group of people (or perhaps a new group) stood in approximately the same formation, this time holding white posters with black letters on them that spelled out something too small for us to read.

For a while, I liked to think of my wife there among

them, holding a candle or a piece of the message, but, in truth, my wife does not like crowds, and it's more likely that she was not.

Within a week, regardless of my wife's involvement or lack thereof, the vigils had stopped, the news reports, I'm almost certain, had stopped as well, and we had become a fixture of the Dallas skyline, no different or more exciting than the neon Mobile Pegasus.

II.

I often find myself considering the man my wife married, by which I usually mean myself, a thought that then returns me to the fact that she has since remarried, and so I am forced to think of the two of us, her husband and I, side by side. This despite the fact that I have never seen him, which leads me, more often than not, to picture myself side by side my other self so that I might consider how the two of us have failed and how we continue to fail as husbands. I have a cataloged list in my head; it grows by the day, and it changes nearly constantly as faults are moved around, given more or less priority, my dirty underwear left on the bathroom floor moved down a rung by the peanut-butter-encrusted knife left for a week in the backseat of my car. When I get into this mood of rearranging faults—real and imagined—I begin to wonder, too, what the other passengers, those who are left, are thinking. We are not friends, any of us. Of course, we were all friends at first, or, at the very least, friendly with those people to our left or our right or across the aisle, as people on a plane tend to be, in that manner of searching for common ground in a book being read, a destination being reached, a vacation being taken. With the underlying sense that these friendships would last no longer than the few hours between Dallas and Chicago, we opened ourselves up to our neighbors. These relationships were made stronger once the plane was hijacked, as we felt bonded to one another by a shared sense of tragedy and uncertainty. Then, as time passed, as we continued to circle, as we realized just how long we might have to share the same space with one another, we—I am projecting now—began to feel crowded, as if there wasn't enough room, and slowly we gathered ourselves inward, pulling knees into our chests, feet onto the seats, curling our arms around our shins, and placing our heads down or, if we could stomach the sight, pressing our faces away from our neighbors and against the windows. Now the plane is still and quiet, and we have been moving with such regularity for so long that I have this sense of perfect unmovement, which creeps into the pit of my stomach and produces there a soft fluttering of wings and a welling anxiety, as if I had forgotten to do some minor but personal thing, or as if I were riding a child's ride at a fair, the dips not enough to be truly belly-rising, but raising, instead, a tingling awareness of gravity, or gravitas, in my arms and shoulders and legs; a feeling that is at once pleasant and upsetting.

When we were still talking—the other passengers and I—the woman who sat next to me and who had once asked that I store some of her bags beneath my seat told me, breath-lessly and as she sat down, officially the last person to board the plane and take her seat, how she had nearly missed the flight and how she had had to beg and argue and plead with the gate attendants to let her on board. I explained to them, she told me, how the shuttle had had a flat and how someone was supposed to have called ahead to tell someone about the situation, and that we had somehow convinced the first tow-truck driver to squeeze us into his cab and drive us to the airport so that we could all make our flights on time, but by then, with rush hour traffic, and even with the tow truck flashing its yellow lights, it took us over an hour to move through the accidents and the stalled cars, and by the time we arrived at the entrance to the airport, I only had fifteen minutes to get my baggage checked and run to my gate, and after all of that, do you believe that they almost didn't let me on the plane? How did you convince them? I invariably asked, to which she replied, Why, honey, with my feminine charm. It was an amazing story the way she told it, embel-lished and repeated often to the others around her as we tax-ied down the runway, and in those first few minutes in the air before the Pilot came out of the cockpit and hijacked us all, and then, much later, she began repeating the story again, though lamentably and with less energy, as if she were recit-ing the Act of Contrition; and with each successive dirge, more and more details of the story were removed until finally, late one night a month or so into our circling, she turned her head to me and confessed that in fact there was no flat tire, no tow-truck driver, no real traffic even, but that she had overslept, and that's why she had almost missed her flight. If only I had slept ten minutes longer, she said, and then she turned her head to face straight again, and, while I'm sure she must have said something else between then and the time she passed away, I cannot remember what else that might have been. Now, however, I repeat her story to myself, having adopted it as my own, except that sometimes the tow-truck driver refuses to carry us in his cab and we are forced to hail down a woman driving with her baby in a station wagon, and she's the one who brings us to the airport on time, and sometimes I will catch myself thinking, *If only she hadn't picked us up,* and despite the fact that the story, which is not even mine, has never been true, I cannot help but feel a keen disappointment in the fact that such an insignificant event has led me to this end.

III.

When the Pilot died, it came to light that he in fact did have a copilot. The pregnant woman's son, it turned out, had been spending more and more time in the Pilot's cabin, learning the technique of flying, learning the secrets of our perpetual oil. At first, we were relieved. The Pilot was gone, we could finally land, and the boy, now a young man, would certainly land the plane, just as his mother had asked him to. But, of course, why should he? In a way, it made more sense to us—perhaps not to the boy's mother—that we continued to circle Dallas even after the Pilot's death. In all of our time circling with the Pilot, we never learned, were never told why we could not land, why we had been hijacked. Now that the boy was in charge, though, what else should he have done? What other world did he know but this one inside the plane? Would he so easily give up its comforts, its familiarity?

Most of us had some memory of what it was like to stand straight, to walk on an object that does not so noticeably move, to breathe air that has not been cycled and recycled a hundred thousand times, and even we were a little afraid of what our lives would become if we were to finally land on solid ground. The prospect of seeing a building up close and from below must have been a devastating and frightening one for the boy. Despite his mother's weeping and crumpled body outside the Pilot's door, he did not alter the Pilot's original course, not even to change the direction of our circle.

Shortly after the Pilot hijacked the plane, he had us pose for pictures taken with a Polaroid camera. As with everything else, he did not explain why he wanted these pictures. The flight attendants had us stand in front of the lavatory between first class and coach, and after the picture was taken and had developed, they let each of us look at our photograph before placing it in a box with the rest of them that was eventually handed over to the Pilot.

The Copilot—he had a name, but since the Pilot's death,

he refused to answer to anything but Copilot—found these photographs and decided to take another series of them, and we lined up again and posed. Once these had developed, the Copilot had his mother give everyone the original photograph and the new photograph. A sizable pile of old pictures with no matching new ones remained in the box, and these, we decided, should be placed in the now empty seats, but once this had been done, we changed our minds and took them all back up and placed them back in the box and returned the box to the cockpit.

I had begun to put on some weight before my trip, and I remember feeling self-conscious about the way my pants had begun to fit. There is a difference of maybe thirty pounds between the first man pictured and the second man pictured. Still, the thinness looks no better on me than the extra weight did. Whereas my clothes once seemed uncomfortably small, they look, in the more recent photograph, ridiculously large. Furthermore, along with the weight, my face has lost whatever charm it once had. Oddly, and this seems to be the case with nearly everyone else's pictures, too, I am smiling in both.

IV.

I often find myself lost in thought, trying to imagine the paths of our lives after we have landed. In this I am, I believe, alone.

Suppose the Copilot falls ill and we are forced into an emergency landing, or simply, as he matures, he experiences an epiphany, a change of heart, a desire to do something more with his life. Whatever the reason, some small part of me would not be terribly surprised if one day the Copilot were to step out of his cabin and ask, nonchalantly, "Does anyone know how to put us down?" I wonder, then, which we will choose: to rebuild our former lives or begin them anew. Is twenty years long enough to wipe away bad marriages, poor career choices, too many long hours spent following someone else's dreams? How many of us will return to our old homes, rented out to new tenants or boarded up or sold, settle ourselves back into old routines now occupied by new people?

Some of us have already made our choices. The former accountant practices sleight of hand tricks for hours on end. He has told me, while pulling quarters out of my ear, while filling and emptying the overhead bins with the wave of a blanket, that he plans to change his name, buy a few costumes, and take up the birthday party racket, or aim for the big time, the comedy club circuit. "Carpe diem," he told me.

For others, the choice seems to have been made for us. My wife has remarried. It is likely that by now my parents have both died. The friendships I enjoyed have surely unkindled themselves after twenty years. I will step out of this plane and onto the tarmac with no human connection but to the people on board with me, most of whom I have not spoken to in months. I am afraid that I will, if I'm not careful, seek out a life that most closely resembles the one I have for twenty years been living. Perhaps when we land, I will buy a bus ticket and ride the Crosstown 404 as it loops through its never-ending circuit. Or I might rent or buy a car and drive to Belt Line Road and continue to circle the city in that way. It would be good to devise a plan to prevent this sort of life taking hold, but no such plan comes readily to mind. In my imagination, then, I often wind up on the side of the road, kicked off the bus by the driver or having run out of gasoline, forced then to continue my course on foot. These thoughts bring me little comfort, which explains, perhaps, why the others have given up such fruitless speculation and why all plans of overpowering our hijacker and taking control of the situation were long ago abandoned.

I will not be here for the more realistic ending, of course. How could I be? Though not yet the oldest person on the plane, I am not far from it, either, and it's not likely that I'll live as long as the Copilot, who seems to be in excellent health. We can hear him perform his calisthenics every morning after he wakes and every night before he goes to sleep, a regimen he must have learned from the Pilot. When we glimpse it, his face has a ruddy glow.

As I imagine it, everyone else will have gone by then, too. Even now there is only the one flight attendant left, and though younger than many of us, she has long since stopped taking her drops, and her once pretty face is gaunt and withered. Soon, then, no members of the original crew will be left, and there will be only the seven other passengers who remain. And once we have all died and there is only the Copilot, what then? It's unlikely that he will land—I doubt he even knows how. But he might become lonely. He might tire of the Dallas skyline, which has changed not at all since we first took off, and seek some new skyscape. Flying straight ahead for some time, east or west, toward sunrise or sunset, perhaps finding himself soon over the Pacific Ocean, wondering what this world is that he's flown himself to, blue above and blue below, until, following the sunset each day, he eventually finds the Asian continent, or perhaps Africa, and then Europe, and then the Atlantic, and the Eastern Seaboard, until he reaches Dallas again, at which time perhaps he will turn left, or right, or continue on straight again, circling the world the way he has for so long circled Dallas. I can't see how it will or should matter to me, since I will have long since died by then, but at times I feel sorry for the boy, sorrier for him than for us. He will fly and fly and fly, until he one day slumps over in his captain's chair, the dead weight of his body pushing the controls forward. I can feel my stomach lurch even as I imagine the nose dipping, the wings turning downward. The plane will break through the clouds, condensation beading up along the windows like rain. The world will rush past below, cars and buildings and trees and people becoming larger by the moment, as if they are rising to meet us, until at last, with great and terrible speed, the Copilot finally lands.

The Miniature Wife

The truth of the matter is: I have managed to make my
wife very, very small.

This was done unintentionally. This was an accident.

I work in miniaturization and it is, therefore, my job to
make everything smaller. I have developed a number of processes, which members of my staff then test. They will, let's
say, make a smaller hatbox in order to test the process that I
used to make a smaller hat. That is simply an example, of
course. We do not actually make hats or hatboxes. I cannot
disclose to anyone, not even to my wife, exactly what I make,
or how small I make it. I can only say that I am quite good at
my job, and I have moved quickly through the ranks and
now head an entire department of miniaturizers.

And let me say this, too: I never bring work home with
me, tempting though it might be. I have set strict rules for
myself, the same rules I enforce with my workers. I can

hardly afford to be seen as the employer who abuses his power. I do not make the boxes in my attic smaller to make room for more Christmas decorations. I have never made our winter wardrobe small in the summer or our summer wardrobe small for the winter. I rake and pile and bag the autumn leaves like anyone else does.

Still. There it is: my wife, shrunk to the height of a coffee mug.

What bothers me most about the current situation (not her size, as I am quite used to seeing normal objects reduced to abnormal sizes, even to the point that I wake up some mornings overwhelmed by the size of everyday objects, alarmed even by the size of my own head) is that I don't quite know how it happened. Otherwise, I would gladly reverse the process, as I have done time and again at the office. But as there are many different means of making things smaller—the Kurzym Bypass, ideal for reducing highly complex pieces of machinery, for instance, or Montclaire's Pabulum, which is the only process by which one might safely reduce inorganic foodstuffs, to name only two—and since this reduction was accidental and I don't know how it was performed, I am at a loss as to how to bring her back.

The irony of this is not lost on me, rest assured. Would that I had an ally in my office, with whom I could brainstorm solutions to this problem, then, surely, she would be returned to normal by now, but I have no one of the sort, and have made no progress on my own. Hence the dollhouse, something solid, fashioned of wood, and constructed with her in mind. The enormity of our real house and its furnishings—craterous bowls, cavernous pockets, insurmountable table legs, and bathroom counters slick with puddle-sized droplets of water—fill me with a great anxiety. I have also, claiming allergies, given the cat to a friend and have refused to let the bird out of its cage. I should like to get rid of the bird entirely, but I know that such a loss would upset my wife, who is, at the moment, upset enough already.

⊛

We were in the kitchen when it happened. It happened and then she screamed. I could see her scream, but I couldn't hear her, though in my imagination it was not so much a scream as a startled yelp. I've learned, since then, to listen for a different register of voice. I have also fashioned small ear-cups that fit nicely around my head and allow me to pick up softer sounds.

So: She screamed, but I couldn't hear her. Then she took her purse off her shoulder and threw it at me. She threw it hard, so it seemed, but a person the size of a coffee mug can only do so much. Unable to hit me, then, and with nothing else in reach, she attacked herself, or, rather, her clothing. In a matter of seconds, she'd torn off her skirt, ripped the shirt off her back, thrashed at her panty hose, and broken the heels off her shoes. Then she grabbed her purse again and dumped out everything in it and, there, found a lighter, and, before I could move to stop her, she set the small pile of clothes on fire, then stamped at them, and then kicked them off the edge of the table.

It was quite a display.

Needless to say, her clothes were ruined.

And my wife, who was very small, was now naked as well.

◈

The thing is: My wife's condition has begun to affect my work.

On two occasions, colleagues have remarked on the sloppiness of my appearance. Generally, I am a very neatly dressed, well-shaved man.

I want to but can't tell them that my wife is a strong climber. That she is resourceful beyond my imagination.

I want to tell them that she has fashioned ropes. That she has forged small tools.

I want to tell them:

To be honest with you, Jim, my face is unevenly shaved because my three-inch wife has climbed up the porcelain sink, hoisted herself up to the medicine cabinet, opened the heavy mirrored door, and has dulled all of my razor blades.

Truth be told, Paul, my miniaturized wife removed every other button on each of my work shirts yesterday while I was in the office. And if we look closely, I mean really closely, with one of our best magnifying glasses, we could probably see her tiny teeth marks in the thread.

I want to tell them this, but I cannot. Instead I spend more time in my office.

And I've had to suspend my open-door policy.

◇

She is not unattractive, my wife, in her miniaturized state. Her best features—her waist, the round curve of her hips, her shapely legs and fine eyebrows—are there still, undiminished by her diminished size. But what's more—and more surprising—her harder, more difficult to reconcile features have softened. The hard, reproachful look in her eyes. The often angry or disappointed set of her jaw. Her rather large feet. All of her should have reduced proportionately, and maybe it all has and this is but a trick of the mind, but one night, as she slept in the small makeshift bed I made for her—matchbox, tufts of cotton, stitched squares of felt—I crept up on her and spied on her with a magnifying glass—I own quite a number of very good glasses—and it seemed to me that something in the process of miniaturization had enhanced the look of her.

As much as I hate to admit it, I felt some pride in this. One of the many complaints we face in my office is that in the process of miniaturizing a thing, we rub out the details of it. For the past two years now, we've been working diligently to develop—across all of our miniaturization processes—an ability to retain the sharp and necessary details, the inherent beauty, the power of a thing's function even when shrunk down to the size of a cup, a blade of grass, a grain of sand.

Gazing down at my wife through my magnifying glass, I could see that we had finally found some measure of success. I must have made some sound, then, or perhaps the simple presence of me looming over her with my magnifying glass was all it took, but regardless, she woke and looked up at me and offered me a disdainful shake of her head before gathering the pieces of felt around her and stomping away. I looked for her but she had disappeared—more quickly than I would have thought possible—and I did not see her again for another two days.

In the construction of the dollhouse, I have not relied on a kit. Instead, I have leaned heavily on blueprints. A kit, so I assumed, would not allow for enough customization. Dollhouses made to order do not account for room size, doorjambs, ceiling heights, are not designed to be inhabited. Not to mention that what I had to build, in order to coax her into it, to persuade her that some kind of life, a temporary life inside it would be an improvement, for it to do what I required of it, the dollhouse needed to be, in miniature, a much better house than our own.

In all, the exercise has been quite enjoyable. There is the smell of sawdust and wood and wood glue, the metallic smell that lingers on the tips of my fingers after handling so many small nails. And of the dollhouse furniture, I have finished carving all but the bed, which I found to be beyond my small abilities. Excuse the pun.

I've asked one of the guys in production to build a bed frame to my specifications, and then I will have someone else miniaturize it for me. Then I will take the small bed home and place it inside the dollhouse and the house will be complete. The roof is already installed. The rest of the house has been furnished, despite my wife's objections, despite her petty vandalisms, the graffiti (nail polish, easily removed), the torn curtains (easily replaced). Despite the fact that she has broken the glass out of the windowpanes, which I decided don't need to be replaced, as there's little threat of rain or snow.

She is against the house now, but once I have the bed in place and have the bedroom decorated, almost exactly as our bedroom is decorated now, I know she will fall in love with it just as I have fallen in love with it. Until then, however, I've closed the house and have blocked the door and covered the windows.

⊚

I miss her, of course, my wife. It's strange, though, since, technically, she is here with me. Is in the house, anyway, though I don't know where exactly, or what she's doing. But in truth, it's as if she has gone away for business—though she doesn't have a job to speak of—or on an extended vacation with a group of girlfriends, though she doesn't have that, either. In any case, I find myself, when not actively building the dollhouse, reverting to an inert state. I do not cook for myself, content to simply order in or to raid the cans of peas and green beans and Chef Boyardee ravioli with meat sauce, which I crank open and dig into with a fork or spoon, without heating it up or tasting it in my mouth.

I find it hard to fall asleep. I do everything within my power to stave off the hour that I must finally go to bed, and when I do, I throw myself into bed in the most uncomfortable positions, my legs hanging over the edge, a bunched-up pile of duvet or a small throw pillow distractingly placed under my side or the small of my back.

The bed is permanently unmade, the kitchen uncleaned. I call in sick with more and more frequency, and then spend the day in my sleepwear watching daytime television when before I did not watch television at all.

The only time I feel like myself is while in the garage, wearing my magnifying goggles, the soldering iron in my hand, or my miter shears, or when using the diamond tip carving burrs I bought only a few days ago. I think of her in these moments, or if not of her directly, of what I'm doing for her, for us, and it's almost as if she is standing right next to me, watching me as I build.

⊛

In my imagination, my wife is training. For survival, for success.

In my imagination, she is strong, much stronger than before. She has taut arms and a strong back and thick legs. Her feet are tough, her hands gloved in calluses.

Since my wife's accident, I have found more than the normal amount of dead flies in the house—on the windowsills, on the kitchen table, floating in the toilet water. Under the magnifying glass—borrowed from my office—most of the flies look to be stabbed through, a small sliver of wood running through an abdomen or an eye. One of them looked caught, tortured, its legs removed, wings twisted back. At normal size, my wife was never this cruel. Her need for survival, I believe, has made her so, and in a way I am proud, am glad that she survives. She is a woman who, before, could not open jelly jars, who was afraid of dogs and open closets and mice and insects. I am not unconcerned, however, that if I do not find a means of reversal soon, she will be lost—to civilization, to me.

Before she had been reduced to the size of a coffee mug—in fact, ever since we have known each other—my wife had been the kind of person to leave notes. Notes of thanks, notes of displeasure. Small reminders of things to be done, gentle and not so gentle reprimands. One night, shortly after we were married and living together for the first time, and after I had gone to bed for the night, she placed a plastic grocery bag full of dirty dishes next to my side of the bed. These were dishes I had used but hadn't yet washed and put away. They were a day old, or no more than two days old at the most. After I woke the next morning and stepped on the bag of dishes and twisted my ankle on them and nearly fell over because of them, I picked up the bag and found affixed to it a small yellow Post-it note on which she had simply written *Yours*.

Often her notes began *Please remember to*, or *Don't forget we need*, or *Did you remember that*. But just as often she dispensed with even these pleasantries and left me notes that read *Laundry* or *Dishes* or *Your shoes on the floor* or *The hairs you left on the bathroom sink.*

Even now, even at the size of a coffee cup, she leaves me notes, though lately I do not understand them, or cannot read them, even with the assistance of one of my many very strong, very good magnifying glasses. Nor do I know where she has found the paper or the pencil with which to write these notes. I find them in surprising, implausible places. Affixed to the bathroom mirror, which seems much too high for her to reach. Mixed in with the little pieces of lint and detritus in my pants pocket or the inside breast pocket of my jacket. At the bottom of my cereal bowl. Stuck to the refrigerator with a magnet.

At first these notes offered some form of communication between us, though there seemed to be only so much for her to say. *Please hurry. I miss you, too. At night I am cold. The ants rarely bother me, but I cannot abide the flies.* But the longer she remains in her miniaturized condition, the less intelligible these notes are. I found one just the other day that read *Puppies make the best mayonnaise.* And another that read *Flies on the living room windowsill.* A third that read *The life you promised me.* I have found some notes that do not contain words at all, but merely doodles or scribblings or diagrams. She will draw on them at times, but, as she is not a very accomplished artist, these drawings do little to move me.

Rarely do I know what to make of these notes. For a while, I thought to keep them, though I couldn't say why or to what purpose. As a needless reminder of this somewhat rocky moment in our marriage? Now, as I find them, I collect them in a small envelope I keep in my back pocket, and at the end of the day, as I undress for bed, I empty the envelope's contents into the trash, and the next morning, I start all over again.

⬡

The house took me nearly two months to complete, much longer than I had expected, but having completed the house, having added the bed and the rest of the furniture, having finished painting the rooms inside and out, I opened it up to her yesterday, only to wait to see what she would make of it.

Already, less than a day later, there are signs of life inside it.

The bed is unmade and there is a mess in one of the living rooms—pillows on the floor, a lamp left on, signs of domesticity, of being lived in. I can't see very well because I am only looking through the windows. I'm afraid to open the house up. If I unhinge the house and pull it apart, I run the risk of catching my wife and splitting her in two. Regardless, there are signs of life, of living. Soon, I should be able to devise a way to return her to normal.

But then again—it is such a nice house. Much nicer than our normal-sized one. Is it possible that she and I could be happy there together? Once a week, I could return to normal size and buy groceries, run errands, make our lives comfortable. I could even continue working—shrinking myself every night after coming home. I could sleep with my wife then. We could be together. Though it goes against my sense of ethics, true, it is so much simpler a solution.

And I have so far tried just about every known process for deminiaturization that I can think of. I have brought home engorgement and enlargement solutions, a number of which I developed myself and know for certain to be fool-proof; I've made her spend four hours inside the Magnifying Chamber, a rather small device itself, small enough, anyway, to slip into my pocket before I left the office for home, breaking, again, any number of laws and office policies; and, as a last resort, I carried her out of the house and drove her to the remote piece of badlands owned by the company and there, uncertain as to whether she would even survive, I pushed her through the Fibonacci Tunnel.

Nothing has worked.

I'll leave my wife a note explaining my idea to her. If we discuss it, I'm sure she'll see the benefits. I'm sure she'll see that this might in fact be the best thing for us.

For a moment, for one single moment, a long but single moment, I harbored a fantasy of what life might be like, what our life together might be like, if I were unable to restore my wife to her original size. If we were to live together in the dollhouse I built for her, which is, as I've said before, a very nice house, a much nicer house. Then I spoke that fantasy out loud, and then the fantasy was ruined.

What I mean to say is: This ordeal has taken its toll on all of us.

Today, I had to fire one of my employees, Richard Paul Wear. He was not the best man—as his actions proved—but he was a very good miniaturist; he was ambitious.

And though his actions are unpardonable, I cannot blame him entirely. I should have known that miniaturizing a phone for my wife would lead to, if not this exactly, something similar. But I was concerned. I had had no word from my wife since I finished the project, and after the first two days, I saw no more signs of life in the house. The bed was made; the rooms were neat and untouched. I left her notes, but they went unanswered. She had stopped leaving me notes long before all of this. My questions about miniaturizing myself were ignored. I called for her, softly so as not to damage her shrunken ears, but my voice did nothing but agitate the bird. The truth is, I sorely missed my wife. The construction of the dollhouse, as it was for her, helped me manage through her absence, and there were little signs of her presence around the house—the flies, the dulled razors, the notes, the torn buttons—and though annoyances, they proved to me that she was still around. Since the completion of the house, I have heard nothing.

Therefore, I bought a cordless phone and miniaturized it. (The depths to which I have sunk!)

I wasn't sure if the signal would work for such a small phone, nor did I have a means of testing the equipment, but I figured there was nothing left to lose. With a pair of tweezers, I placed the tiny phone on the coffee table of the downstairs living room of the dollhouse, where my wife could easily find it. Three days passed without word from her. I called home once or twice a day. The phone must not have worked, I thought. Or she has left me—even if she had not yet left the house—or she was dead.

On the fourth day, I came back to my desk from a meeting and found a message on my phone. "Come home for lunch, dear. I've missed you so."

Until that moment, I hadn't realized just how much I had missed the sound of her voice, full and loud and loving. Why hadn't I thought of the phone before? There was nothing small about her over the phone line. I did not hear the voice of my shrunken wife, but rather the voice of the woman I loved, the woman whose touch I missed. The sound of it brought tears to my eyes. I felt faint. I wanted to leave immediately, drive home, meet my wife, tell her how much I loved her. I grabbed my jacket and was about to leave when one of my technicians came in with a problem, an accident in the lab, which, in the end, took me until lunchtime to correct. As soon as I could, though, I sped home, my heart in my throat.

Only in hindsight did I find it odd that the door was unlocked. I expected to see her waiting for me on the kitchen counter or on the coffee table. I stepped gingerly through the house, the cups around my ears so that I might hear her. Then I heard a noise from the upstairs bedroom, where I kept her dollhouse. *Of course*, I thought. *The dollhouse!* How silly of me to have forgotten! I took the stairs three and four at a time, reckless and youthful in my haste. I burst through the bedroom door and threw the house open, completely forgetting in my excitement that I might harm my wife, might split her in two.

And there she was.

In the dollhouse. In the bedroom. On our bed.

Naked.

And there, on the floor next to the bed, inexpertly covering himself with a pillow, was a cowering and miniature Richard Paul Wear.

My wife smiled at me and then leaned over to him, tousled his hair, and gave him a peck on the forehead.

Sleeping with my wife aside, Wear had broken company policy. Not only did he use his knowledge of miniaturization outside of the workplace, he did so on himself. Granted, I have made my own innumerable missteps, but surely anyone can see the difference between miniaturizing yourself so you can step out of the office for a nice go-around with your officemate's miniaturized wife and stealing engorgement solutions and deminiaturizing machinery and using office resources to miniaturize beds and whatnot in order to make your (accidentally) miniaturized wife's (temporary) miniaturized existence more comfortable.

But more important even than that, he knew about my own situation. Such knowledge could find its way back to the office, could spread among my employees, could result in my termination, an investigation, police reports, legal action.

So what else could I do but cover him in honey and seed and then feed him to the bird?

◇

A conflict has arisen between my wife and me.

I destroyed the phone, lucky that my wife had not called the police, or worse yet, my supervisor, had only called Wear, whom she had met briefly at the last company picnic. Once the phone was destroyed, I locked my wife inside the dollhouse and covered it with a drop cloth.

"Live in darkness," I yelled. "See how you like that."

I came home to find the dollhouse burnt to the ground. Nothing else in our house had been damaged, aside from the tabletop scorched by the fire. I do not know how she managed to free herself from the dollhouse itself—I had nailed it shut, had covered the windows with squares of cardboard that I glued and then duct-taped to the outside of the house, had weighted down the drop cloth, had made it impossible to escape from. Nor do I know how she controlled the fire such that the house itself burned but nothing else. Yet there it is, or, rather, isn't: The house, and everything inside of it (excepting, I can only assume, my wife), is gone.

I am not unprepared for this. To be honest, this is not unexpected. I am the kind of man who thinks through all possible courses of events. Horrifying or not, I did at one point imagine this might come to pass, or if not this exactly, something like this.

If she can burn down the dollhouse even as it sits inside our real house, then she is capable of almost anything. For this reason, I wear headphones and swimming goggles to sleep. I tie down the sheets, layer the bed three and four blankets thick. On far too many nights have I woken up only just in time to see the small figure of her jump from the top of our mattress and scurry beneath the bedroom door and into the hallway. Taking these precautions allows me to sleep peacefully, but when I wake in the morning, it is to the sickening smell of a dead cockroach, speared through its abdomen by a tiny metal skewer, the tip of which has been shoved firmly into the soft wood of our nightstand. She has set the whole thing on fire, hence the smell.

This is, unmistakably, an act of war.

In response, I am starving the bird. I haven't fed him since I fired Wear. Tonight, before I go to sleep, I will set him free in the house.

◈

This morning I woke to find the bird (dead) on my side of the bed, covered so that he appeared to be taking a nap. Either she guessed my next move or she had been planning this move all along.

How did she kill him? How did she manage to move him—he's well over three times her size—and settle him on my pillow? How did she loosen the sheets, and when she did, why did she not do more to me? Questions I cannot answer, though I am not without my own next move. On my way home I will stop by our friend's house and retrieve our cat.

◇

Not just the cat, now; we also have a number of spiders and cockroaches that I set free to wander through the house. I like to picture my wife as Jason or one of his Argonauts, a sword in hand, fighting large and mystical beasts. Hordes of skeletons. Giant cats.

I have, furthermore, flooded the bedroom. The bed now sits on stilts. I have waders sitting just outside the bedroom door for when I come home and want to go to bed. The water is about a foot and a half deep. It is an unnecessary precaution. The cat will find my wife eventually if he hasn't done so already. But one can never be too careful. With a large sheet of plastic spread along the perimeter of the room, I've built a miniature pool, a moat of sorts. Now that the room is flooded, I've stopped wearing my goggles and headphones. I sleep, some nights, without covers at all. And when I dream, I dream of the cat charging down on my wife. He has no front claws, but he has teeth. He has plenty of teeth.

I've also developed the habit of checking the house for spiderwebs and checking those webs for wife-shaped mummies. I have only found a fly or two. I scour the kitchen and the living room for the remains of my wife, but, again, nothing.

I've found nothing and have heard nothing.

◇

Jason and the Argonauts. It is almost as if, by making the comparison in my head, I have brought this all upon myself.

Now I am blind in my left eye, and the cat is drowned, floating next to the bed.

She loved that cat.

It all happened while I slept, of course. Though the cat must have been dead before it was drowned. Surely, the sound she would have made while struggling to drown her cat would have woken me.

I knew that she was still in the room. She must have been. She was somewhere hidden, her boat—how did she learn to make a boat, and where did she find the materials for the hull, the rudder, the oars, the sail?—safely anchored next to the bed. There was a good deal of pain after she stabbed me through, but partly I was acting as I writhed about the bed and tossed around the room, my hand cupped over my eye. While one eye bled, the other searched the room for signs of her.

I stumbled from the bed to the dresser to the closet, looking for threads, tiny ropes, anything she might have used to cross over the water. Nothing. She must have swum for it in those first moments when I was distracted by the pain. The waves thrown about by my stamping feet might have carried her even faster to the water's edge.

Or perhaps she is even cleverer than that.

Perhaps she is still in her boat or just beneath it, bobbing just under the surface of the water, a small tube feeding her air.

With a quick swipe of my hand, I smash her ship, slam it under water and into the bedroom floor. Smash at it again and again and again until my hand is sore and bruised.

When I stop, the pieces of the boat float to the surface, but, sadly, my wife is not among them.

◌

My wife is stronger than I am. I am ready to admit that now.

You are stronger than me.

I haven't slept in three days.

Can you see the white flag, dear? Am I waving it high enough for you?

Part of the house, now, is entirely hers. She has set traps, trip wires. She nearly took me down the other day as I ventured into the kitchen, feeling all at once like Gulliver brought down by the Lilliputians, as thin but strong hemp twine twined its way around my ankles, my waist, my wrists. I stumbled into the stove but then shoved myself back and out of the kitchen, landing flat on my back, but with enough force to break the twine around my ankles, and quickly, then, I stood and kicked and screamed, in case she was nearby, ready to pounce again.

She has stuck tiny spears into the carpet, has formed a perimeter around her camp. Small spears bearing the heads of a spider or two, and some cockroaches, and at night, I can see a small bonfire and I stare at it, transfixed, wondering what she is burning. Pieces of carpet? Or insects? Or what?

Her camp. That's where I am headed now. I will follow in her footsteps. It will be difficult and, small now as I am, blind in one eye, weak from lack of sleep, I doubt that I will make it very far, certainly not to her camp, and if I do make it through the living room and across the cold landscape of the kitchen and into the den where she waits for me, then I can only guess at the fate that awaits me there. But I will do everything in my power, will fend off hordes of spiders or cockroaches if necessary, will sacrifice my right eye if only it will allow me even the one last opportunity to creep up on her as she sleeps, wrap my hands around her thick neck, and strangle the life out of her tiny body.

William Corbin:
A Meritorious Life

CORBIN, WILLIAM (1570–1660). Clown. Place of birth: Manchester, England. After he died, William Corbin's body was taken, in secret and at great peril to his acolytes, back into the heart of the Klounkova Territories, where, on a modern map, one might now find Moldova, though at one point, the Klounkova Territories ranged from the edge of the Black Sea and westward into the European continent, cutting large swaths through the Ukraine and Romania and parts of Bulgaria. Corbin was interred in the southern flatlands of Moldova, though it had been his wish to be buried deeper in, nearer the center of the Klounkovan encampments. In the end, his friends and followers dared not risk discovery by the nomadic and restless Klouns.

Corbin owed his fascination with Klouns to his father, a village constable, who often took his three sons (of which William was the youngest) to variety acts and lowbrow, death-defying street shows, carnivals performed by traveling circuses hailing from Eastern European regions near or bordering the Black Sea. Inevitably, performing as part of one troupe or another, would be a Kloun, who, big-footed, of pale complexion, and with an over-expressive face, would often steal the show through popular movement skits and drama tumbles and the performance of ineffable sleights of hand. Although Corbin's father detested the antics and the appearance of Klouns, William was enthralled by the graceful movements achieved by their curious and oblong shapes. Time and again, William would sneak past his father and watch with fascination, as "even their emboldened eyebrows danced along the contours of their paper-white faces."

One day, a young William broke from his family, found his way to a small congregation of Klouns, separate from the amassing crowd, and offered himself to them as an apprentice:

Only after meeting them face-to-face, standing not two feet away, did I realize the truth of their size, speed & strength. Clearly, they stood a head taller than my own father, if not taller still, and were fit with powerful legs & exaggerated forearms. Silent they were as three stood & before I knew they had yet moved, surrounded me & lifted me above their heads. One supported my legs, the second my neck & shoulders, while the third walked alongside & beneath me, & they turned me over & over again, as if I were a spit hog, cooking over an open flame.

The Klouns stripped the boy of his shoes, replaced them with a pair of their own, large and ridiculous, and then smeared a chalky substance across his face in uneven clumps before setting him back down and roughly pushing him back toward the crowd, whose attention had turned from the puppet show to the performance of the Klouns and Corbin.

"Yet the whole time, not once did they speak, nor never did one even so much as smile."

At the age of sixteen and disillusioned but not swayed by this encounter, William Corbin began in secret to learn the actions, attitudes, and performances of Klouns. Spending long hours watching carnival sideshows where Klouns most frequently performed, William put to memory many of the more well-known Kloun acrobatics, such as Bênchï's Ten Facial Forms and Coefçneuçi's Six Corporal Attitudes, which he then practiced at night in an abandoned shed some miles outside of town. When not practicing the foot steps and body rolls of Klouns, William occupied himself with the design and construction of authentic feet—"overlarge and made of flesh-colored sap, fired and molded to a shape that, when placed flush to my own foot, fits so that one cannot tell that my feet are, in relation to most Klouns, abbreviated, and made of such materials, and with accurate texture and design, so as to act not as simple props, but to act as feet act." He also spent his time mixing face powders with plant resins to produce makeup to pale the color of his face and redden the surface of skin around his cheeks, the recipes of which have long since been lost or forgotten. He worked for over three years to develop a mixture that would not fade or smear despite "sweat, the heat of a noonday sun, the salt waters of the Atlantic, nor the simple, casual touch of a child's finger, drawn along my cheek to see if I am real, to see if I am in fact a Kloun."

At nineteen, confident in his appearance and the craft of his movements, confident, too, in his ability to pass as a Kloun, William Corbin began performing in the town's main square, never once recognized by his neighbors or friends or even his father. He continued performing for six months before he joined a small traveling show that was headed back to mainland Europe with plans to return to Romania and hopes of performing along the way. He traveled for two years without incident or discovery, further honing his skills as a Kloun and learning the now extinct language of that people. Once in Romania, Corbin left the troupe and traveled into the Klounkova Territories, which had begun to shrink little by little, year after year. To his surprise, he was easily accepted by a highland tribe, with whom he traveled for two years, and where he married and he lived peacefully, and soon he began to feel not that he was disguised as but was in fact a Kloun.

Although he kept a journal of his life from the time he left England, his entries are written almost exclusively in Klounkovan, a singular and indecipherable language, and so it is that no one knows how his charade was discovered, only that it was. In 1640, William Corbin was violently expelled from his tribe and was forced to leave the Territories. He was separated from his wife, who, it is believed, was pregnant, and he was often forced to hide even after crossing the border separating Klounkovan lands from the rest of Europe, even as he traveled back to England, shadowed as he was by a small, independent band of Klouns who believed exile too lax a punishment for Corbin's crime and betrayal.

Once he returned to England, Corbin continued to perform under different names and bearing different guises, and in time developed a system of training others in the movement arts of Klouns. Every week until his death, a small group of men (no more than ten at any given time) would gather at night and in secret in the chill and damp fields on the outskirts of town to learn Corbin's craft. While these men's movements paled in comparison to those of the original Klouns, and could not compete even with the inestimable power and abilities of Corbin himself, they continued to practice his craft nonetheless, and passed on his knowledge to others, and their descendants continue to perform even today, having, over time, outnumbered and then replaced the race of Klouns, which disappeared some few years after Corbin's death and whose storied past has long since been forgotten.

The Sounds of
Early Morning

She sat up in bed but couldn't find her husband, then found him lying ("Poor exhausted bunny") on the floor at the foot of the bed, the surgical mask still wrapped around his head, twisting around to cup not his mouth but his ear. If she squinted at him, he looked scrubbed and fresh and like a boy playing doctor, but she had to squint.

How funny, she thought. *How absolutely wonderful.*

Moving through the house to the kitchen, she noticed the cracks in the wall were bigger today than they had been the day before. They would have to move soon, or else repaint.

In the living room, the dog was barking, and though she couldn't hear him, the force of his barks made her chest feel rubbery and beat upon, and so she moved quickly through the room, crouching behind the couch so that its cushions, already torn beyond repair, would absorb the brunt of the animal's timbral and violent voice.

There were still dangers, she decided. And if her husband continued to refuse to send the dog away, something else might have to be done. For their own protection.

Once she had made it through the living room and into the kitchen, forgetting for the moment that her ears were protected, she moved gingerly among the items on the counter and the appliances in the cabinets, lifting pots and pans by two fingers instead of four, cracking the breakfast eggs the old way, wrapped in nonreactive plastic towels, rolling them under a heavy, padded, cast-iron pin so that the shells were crushed fine, would not be as noticeable when eaten. She had become so adept at her routine, so careful, so quiet, that it wasn't until she dropped a dish that she remembered being protected, remembered her husband's tiny knife, the sharp pains, and now the blessed, blessed silence.

She smiled.

❋

The first task, she decided, was to take care of the dog. She was reluctant, but she couldn't rightly avoid the dog forever.

She wrapped herself in her afghan. She tightened her hood. She wore her mittens. The dog had chewed the goggles into a useless mess, so she approached him with her eyes closed, rapidly blinking at intervals to check her progress, his movements. Grabbing him, she covered his snout and threw him outside, and then beat him back with her voice until, with what she imagined was a whimper, he scuttled off. Better, she would explain to her husband, than cutting its vocal cords. No need to be cruel, she would explain. Can't leave the poor thing defenseless.

Then she made the bed.

She did so stepping carefully over and around her husband.

She hoped her screams hadn't caused him serious harm. His skull had always been soft, delicate. Normally he wore hats, hats she had knit for him out of a fibrous copper material he'd brought home for her after the last time he had gone scavenging. He should have worn one of his hats before he performed the operation. She should have reminded him, but in her excitement, she'd forgotten all about it. All about him.

She finished the bed and then looked at her husband, still on the floor, still breathing, but only barely, and she worried.

In an hour, she thought. *If he is not awake in an hour, I will wake him.*

She fixed herself a cup of coffee, and moved to the back porch. So much time had passed since either of them had dared step outside that the vines had brambled—perhaps a defense mechanism—across the patio furniture, so that it took her not a few snips with her shears to cut out a space for sitting. She carried the afghan outside with her, just in case. One can never be too careful. A swooping, cawing blackbird. Claps of thunder. Yelling, rambling children. Very real dangers, all of them. But, in truth, she didn't expect to use the blanket and was, after a moment, quite frustrated at herself for being so cautious, for bringing it along at all. It snagged on the thorns.

After a time, her coffee went cold. The wind picked up and was, no doubt, howling. She could feel the sound of it against her cheek. Rather than cover herself, though, she gave up on the morning and, back inside, sat down to wait for the afternoon.

Her husband looked vulnerable, like a pile of leaves. He still hadn't woken, but his lips moved slightly when she moved him from the floor to the bed. She tied him there, anchored him to the bedpost. She removed the mask from his face and covered his ears with the pieces of foil left on the nightstand. *Too little too late*, she thought to herself. She set his head against a pillow and pulled the sheets to his chin. She pinched his nose, hoping he might wake. He had been against the operation from the very beginning, and now she was afraid he might have been right. They had torn through twelve notebooks arguing back and forth about it, until, finally, she had worn him down.

She lightly touched the bruises on his cheekbone, bare patches high on his face, which had not been quite protected by the mask. She mussed his hair, careful not to pull any of it out. He had been against the operation, but he hadn't offered any other viable solutions. They had already replaced three windows, and this in just the past week. The dog could not be placated and had become so harmfully loud, neither of them could approach him without suffering bruises and cuts. Children from other neighborhoods and looters, with all their shouts and threats, their powerful voices shuddering chips of paint and loose pieces of drywall onto their heads—the world had become wholly unpredictable and loud. She and her husband had to do something.

She looked at her husband, at his bruises, his cuts, his now misshapen nose. It had been such a nice nose. She touched his cheek. She pressed the flat part of her palm against it. She pushed his head gently to the side. She could get a mirror, she thought. She could find her compact in her purse and hold it under his nose, like she had seen someone do once in a movie, although in the movie the man was trying to make sure a person was dead, and she would be trying to make sure a person was alive.

She shook him softly by the shoulder. She wanted him to wake up. She wanted him to wake up and to make her believe everything was going to be okay. She pressed her hands into his stomach, leaned into him, not too much, just enough to make him open his mouth, to force air out of him, to elicit even the smallest breathy rasp of his voice. But even if he had made a sound (and maybe he did), she wouldn't have been able to hear it. And then the reality of this—she couldn't hear anything at all—slowly became real to her.

My, I'm jumpy, she said.

She said this thinking she should at least be able to hear her own voice inside her own head.

Anxious, she said.

Anxious, she said again.

Anxious, she said. And again. Louder. And louder. Straining her throat. Yelling, screaming.

She closed her eyes and cupped her hands over her ears as if she were in a concert hall and yelled as loud as she possibly could. Tried to imagine what her voice, so loud, might sound like.

Nothing.

She opened her eyes then, and, seeing what was left now of her husband's face, she let out a small gasp and then covered her mouth, afraid even the softest sound might ruin him beyond repair.

◊

Housework, her mother always said. Tidy up your house, tidy up your soul.

So she moved into the bathroom. Scrubbing the grout, tearing mildewed strips from the shower curtain, polishing the marble countertops—these actions calmed her. But.

She rather missed the dog now. She wouldn't quite admit it, but she rather missed the noise.

She wouldn't mind, she decided, even if one of the children or a looter came to stand outside and shout at the walls.

Then, after a moment, she realized that they just might be outside that very moment and that, unless she looked, she would never know.

So she looked. And sure enough, eight boys stood in a semicircle in the front yard. Their shouts, amplified (or so she imagined) by hollowed-out plastic drinking cups, warmed the air around her house. Standing on the porch, she removed her sweater.

They must be very young, she thought. *Their voices haven't changed, or else they are hoarse from hours of shouting, weeks of shouting.* The damage their voices caused was negligible.

Still, the grass at their feet browned, and the plants closest to them wilted under the weight of their breath. It was obvious they were trying their best. But in the end, their wasted efforts only depressed her further.

⊙

Dressed in her space suit, she walked protected through the neighborhood for the first time in months. She waved at her neighbors' houses. She smiled at the sunshine. Twice, she stopped her walk to bend down to the earth and unroot the small blades of grass pushing through cracks in the sidewalk.

If looters whistled at her, she took no notice. One or two children ran up to her, throwing their voices at her, and then ran away, unsettled, frightened when nothing happened, when she showed neither sign of fear or anger.

The suit wasn't meant for space, she knew, but *space suit* had become a loving term between her and her husband. *Put on your space suit and we can sit outside,* he'd say. *Let's put on our suits so we can make love.*

There were no real space suits, just as there was no real space.

But before, even wearing the suit, even wearing two suits, she wouldn't have dared walk outside for such a prolonged time. No matter how protected her body, no amount of fabric or material could protect her ears. The small predatory birds, in order to survive, had learned the construction of angles and reflection, refraction of sound that could pierce even the most secure ear-covers. Furthermore, the rustle of leaves, the crack of twigs, the rushing sound of a strong wind—any of these could be harmful, or fatal, even.

How the children and the looters had survived these past few months, she never managed to discover.

◉

The wind swept tattered pieces of soundproofing and insulation past her and down the street. She looked at the other houses surrounding hers, which seemed as cracked and chipped and crumbling as her own. At one point, a small bird fell from the sky to land just feet away from her, knocked unconscious, she assumed, only then to be jawed by an emaciated cat, which must have screeched and hissed the bird out of the sky. She had hoped getting out of the house would have done her some good, calmed her down, made her feel somehow less guilty, but being a witness to all of this had only exhausted and saddened her. She was glad her husband couldn't have come with her.

She had decided to turn around and walk home then, to go back to him, to tend to him as best she could, when something struck her in the small of her back. She turned around, startled, expecting to see someone with a bullhorn or some other voice amplifier, something strong that could punch through her suit. Instead she saw a huddle of boys with rocks and sticks, made timid by the unfamiliar speed of thrown objects. They stood silent at her. Then, one of the boys lifted his hand and threw, his rock glancing her shoulder, then another boy, and then the rush of them, like a dam bursting open, each of them picking up new stones or collecting those already thrown, flooding over her, each with his mouth closed.

The Artist's Voice

I.

I first met Karl Abbasonov after he had been transferred
from the small paralytic ward of a privately owned Episco-
pal hospital, St. Ann's, located in upstate New York, to an
assisted living apartment back in Texas, the state where he
was born, and where he is cared for by a rotating staff of
three nurses and occasionally transferred to a sanatorium
whenever his health takes a drastic turn for the worse.

His first words to me, after I introduced myself, were,
"You are an ill-used clarinet."

Abbasonov's voice is rich, deeply timbralled, and surprisingly strong. Abbasonov speaks slowly and often tends
to overenunciate, and the letters of each word round out
smoothly, as if themselves part of a song or a melody. He
does not look at you when he speaks because the muscles in
his neck (the semispinalis capitis, the semispinalis cervicis,
the multifidi, and the rotatores) cannot move and because

his ciliary muscles (those muscles of the eye whose contraction changes the shape of the lens to accommodate objects
of varying distances away) also cannot move, and so he does
not know what anyone looks like, hasn't known in almost
twenty years, and his best judge of people, how he remem-
bers who is speaking to him or who is in the room with him
without ever seeing the person's face, is through the sound
of the person's voice, and when he or she does not speak,
then by the tone of the person's breath. Abbasonov claims
to hear every sound as a note, and cannot abide large crowds
of people (the kind one might find in restaurants, at bus sta-
tions, cocktail parties, or rock concerts), the din of their
speech a cacophony of flats, sharps, discords, and sad melodies of songs he does not wish to remember.

The muscles in his body, all of them, are by now so
tightly contracted that his heart beats and his lungs breathe
with the aid of a small metallic box, Abbasonov's Gray Box,
created for him by Nicholas Tremmont. Tremmont refuses
to take full credit for the design and construction of Abbasonov's Gray Box. "The original idea was his," said Tremmont, when I spoke to him at his office, "and he's the one
who approached me about its design, maybe fifteen years
ago. He'd sketched out something very minor and vague on
the back of a cocktail napkin, and the lines were shaky
because, I found out later, he'd just started working on the
piece that he's been working on for twenty, twenty-five years
now. I took an interest in the idea of a small box that could
not just monitor the heart, lungs, stomach, kidneys, what
have you, but also make them function simultaneously, like

they do when controlled by the human nervous system. It took over ten years to finish even a prototype, and it's lucky for him, too, I guess, that I even got that out, and that when we plugged him into it, the whole damn thing started working right, though there were a couple of bugs right at first."

Like what? I asked him.

"Well, for one thing, we didn't think of installing a surge protector, and that first night an electrical storm blew in from the southwest, which, though nothing happened, gave us both a big scare. What really scared us, or me, since I never told him exactly what almost happened, is that I'd miswired the heart mechanism at first, and only realized my mistake just before plugging him in; if I hadn't, I'd have had his heart drawing in blood—all the blood all at once, all of it to his heart—which, most likely, would have caused his heart to burst from the pressure." The box, still just an early prototype, manages to control all internal muscular functions—the pumping of blood, the circulation of oxygen, the excretion of waste—but is not sophisticated enough to de-contract or relax the musculoskeletal system whose near-permanent contraction relegates Abbasonov to a wheelchair. With this knowledge, it is surprising that Abbasonov is still alive, but even more surprising that he is able to speak, a fact which has, until just recently, confounded every doctor in America and Europe who has treated or tried to treat his affliction.

II.

Isailo Abbasonov moved to Ben Ficklin, Texas, in 1938.

In the late fall of 1936, he and his wife, Fabia, left their home in Albania on a steamer bound for New York City. They spent two years in New York, where Isailo, a skilled accountant, worked as a line cook in a Russian kitchen, and Fabia worked as a housekeeper, washing clothes and dusting bric-a-brac. Then the two moved to the small town of Ben Ficklin, where Isailo's uncle, Milorad, lived and made decent money constructing crude machinery that was then shipped to Mexico and used to sew rough-hewn blankets and trousers for the campesinos to wear while working in the fields picking cotton.

Less than six weeks after their arrival, Milorad died, bitten by a rattlesnake while demonstrating to Isailo how the thick material of the machine-produced trousers protected workers from burs, thorns, scorpion stings, and snakebites.

Isailo, who knew nothing about metalwork or simple construction, who had in fact been called down to Texas to help his uncle with the accounting side of his growing business, suddenly found himself in charge of an operation that consisted of a house-sized garage littered with greased machinery—cogs, springs, belts, the like—and a small staff of four. His uncle, afraid that his workers, after learning the design of his machine, would steal the design and leave his workshop to start their own businesses, taught each man how to build only one-fourth of the entire apparatus, the four separate parts then pieced together by Milorad himself, in secret. No one, it turned out, knew exactly how to connect the four parts into one whole. After six weeks, the machine parts still not fitted together, Isailo was forced to fire the four men who had worked for his uncle and close the machine shop.

By this time, Fabia was pregnant. "It was a tough time for my parents, then," Abbasonov told me. "My dad found another job as a line cook, and my mom had gone back to work cleaning houses, and she did that until about the time I was born, and then went back to it less than a month after, and since they couldn't afford to pay anyone to take care of me, she took me with her. The thing was, my father could have worked as an accountant, but nobody would hire him in the States, at least not in Texas, until they had some proof, some certification that he wouldn't run off with their money. He was from Albania, and no one in Texas had heard of Albania, knew what Albania was. Most of them thought, because of his color, because of his features, that he was some mixture of Mexican and black, although nobody thought it strange that he didn't know how to speak Spanish. But that's how he found work as a cook, because everyone thought he was mestizo. He was working the morning shift cooking breakfast for field hands, county deputies, and farmers." A small amount of luck befell Isailo when the restaurant owner's husband, who managed the restaurant's finances, was bedridden by a stroke that incapacitated the left side of his body. In order to care for her husband, the owner considered closing the restaurant, but Isailo, unwilling to look for yet another job, offered to work extra hours managing the office for free if she could find someone to run the kitchen and the restaurant floor.

Three years later, Isailo bought the restaurant from the owner, who moved her husband to Santa Fe, New Mexico, in hopes that the heat and the dry air might better suit his physical needs.

"After that, my mother quit cleaning houses, and the three of us spent most of our time there, at the diner. Most of my memories are of time spent in the restaurant, in the kitchen sitting on a worktable, or on the floor behind the counter. It was called the Olympia Diner, after the woman who owned it, and my father never changed the name. He never changed the menu, either, and when he painted the dining room walls or retiled the kitchen floor, he kept the same colors and the same pattern, the same tile, the same everything. One year, the owner—this was after her husband died—came back to visit her family, and she stopped by the restaurant to see what my father had done to it, and when she saw that it was almost exactly the same, she started to cry. She didn't sob or gush or anything like that, but there were tears in her eyes that sometimes slipped down her cheek and made her face wet. She didn't know what to say. She ordered a cup of coffee and a piece of pecan pie, and when my father wouldn't let her pay for either, she just stood up from the counter and left. That was the last we saw of her."

Just before their son's eighth birthday, Abbasonov's parents sold the Olympia, and the three of them moved to Dallas, Texas, where they used the money from the sale of the restaurant and the money that Fabia had saved to buy a house, a piano, and to pay for piano lessons for Karl, who had been begging his parents for music lessons since the age of four.

III.

The 1693 edition of Blancard's *Physical Dictionary* contained the first written record or mention of tinnitus aurium, defining it as "a certain Buzzing or tingling in the Ears." The American Tinnitus Association (founded in 1971) further defines tinnitus as "the perception of ringing, hissing, or other sound in the ears or head when no external sound is present." According to statistics collected by the ATA, an estimated 50 million Americans suffer from some varying degree of tinnitus, and over 16 million Americans suffer from tinnitus to such a degree that normal, day-to-day living becomes impossible.

The human ear is divided into three main regions: the sound-collecting outer ear, the sound-transmitting middle ear, and the sensory inner ear. The outer ear is separated from the middle ear by the tympanic membrane, and the middle ear is, in turn, separated from the inner ear by membranous fenestrae. The sound-collecting compartment of the outer ear is conical and called the pinna. This cone functions poorly for most people, which is why the elderly may cup their hands to their ears when they want to improve their hearing. The middle ear specializes in transmitting the sound from the outer ear to the oval window opening of the inner ear through the vibration of movable bones called ossicles. The inner ear then conducts this information to the receptor neurons.

The inner ear serves a second function (through the intricate vestibular system), which is to tell the rest of your body where your head is and what it is doing at all times. The vestibular system satisfies this function through two main processes: angular acceleration, necessary for shaking or nodding your head, and linear acceleration, necessary for detecting motion along a line, such as when an elevator drops beneath you.

The auditory and vestibular systems are intimately connected; the receptors for both are located in the temporal bone in the inner ear, in a convoluted chamber called the bony labyrinth. A continuous membrane is suspended within the bony labyrinth, which creates a second chamber within the first, called the membranous labyrinth. The inner ear has two membrane-covered outlets into the middle ear—the oval window and the round window. The inner ear and the middle ear are connected through the oval window by a small bone, the stapes, which vibrates in response to vibrations of the eardrum, and which then sets the fluid of the inner ear, called perilymph, sloshing back and forth, which in turn causes the round window to vibrate in a complementary rhythm. The membranous labyrinth, caught between the oval window and the round window, bounces up and down in all the sloshing.

Located within this sloshing mess is the organ of Corti, which rests on the part of the membranous labyrinth called the basilar membrane, and it is here, finally, where the trans-duction of sound into neural signals occurs. Auditory hair cells sit within the organ of Corti—inner hair cells, which are the auditory receptors, and outer hair cells, which help to "fine-tune" the pulses of sound. The sensitive stereocilia (sensory hairs) of the inner hair cells are embedded in a membrane called the tectorial membrane. As the membra-nous labyrinth bounces up and down, the basilar membrane bounces up and down, and the fine stereocilia are sheared back and forth. When the stereocilia are pulled in the right direction, the hair cell depolarizes and releases a signal. This signal is transmitted to a nerve process lying under the organ of Corti, and is then transmitted back along the auditory nerve to the brainstem, where it is read, finally, as under-standable sound—car horns, voices, jet engines, or music.

But why should any of this matter?

Bear with me for just a moment longer.

The outer hair cells of the organ of Corti help to "sharpen the tuning" of the frequencies of sounds we hear. Outer hair cells can change length in response to nerve stimulation. By pushing the basilar membrane up and down, the outer hair cells can amplify or dampen vibrations, making the inner hair cells more responsive or less responsive. The theory, then, is that if the outer hair cells can move the basilar mem-brane (and it has been proven that they can), then they can, in special cases, also move the oval window, and then, pos-sibly, the eardrum. And in severe cases, by shifting the eardrum, the outer hair cells can make the ear work in reverse so that the ear acts, in essence, not like a receiver, but, rather, a speaker. Even before Abbasonov, there have been many cases in the history of medicine of a patient complaining of persistent whispering in her ear, dismissed as crazy until an obliging doctor finally places his stethoscope to her ear and listens, only to discover that he can hear the whispering, too. It is this phenomenon, of the ear reversing roles, that most doctors use to account for the constant ringing or roaring that plagues sufferers of tinnitus.

What I have just presented here is almost word for word the same anatomical lesson I was given by Dr. Larry Franklin, a tall, emaciated, and young professor at the Washington University School of Medicine, who was, according to most experts, the first doctor to understand and then explain how it is that Karl Abbasonov can not only speak, but speak well, even though every muscle in his body is contorted in such a way that even the simple act of breathing is, for him, performed by a machine. At the end of the lesson I was, to be honest, almost afraid to ask the next logical question:

"So, Dr. Franklin, what does all that mean?"

"What does it mean?" he said. "Well, simply put, it means that Karl Abbasonov communicates, verbally, through his ears."

IV.

The piano in Karl Abbasonov's living room is an old, wood-finished Steinway upright. The legs are scratched, and there are spots along the body and on the bench and on the lid where the finish has been rubbed away. "Those come from water damage," Abbasonov told me. "My mother had a goldfish in a small fishbowl on the top of the piano for a while—which, in hindsight, doesn't make much sense—and I accidentally broke the bowl against the wall, sometime during my Beethoven phase, a year or so into my piano lessons." He paused for a moment before concluding: "I was very exuberant about Beethoven."

His parents had bought the piano from a woman who had wanted to learn but who had quit playing after just three lessons. No one plays the old piano anymore, as most of the hammers have been worn away through Abbasonov's exuberance, but he has kept it as a memento of his parents, his childhood. On more than one occasion, a music fanatic or a freak show fetishist has offered to buy Abbasonov's old piano from him, and one woman from Wyoming once offered to buy, for fifteen thousand dollars, his entire collection of piano lesson books, the kind of by-rote scale books used by elementary school children when first learning to play. Abbasonov's, the ones he showed me, looked untouched.

Abbasonov's piano and piano books, however, aren't the only thing collectors and museums have requested. The Mütter Museum in Philadelphia has offered, in the event of Karl's untimely or unexpected or, even, natural death, to preserve his body in the exact position in which it is left at the time of his passing. And though they have assured him of "star treatment"—his own exhibit complete with a piano and copies (if not the originals) of his musical scores—they haven't offered him any financial compensation.

"I haven't told them one way or the other yet. Partly I like to string them along, but mostly I just don't think about it. Really, in the end, all of that will be left up to either Dr. Franklin or Dr. Johnson. Though I'm pretty sure one of them will keep the piano and at least some of my old music books and all of my own music. But who knows what they'll do with me."

His parents and his first piano teachers faced a similar problem—What should we do with Karl?—once he began taking piano lessons. He started with a forty-five minute lesson once every week, on Wednesday nights. Western music comprises twelve diatonic major scales and twelve diatonic minor scales. Of the minor scales, there are three different variants—melodic, harmonic, and natural. The natural minor scale is, note for note, the same scale as a major scale, except that it begins with a different starting tone and results in a different interval pattern. These forty-eight scales are the standard for Western tonality, formed and used extensively between the seventeenth and nineteenth centuries. In the six days between his first lesson and his second lesson, Abbasonov had mastered the complete range of diatonic scales, all forty-eight of them, this after being taught only the very first, C major. His piano teacher, after she heard him run flawlessly over each, was speechless. His parents increased his lessons to two a week. After a month, though, he had to find a new piano teacher, one more advanced and who might be able to keep up with him. Three months after that, Abbasonov moved away from piano teachers altogether and moved into the Southern Methodist University's conservatory program, where he took daily lessons from professors of musicology, music theory, and advanced piano, and where he first took up the violin.

"I was in heaven. I felt so completely submerged in music. There I was, an eight-year-old kid who didn't have to go to school but for a half day, who could spend his days around instruments and around music. Sheets and sheets of music. I've always been a fair sight reader, and so I used to play through whatever I got my hands on. It frustrated my teachers no end, because I would jump from new piece to new piece, and it took all of their energy to get me to focus enough on one piece to really polish my performance. But after a while, they just let me go, figuring that I was only eight and that I would settle down with age. I didn't care what was placed in front of me, I would play through it, and maybe play through it again if it had been particularly difficult, like a Rachmaninoff or a Liszt, both of whom had larger than average hands and much larger hands than mine, and so I had to improvise while playing their music to get the full range of sound that they could produce. Life was perfect, and sometimes I like to think that, if I hadn't been introduced to music composition, life would have stayed that way, but I'm sure, after a while, I'd have stumbled into composition on my own, and then it would have happened anyway."

The "it" happened just before he reached his tenth birthday, when one of his professors gave him a small book of blank score sheets "for those melodies, he told me, running through my head that might be mine and that might be lost if they're not written down. At first, I didn't know what he was talking about, had become so caught up in Bartók and Mozart and Schubert to even think about my own notes, but then, once the notion was pointed out to me, the notes just followed. That's when I had my first seizure. A short one, to be sure, since the melody I thought out was short and simple, very much a nine-year-old melody, so it was less of a seizure, more of a stiffening, and not throughout my whole body, but in my shoulders. Back then, it always started at the base of my neck and in my shoulders."

Abbasonov never thought much about his stiff joints and minor seizures. It was, in fact, his parents who noticed their son shuffling through the house in a slightly hunched and stiff-hipped manner. When they asked him about it, he shrugged them off, told them he was busy, that he was in the middle of thinking through a song, that he had almost fin-ished it, and that he needed to start writing it out. When he came back out of his bedroom, the piece finished, he would be fine and fluid again, and he would claim that he didn't know anything about the way he was walking, and, no, he didn't remember being in pain.

"The next time, though—long before we figured out that it was in any way connected to music—I had started work on a scherzo, playful and fun, but longer and more compli-cated than anything else I'd tried to compose, and then it was unignorable, unavoidable. I couldn't get out of bed, and after a while, I couldn't move even my eyelids. My parents had no idea what was wrong with me. The doctor, when he came to the house, couldn't figure it out, either, other than to say that I'd had some sort of fit or seizure. They hooked me up to an IV so that I could get food and water, had a nurse come to the house to stay with me, because no one knew what this was, much less how long this was going to last. I'd been working on the piece for about two weeks, and I wasn't bedridden until the last three or four days. It was a longer score, but not that long, really. And so, I wasn't even scrunched up, nothing like the way I am now. I was just flat on my back, stiff as a board, stuck in bed, while I ran through the music in my head.

"I knew, part of me knew, that what was going on was caused by the music in my head, but I didn't want to think about it that way. Instead, I thought that the music was what was helping me through these strange seizures, thought that I was occupying myself by thinking about the music and nothing else but the music, and that if I could make it through this melody in my head, see it all the way through, picture exactly how it should sound, then I would pull myself, or the music would pull me, through this seizure, and the next seizure, and the next."

Soon, however, the seizures began to attack Abbasonov with alarming frequency.

Karl Abbasonov is one of five known sufferers of the musculoskeletal and neuropsychological disease locomotor ataxia agitans libertætis. In this affliction, a kernel of an idea infects the brain, like the spore of a fungus might infect the brain of an ant. In Abbasonov's case, this spore comes in the form of an original piece of music—and as the kernel grows, neurotoxins develop that in turn affect either norepinephrine or acetylcholine (the doctors aren't sure which in these cases), causing these neurotransmitters to send incorrect impulses across incorrect synapses. This causes a slow and simultaneous arthritis, contraction, or paralysis to occur, so that the body, in effect, involuntarily contorts. Visually, if one were to video record and then watch it at a higher speed, the progression of this disease, from the time the kernel enters the brain through to the final contortions of the body, resembles the wilting of a flower or a weed under a hot sun.

The first known case of locomotor ataxia agitans libertætis was described in late 1942 by Dr. Phillip Koepkind. His patient was one Adam Shy, a minor artist whose paintings were acrylic abstracts, angular and uncomfortable to look at, done in browns, blacks, and reds, each one a tightly concentrated patch of colors and lines roughly the size of a quarter, sometimes as large as a silver dollar, painted onto unusually oversized canvases. Dr. Koepkind found that hypnotism and subliminal suggestion partially cured Adam Shy, whose artistic endeavors paralyzed the left side of his body from the neck down, and his entire body from the waist down. "In the course of a month," wrote Koepkind in 1944, "not once did Shy suffer from what had, before treatment, become almost hourly paralytic attacks. It seems, however, that the suppression, through hypnotic suggestion, of Shy's artistic urges must be maintained through monthly sessions, otherwise the urge to produce slowly resurfaces and the paralytic attacks return."

Although Abbasonov has been through over ten hypnotic sessions with six different hypnotherapists, psychologists, and musico-therapists, he still has not lost the urge, the need to compose.

V.

Of the two doctors most invested in the case of Karl Abbasonov, Dr. Johnson and Dr. Franklin, Franklin has known him, or of him, the longest.

Dr. Larry Franklin knew of Karl Abbasonov long before the two ever met. Dr. Franklin's mother, June, a recently retired piano teacher and the current conductor of the church choir in Larry Franklin's hometown, considers Karl Abbasonov one of the greatest American composers of the twentieth century—June and Karl were friends during high school.

"Once," she told me, "he wrote me a song during algebra class. Took him about five seconds, scribbling it on the back of one of our pop quizzes. I've still got it here, somewhere, in the attic or in a box, I'm sure. I remember, though, on the quiz he'd gotten a D. And on the back, he'd written me this short little trill of a song, like a birdcall, in the key of D." Puckering her lips, she whistled for me a thrilling conversation of notes that sounded, truly, like a birdcall. "Of course, I didn't read music back then. Didn't know what he'd given me, and when I asked him about it, he just smiled and said

I'd have to figure it out for myself. Really, that's why I started taking piano lessons. I took the little scrap of music to the school's music teacher to ask her what it was, and she played it for me on the piano. I liked the sound of it fine, but just listening to it, I didn't feel satisfied. I wanted to know how to connect what he'd written on the page to what the music teacher had played on the piano, so I asked her to teach me the notes so that I could play them, too. After she did, well, I just fell into the trap, and I'm still playing piano to this day."

Abbasonov left school before June could play for him what she'd learned. "He just stopped coming to classes. He'd been sick for a while, on and off, always in the nurse's office, and then his parents sent him down to Houston for some special surgery or something, and after that, he just stopped coming to school altogether.

"I went off to college, received my degree from North Texas State, music pedagogy, and that's where I met Richard, and the two of us were married just after we graduated, and then we moved to Oregon. We settled down, and then Larry came along. By then, I was teaching students out of the house. My life had settled and I was happy, but I never really stopped thinking about Karl. Every once in a while, I would walk through record stores looking for Glenn Gould, or Horowitz, but also, in the back of my mind, hoping that I'd see Karl's name on a compilation tape or on a record, the composer of some Hollywood score, anything, but I never found a recording of his music. Not in Oregon, anyway. I once flew out to New York for a music conference, and while there, I found this small, eclectic classical records store, and

I stumbled across one recording of him, but it was him playing Bach fugues, and to be honest, it wasn't all that good. I
don't know if I even still have it."

Abbasonov recorded that album in October of 1969 on a
small label that no longer exists. The year is important to
Abbasonov. That year, in February or March, he began composing his most ambitious score to date. Before then, he had
been writing pieces for string quartets or short symphonies
or complex piano pieces. They were light and playful and,
God willing, short. He hadn't produced anything, anyway,
that had taken more than a few weeks, or at most a month,
to compose in his head, for he is unable to begin writing
the piece out until it has been finished inside of his head, and
the longer it remains there, the more complex the piece is, the
more his body works against itself. At the time of his Bach
recording, however, he had been working on the same piece
of music for over six months.

"Frankly," he told me, "I don't even know how I recorded
that session. We laid it down in one take, and I haven't listened to it but two or three times my whole life, mainly
because, even knowing the circumstances, I think it's awful,
but what I do remember is that the end of the session sounds
smoother, sounds more controlled than the beginning of the
session. I think that by the end I was concentrating so hard
on making my fingers play through Bach's fugues, which are
complex and brilliant, that, for a moment, I forgot about my
own work." I asked him how he was able to play at all, for
surely after six months of composing his body must have
been almost fully paralyzed. "My arms and hands have

always been the last part of my body to even begin to stiffen, and I'd never worked on a piece long enough for them to freeze up completely," he said. "And then—a good friend of mine set up the sessions, and after he saw how I was, he rigged up a studio that made it possible for me to play without sitting up or moving anything but my hands. The studio looked bent out of shape, had been made into some weird contraption of pulleys and rope and levers, and in the middle, hanging from the ceiling, impossibly, was a piano. A Steinway grand, six feet, nine inches. I've got pictures somewhere."

And so he recorded Bach and then June bought it, and, even though she didn't like the recording, she felt compelled to reconnect with Karl Abbasonov. She called the record label, and they gave her an address. She mailed him a letter. Two weeks later she received, instead of a reply, sheets and sheets of music. "All of them Karl's, all of them short pieces. Scherzos, mazurkas, piano exercises, compositions for strings, some concertos, some pieces for harpsichord, even small, complete operas. But everything short. Even the two or three symphonies, minutes long. And yet some of them so complex, I still can't figure them out. Piano pieces that seem meant for two or three pianos, string quartets that feel made for full orchestras. I still haven't figured out the real complex stuff, but some of the simpler pieces I play over and over again. Some of the exercises—the simplest ones, anyway—I gave to my students. But mostly, I played Karl's piano pieces for Larry when he was younger."

VI.

I met Dr. Harold Johnson at a small medical convention held
in Austin, Texas, some few weeks after my initial meetings
with Dr. Larry Franklin and his mother. Dr. Johnson is cur-
rently the resident director at Baylor University Medical
Center of Dallas. I mentioned that I was interested in his
thoughts on the Karl Abbasonov case and made an appointment with him for breakfast at one of the small taquerias
along Congress Avenue. After we ordered, I explained to
him Dr. Franklin's theory about Abbasonov's ears, and then
I asked him for his opinion on the matter.

"Bull. Shit" were the first words out of Dr. Johnson's
mouth.

Dr. Johnson graduated in 1967 from Rice University and
then entered Baylor College of Medicine in 1970. After graduation, he moved to Boston, where he completed his resi-
dency, and then moved to New York, where he lived for four
years and where he practiced neurosurgery at St. Luke's Hospital. He is a big, bull-necked man with a large voice and large,
Texas-sized hands that, when they grab your own hands in a
handshake, are surprisingly soft and quick, as well as strong.
"Bull. Shit," he repeated. "That's exactly what I would've told
you a year ago, hell, six months ago, if you'd come in here
with some damn fool idea about Karl talking out his goddamn ears. 'Cause that's exactly what I told Lare [Dr. Frank-
lin] when he came in here and explained the whole thing to

me. Hell, we can call him up right now and you can ask him yourself. He'll tell you my exact words. Bull. Shit. But he wouldn't let go of the idea, and just kept pestering me about it until, finally, he said, 'Look, Harold, if you don't believe me, we can just go test the goddamn theory out right now.' I'll tell you, that boy makes a powerful and persuasive case."

Dr. Johnson became interested in Karl Abbasonov while living in Manhattan. In 1989, Abbasonov's partner, Annie Ashbury, contacted the ten best neurosurgeons living and working in New York City, and Johnson was number ten on her list. The ten of them were invited to Abbasonov's apartment, where they were served lunch and cocktails. All of the doctors knew one another, but only one of them, Dr. Richard Iovinelli, had ever met Karl Abbasonov or Annie Ashbury, and during lunch and over drinks, the other nine surgeons plied him for details about their mysterious host. It wasn't until after cocktails that Abbasonov made his appearance.

"The whole time we were there," Dr. Johnson told me, "eating lunch and having a quiet drink, we'd been listening to music over some speakers. Short, tense, complex music. Never heard anything like it, wasn't sure who it was, or when it was from. Turned out it was Karl's stuff, and Annie had put it on for us, but then, before she wheeled Karl into the room, she must've turned it off.

"It was quite a shock to see him. It seemed that Karl had worsened since the last time Richard had seen him, so even he was pretty quiet there for a while, just looking at poor old Karl. Supposedly, nobody knows for sure these days, the man stands at about six-two, six-three, and there he was in that wheelchair, taking up the space of a four-year-old, his body all wound in tight, except for his left arm, which for some reason had contracted differently from the rest of him, so that it stuck out of him, like a dead tree trunk sticking up out of the ground.

"They had this crazy idea of some kind of tag-team surgery, where the ten of us would work nonstop in shifting rotations, trying to rewire his whole damn system. If you ask me, certainly not one of Annie's better ideas, though you can't blame her for trying. By that time, Karl'd been paralyzed for just over two years, and he'd been working on this piece of music for going on twenty, and it looked like he was only going to get worse, stuck in a wheelchair with that little gray box of his. Frankly, none of us figured that piece of shit to last for more than a week at the most. And she was such a nice woman, and anyone could tell just by looking at her how much she loved him, and she kept baking us cakes and cupcakes and muffins. So it broke our hearts to have to tell her that it wouldn't work, the ten of us digging around in there at different times, during different stages of the operation—too much possibility of error. And for a while after we told her no, Annie stopped talking to us altogether, all ten of us, and it wasn't but a few years ago that she called me up out of the blue one day after she found out I'd moved down to Texas. Karl, you know, is from Texas, and this was when they first started thinking of moving him back home. Of course, then, six months later, she passed away. Funny how, with all that attention we were paying to Karl, none of us knew a damn thing about Annie's condition—heart murmurs, high blood pressure—makes sense that the stress of caring for Karl would catch up to her, but still, it took us all by surprise."

Dr. Johnson was quiet for a moment, tipping back the last dregs of his coffee. "Nice woman," he said. "True salt of the earth."

Then I asked for the check, and despite my objections, Dr. Johnson paid the tab. As we were walking out of the restaurant, I couldn't get the nagging feeling out of my head that something was missing still.

"But wait," I said. "You're telling me that Dr. Franklin's theory holds up?"

"Holds up? Oh, hell yeah. No mistake. It's the only theory that makes any sense. I might've been skeptical at first, but that little bastard Franklin's right. Karl's talking out his goddamn ears. The only thing left to figure out is how the hell it all works—does he talk out of both ears or just one? Is there some kind of internal, neural mechanism that lets him talk one minute and listen the next, kind of like your intercom system, or what? And then, how do those synapses connect? What's sending what signals and where, that kind of thing. It's funny how nobody ever really questions it, though, when they're talking to him. It's not something you think about right at first. You just talk at him and he talks back and so you know he heard you and you already know that you can hear him so it never really occurs to you to ask yourself how it all happens even though he's crumpled up like some kind of leather knot. Hell, I've known him for going on eighteen years, and it sure as hell wasn't me that said,

Hey, fellas, how the hell you think old Karl talks when he can't even move his jaw? It was Larry who first wondered about all that."

VII.

"What's funny is that even I didn't think about it." I'm sitting in Abbasonov's Texas apartment. "Nobody did. Not even Annie. And then Dr. Franklin came to the house, showed up without warning, flew in from Washington and rented a car and found the house and knocked on the door. That was when we were still living in New York."

Listening to Abbasonov, I'm trying to make myself hear the words come out of his ears, trying to make myself believe how it all really works, but the illusion of it all is too strong. I feel like a child again, handed a sheet of optical illusions— a candlestick holder or two faces? An ugly old hag or a beautiful young woman?—and, as a kid, once I knew what the second image was, I could always make it come back. But this—is he talking with his mouth, which is impossible, or does he speak through his ears, which is equally (or so I thought) impossible?—this defies my ability to reason. Furthermore, there is no physical movement to make it clear one way or the other. His ears don't flap around. His Adam's apple does not move up and down. And yet, somehow, he's talking. I can't make the first illusion fade, can't bring the second one to light, and so I give up trying.

What makes it all the more difficult, makes it worse, even, is the discomfort I feel simply looking at him. He is a painful thing to look at, wrenched into violent knots, cramped into himself, smaller now, even, more tightly constricted than when I first met him only a few weeks before. The question I want to ask him, but don't have the heart to, or don't need to because I feel like I already know the answer to it, is this: Is it worth it? This piece of music you're composing in your head, will it really be so good that it is worth all of this?

"Larry came over," he continues, "and we were surprised, Annie and I, but it was a pleasant surprise. All he said was that he wanted to run a few tests. I was used to testing by then, and Larry's always been a nice young man, so I told him that was okay, and then I asked him what he was testing me for, but he wouldn't tell me, said that he'd tell me just as soon as he was done. Then he opened a bag of cotton balls and told me not to mind him, to keep talking while he was setting things up, so I kept talking to him, mostly small talk, about his flight, about the weather, about why he was stuffing cotton into my ears."

To clarify, many people are under the false impression that Karl Abbasonov is paralyzed—that his nervous system doesn't work properly, which is correct, and that he has no sense of touch, which is incorrect. His nervous system is not deadened or numbed, but, instead, overactive, which makes his skin extremely sensitive, which is how he was able to feel the discomfort of all these cotton balls pushed into his ears.

"But he didn't say anything," Abbasonov tells me, "and he kept stuffing cotton in my ears until I guess he must have pushed ten small balls of cotton into each ear, and I told him, Look, Larry, I don't think my ears can hold another piece of cotton, but he was ignoring me, or so I thought, and anyway, he'd stopped talking to me, stopped answering my questions. And I must have been that way, twenty balls of cotton stuffed in my ears, for about ten minutes, maybe longer, until he finally took the cotton out, and it was then that I realized that he hadn't stopped talking to me but that I hadn't been able to hear him because of all the cotton. I couldn't see Annie, but I could tell something was up by the way her breathing had sped up, could tell that she was excited about something. Then Larry said to me, 'Karl, that's amazing. How do you do that, and why haven't you told anybody?' And Annie was going on about how she never even thought about it, and why didn't she notice it, and it's all so obvious that, of course, I couldn't talk with my mouth. By that time, I was thoroughly confused, which is, I think, the reaction Larry was looking for. He was pretty sure I didn't know that I didn't talk normally, and he was right. When he explained it to me, how my voice had been muffled even by the very first piece of cotton and how my voice had disappeared almost completely by the end (he claims he only put four or five pieces in each ear, but that's a lie), and that neither he nor Annie had heard me tell him to stop stuffing cotton in my ears, I was pretty excited. I mean, that's a pretty big deal, speaking out of my ears, and when you're in a condition like mine, any new development or new discovery is a big deal, so this kind of thing was huge. Funny thing is, after that, I couldn't talk for almost six months."

"Six months?" I ask him. "What happened?"

"If you play the piano," he says, "or if you play baseball, you'll see this kind of thing happen to you, sometimes more often than you'd like.

"Say you're a baseball player and you've been playing baseball since you were young, say, since you were five or six. And, as you grow older, you become a great catcher, a natural, and you've got a great arm to second, and then it happens—and I don't know why this happens, maybe someone says, 'Hey, you've got a great arm,' or says anything to you about your technique—but you start to think about what you're doing. Then you miss the throw to second. Well, you tell yourself, it was just once, nothing to worry about, but you worry about it anyway, and you miss the throw again. Now you're thinking about it more, and you're starting to really worry. And then you miss the throw to the pitcher. This is something you've been doing for almost twenty years now, something you could do with your eyes closed (and, really, that might help), and before, you'd never thought about how you were doing it, you were just doing it. And after a while, the manager tells you to put in more practice hours, and then after that, he benches you because you haven't been able to throw the ball to the pitcher in last five games. And you can't figure out what the hell happened to your arm, and you're thinking about it all the time. In your mind, you're going over the basics of throwing a baseball, techniques you learned when you were too young to know you were learning anything. The whole time, you never realize that the thinking is the problem, that your brain's getting in the way of what your body already knows how to do.

"Well, when it came to talking out of my ears, that's what happened. As soon as I found out, I thought myself out of being able to do it. It was Larry who figured that one out, too. And he came over the same way, without a word of warning, and I was depressed this time, and Annie was always crying because I couldn't say anything to her, and I could hear her, but after a while, after a few months, she had stopped talking to me because she said it was just too depressing, like she was talking to herself, or like I was dead. Larry came over with this IV bag of clear fluid—it turned out to be nothing but a sugar-water drip—but at the time, he told us it was a new drug that might loosen my muscles up, might help reconnect the nerve bundles the right way, and so he set everything up and after a few minutes, he told me to try to move—my arm or my leg or my head, or even just try to focus my eyes again, so I could see clearly—and I tried and I tried, but I couldn't get anything to move and it was frustrating, this on top of losing my voice, and Larry kept egging me on, and I wanted to tell him that I couldn't do it, that it wasn't working, and that I was worn out from the effort—my whole body was wet from sweat afterward—but I couldn't tell him anything because I couldn't get my ears to work, and then, suddenly, I was talking again. 'Goddamn it, Larry, shut the fuck up. I can't move a goddamn thing, you goddamn hack.' That's what I told him. He'll never let me forget it, either."

Since that day, Abbasonov's been able to speak clearly and effortlessly, and not once in our conversations did he stumble or falter. "Not thinking about how it worked became easier after that. And even now, talking to you about it right now, I'm not really thinking about it, not about the process, anyway. Not about any of it, really. No. For the past hour or so, I've been trying to move my right arm two inches to the left."

Henry Richard Niles:
A Meritorious Life

NILES, HENRY RICHARD (b. 1940). Poet. Place of birth: Cleveland, Ohio. Born to Polish parents, Henry Richard Niles did not speak his first words until the age of seven. Originally, his parents had assumed that their son was born deaf, but hearing tests disproved this theory, and doctors suggested that the boy's vocal cords didn't work properly. The doctors then suggested that his parents teach him to read and write, and that the best way to communicate with their son was by way of pad and pencil. Rather than subject the mute boy to the ridicule and mismanagement that he would surely encounter in any school system, whether public or private, his parents kept him at home to teach him themselves how to speak, how to read, how to write, how to calculate numbers, and the uses of shapes. Niles could understand only the basics of the Arabic numbering system, never quite cognizant of the numbers past seven, and was oddly more adept at Roman numerals. Furthermore, as a child, he was unable to work either his left or right fist around the nub of a pencil comfortably enough to scratch out those words predominant in (and necessary for) communication through the English language—*the, and, to want*—and although he was able to place vowels correctly in between consonants and was able to place consonants correctly alongside one another, the combinations formed by his hands were both illegible and indecipherable as spoken language.

Niles's first words were *oeghene lachen*. And from there, he let loose with a string of vowel sounds, grunts, and guttural whines released at an imperceptible and near constant speed. "The sound of it hurt our ears," his father said. It would be another three years before his parents would learn that his first words, when translated into English, were *eyes laughing*. Some believe this to have been Niles's first poem.

According to James Avara (*Journal of Linguistic Studies*, 1971, 46–52), Wulfila Jutes was the last speaker of the Germanic language Ostrogothic, and it is from Jutes that linguists were able to piece together the small and incomplete list of one hundred vocabulary words that we recognize and can translate today. Wulfila Jutes died sometime in the early nineteen hundreds and was by no means a fluent speaker. The last fully fluent speaker of Ostrogothic is presumed to have died over a century ago. It is now widely assumed that Henry Richard Niles is the only living fluent speaker of Ostrogothic and the first person to speak this dead language in over one hundred years.

Once the root of Niles's speaking problem had been discovered, his parents placed him with well-respected and
renowned linguists in hopes that they could 1) discover the
origins of the language that he spoke, and 2) teach Henry
Richard how to speak properly and in English, if possible,
but at the very least in French. Niles remained with the linguists from his seventh until his eighteenth birthday. Despite
intensive lessons in English, Spanish, and French, and
although perfectly fluent in each (he is more than able to
read and understand technical manuals, financial reports,
and newspaper headlines), Niles cannot express himself
(poetically) in any language other than Ostrogothic.

Armed with a vocabulary that grows daily, Niles has produced some six hundred poems, ranging in length from a
two-word verse to a one thousand–line canto, of which only
segments can be translated through the use of the one
hundred–word vocabulary list once provided by Wulfila
Jutes. Much of his poetry, when translated, looks bullet-
ridden, torn, and scooped out, though when heard in their
original language, read aloud by the author—there exists but
one recording of Niles reading a series of short poems made
twenty years ago—these same poems, while unintelligible,
have been known to make the listener weep and thereafter
dwell on a history of lost opportunities.

Cash to a Killing

We had spent the past hour burying the body and were on our way to grab a hamburger. I had been worried at first that the body would be too difficult to lift. I'd only had Roger with me, and he'd never done this sort of thing before; usually I've got two other guys, big guys, for the heavy lifting. I'm not a big guy and neither is Roger, and I've heard that deadweight is really heavy. When Roger moved, then, to the midsection of the body, wrapped his arms around the guy's waist, I told him, No way, man, you've got to pick him up from one of the ends, head end or foot end, not the middle, but Roger's always been good at ignoring whatever he doesn't want to hear, and so, when he continued with his flawed plan, straddling the body, wrapping his arms around the waist before changing his mind and grabbing the guy by his belt loops, then bending his knees—he had a bad back from when he worked at an ice-cream shop—and heaved, I expected him to topple forward, maybe land inappropriately, but humorously, on top of the guy, in a lover's embrace, you might say, or at least flip over and land flat on his back on the ground. But either Roger had been working out and was much stronger than he looked, or dead bodies are a lot lighter than everybody says they are, because Roger pulled the guy right between his legs and flipped him up over his shoulder before turning to me and asking, So, where are we going to put this guy?

I wish I could say that killing the guy was an accident, and maybe if you were to take the long view of the situation, take into account the events of his life, those of my life, of Roger's, the arbitrary successes and failures that befell the three of us, or, even further back, befell our parents and grandparents, great grands, back to our oldest ancestors, and determined that it was some accident of fate that he ended up who he was and I ended up who I am, and Roger ended up as Roger, you might say it was an accident. But taking the short view of things, we killed him deliberately and for a specific purpose. And despite Roger's argument, just because we killed the wrong guy doesn't change, for me, the fact of the matter. He was the guy we intended to kill, we killed him, end of story.

What pissed me off more than the wasted time—staking him out, waiting in hiding, killing the guy, and then burying him—was the fact that now I'd not only killed the wrong guy, but that I still had to kill the right guy, as well as the guy who gave me the bogus information about the guy I just killed. That's three guys, when I'd only planned on one, at most two, depending on how I decided to handle Roger after it was all said and done, effectively tripling my work, which was all I could think about as we walked back to the van, that and how hungry I was, which is why I suggested we grab a burger, maybe a soft serve, too, on the way back home.

It was about the time that Roger pulled into the Whataburger that he realized he'd dropped his wallet. Uh-oh, he said. Uh-oh what? I said. No wallet, he said. Don't sweat it, I said. I'll cover you. No, he said. That's not what I mean.

I'm not sure why the jerk brought his wallet to a killing in the first place, as it seems common sense to me: Bring cash to a killing. No credit cards, no license, no ID, unless it's fake and it's got a bogus picture on it. But your entire wallet? Roger's always been a nice guy, but was never much for common sense. So we drove back to where we buried the body, hunted around for Roger's wallet for about twenty minutes, until he comes to the conclusion that he must have dropped it into the hole. Into the hole, I said. You're positive? I'll go get the shovels, he said, instead of answering my question. After another hour of slow digging, slow because we didn't want to accidentally dig up and throw back Roger's wallet with the dirt and muck, we hit the body, only for me to then realize that it was the wrong body, entirely the wrong body, at which point, so we didn't keep digging pointlessly and so Roger wouldn't hop into the hole himself, I said, This ain't him.

What? Are you kidding me? Roger said. How many bodies you think are out here? he said, not really believing me, hopping down into the hole to make sure I hadn't made a mistake, which I hadn't, or, rather, I had.

The thing is, the entire field's on a grid system, the entire plot of land, my great grandfather's, all laid out on this grid, not written down, of course, but kept in my head, with the locations of all the different guys, each buried in his own logical way—it's a mathematical system, foolproof—but I must have been flustered, pissed as I was, and hungry, and so I must have transposed a couple of the locations, which, fine, no big deal, just refigure it out, cover this guy up, go find the right guy, and there you have it, right? Sure. But for the monstrously fucked-up fact that the wrong guy we dug up was Roger's brother, Roger not knowing he was dead and buried in my grandfather's land, thinking, in fact, that he'd skipped off to Vegas to become a blackjack dealer, due in part to the forged letter I'd left for him that said *I've skipped off to Vegas to become a blackjack dealer.*

It ain't him, I said again, a bit more urgently. Come on, I said. We have to cover him back up and go find the right guy, not to mention your damn wallet. But it was too late, and I could tell it was too late by the way Roger's body went stiff, and by the way his throat started churning out this wicked snarl. I brained him with the shovel, right there and then, before things could get out of hand, but my heart must not have been in it, or maybe I just didn't have good footing on the loose earth, and I only grazed his shoulder, knocked him back a bit. Then he just about jumped straight out of the hole and came rushing at me. I'm ashamed to admit it, but I started babbling on about how it was an accident, a mistake, but I knew I was lying and what was worse, so did

Roger, though I like to comfort myself with the thought that he probably didn't even hear me.

I'd heard that if you hit a man in the nose hard enough, you can kill him instantly, and so I tried that first off because I like Roger and didn't want him to suffer. I'll tell you now that it doesn't work or I wasn't doing it right, but as fast as he was coming and as much as my hand hurt afterward, I figure I hit him damn hard enough. He hardly flinched, though, mad as he was, and knocked me flat on my back, lunging right after me, as if to jump on top of me, maybe to gouge my eyes out or strangle me, but I rolled out of the way, figuring Roger, in his anger, had forgotten the gun in his jacket, figuring, too, that trying to strangle the life out of me would be his next logical move, and when he landed on his face in the dirt, I scrambled to my feet and grabbed the shovel and hit him good this time.

Of course, two weeks later, washing the van, vacuuming the seats and such, I found Roger's wallet wedged between the driver's seat and the cup holder. All I can say is, goddamn jerk. Goddamn fucking asshole.

Harold Withy Keith:
A Meritorious Life

K EITH, H. W. (1839–1905). Inventor, scientist (botany, zoology, orismology). Place of birth: Asheville, North Carolina. Full name: Harold Withy Keith. One of two brothers, twins. According to hospital records, Harold and Martin Keith were born simultaneously, and, never quite the younger or the elder twin, H. W. Keith was referred to by family members as the Left Twin.

As young children, Harold and Martin spent their days in their father's cellar working with grains, ground cornmeal and rice flour. As shown by the extensive notes found in Harold's diary, the brothers made certain progress in their experiments to create a food "that would satisfy hunger without inflaming the passions" in the tradition of Graham and Kellogg. Their experiments, however, came to an abrupt and incomplete end when overshadowed by a young and healthy competition over the affections of the handsome Margaret Lillian Mauve.

Little is known about the courtship of Margaret Lillian Mauve, only that, in the end, Harold won Margaret's heart, and the two were married in 1860. Harold's twin, Martin, served as best man, and it was shortly thereafter that the two brothers again began experimenting with grains. On his own, however, unsatisfied with the repetition of grinding grains and baking crackers, Harold Keith began exhaustive scientific and medical research into unknown viruses and bacteria and the possible causes of sudden and painful deaths. It was during this time that H. W. first envisioned the need for the invention and construction of human organ substitutions. "Clearly," Harold wrote, "if a man's liver and kidneys and stomach fail, he will die."

These experiments in organ substitutions, as far as historians can tell, took place in secret and in a separate laboratory. Some have speculated that H. W.'s work was commissioned by the leading generals of either the North or the South, though this theory appears unlikely since Keith's work continued well past the end of the Civil War. Diagrams copied out of early journal entries show that Keith initially hoped to build organ substitutions using the shells of squash—acorn, snake, spaghetti—scooped out by hand and then internally supported by a collapsible yet sturdy construction of miniature wooden beams. After six months, though, this idea was abandoned, although historians are not sure why, as the subsequent journal pages are missing, presumably removed by Keith.

Intrigued by the newly discovered and recently named vascular system of plants (1861), H. W., following the schematics of various complex plant forms, then constructed a life-sized prototype—colored tubes pinched together with clips and impeccable knots—which he then used to represent the intricate system of translocation, storage, support, and conduction that are the major functions of xylem and phloem. His idea involved the installation of vascular bundles in place of or to help compensate for failed organic functions, "for do not plants perform the same basic functions of life in that they consume, store, and then release energy as food, calories, and waste?" A large mimetic reconstruction of this system—built late at night and early into the morning, each section conceived of and molded in the kitchen of his and Margaret's one-bedroom house, the sections then pieced together in a nearby and abandoned toolshed—provided a model from which he designed an apparatus suitable for surgical insertion into a test subject. In his mind, a vascular system performed more effectively than the bulky system of organs already in place: If part of an organ was pierced or somehow punctured, the organ required immediate repair or else would possibly cause failure in the functions of the body, whereas with a vascular system, any number of strands could be cut, punctured, or lost and, so long as there remained other strands, the system would continue to function, albeit at a lower rate of efficiency.

During this period of time, Margaret gave birth to two sons and a daughter, Solomon, Jeremiah, and Mary Ann. Harold's twin brother, Martin, would, in years to come, take their schooling into his own hands. He would, in fact, come to take the entire household into his own hands, and, eventually, the five of them would quietly become a closer family than ever they were with H. W.

Once his prototype was completed, H. W. Keith then outlined a three-step procedure that involved, first, surgically lining the body with the redesigned vascular system, one which would be appropriate for *Homo sapiens*, in which the bundles of human xylem and phloem would run throughout the body and would, if possible, be attached to the blood vessels already present. Appropriate numbers of bundles would be installed in the esophagus and around the stomach and the intestines, near the kidneys, the liver, and connected to the urethra. The second stage involved the patient's adjustment through a new and scientifically formulated diet of liquids and soluble nutrients suitable for the human vascular system, in order that the new system learn its functions (in part by mimicking the old system). For this, he strayed from his earlier experiments in grains, concentrating instead on the nightshade family of fruits and vegetables, e.g., tomatoes and eggplants. The diet would be gradually increased to include more solid foods of the kind normally taken in by the traditional organic system. Once a normal diet had been achieved, the third stage could proceed, which involved the systematic removal of the traditional human organs, "not to include the Heart, which was, of course, the storehouse for the soul, and which was that organ which separated, in the end, Man from Plant." The completion of this project became H. W. Keith's lifelong obsession, everything else—Margaret, his brother, Martin, experiments in grain, his children—all in turn forgotten. It would be nearly forty-seven years later before the work would be finished, and the Human Vascular Bundle System ready for surgical insertion.

H. W. Keith was the first recipient of his patented Vascular Bundle procedure. Twenty minutes into the procedure, as documented by Keith himself, the young man assisting him in the surgery fainted. Undeterred, and with the help of a large beveled mirror of his own design, Keith made one incision after another, and then, feeling light-headed but "confident and with steady and unhesitating hands," completed the operation. Yet due to complications unexplained and unforeseen, he passed away shortly thereafter.

The Animal House

Wendy claimed she found the house on her way home. She claimed she could smell it from the sidewalk, and maybe she could. Her nose was better at smelling things than mine was. As it was, I couldn't smell anything even standing on the small cement porch out front. Only after she opened the door and I stuck my head inside did the smell hit me. It was thick and damp, full of hoof and fur, though when I mentioned this to Wendy, she told me, "None of these animals have hooves."

The noise was such that I was surprised we couldn't hear them bawling and cawing and thrushing in our own house, two blocks away. The animals were caged, and I asked Wendy, "Where did those cages come from?"

She shook her head. "Animal shelter?"

"I thought the shelter closed," I said, but she only shrugged.

Then we walked through the house. There were ducks and grackles, a couple of squirrels, a few feral cats, a litter of rats, and two brown animals I didn't recognize that Wendy said she thought were nutrias, which didn't sound like the name of an animal so much as a sinus medicine. In larger cages outside in the backyard, she told me, there were three stray dogs. She showed them to me, all of them, gave me a tour of the house and all its residents, and for a moment she acted as if they were her animals, her responsibility. And then she bent down to one of the cages and I asked her what the hell she was doing and she said, "I want to hold one of them."

"No," I said. "I don't think you should."

She gave me a sharp and disapproving look and then shook her head and opened the cage and pulled out one of the nutrias, which climbed into her arms. She petted it on the head and cooed in its ear and lifted it out and held it for me to touch, and when I told her no way, no how, she told it not to listen to the bad man.

◈

When I first met Wendy, I was lying in the middle of the floor of an empty house and it was dark and she was standing over me. A house I should mention I had broken into, thinking it could be a place I could live. She was brandishing what had at first looked like a shotgun, but which was a floor lamp, held not like you'd hold a gun, but like you'd aim a cattle prod or a spear. She was the first person, aside from my parents, I'd had any real interaction with since moving back.

I'd moved in with my parents, and I was short of cash, having used the last of it to work my way back to my home-town, which I came to discover had been all but abandoned for no other reason than that, for most people, it seemed like a good time to move on—to some other small town, or a city, maybe—and then, of course, some of the people didn't move on, but instead passed away, which more or less had the same effect. In any case, it seemed like as good a time as any to move back to my parents' house, my parents being some of the few who decided to stick it out, and there get my bearings straightened out, or oiled, or whatever thing you do to bearings to make them work again. After a short while I figured I needed to find my own place, but I still had no money and there was a shortage of jobs, so I found it dif-ficult to scrounge up enough money to move out. But the town was sick with empty houses, old and run-down, and I figured they couldn't be in such bad shape I couldn't pull one of them together again and then live in it, and so I began to wander through town and study them with a critical eye.

The one I'd finally picked, though, turned out to be Wendy's, which I discovered the first night I spent there.

The sight of her, silhouetted against the front window, faint moonlight filtering in through the threadbare shades, made me feel drowsy and unhurried, and for a moment I considered going back to sleep, knowing she'd stay standing over me until I woke again.

"That's not how you hold a gun," I told her.

"It's not a gun," she said, knowing, as she said it, she should've lied. "What are you doing here?"

"Is it a cattle prod? Or a spear?" I asked.

"A cattle prod?" she said, and in her voice I sensed that she wanted to laugh at what I'd said. Instead, she slammed the lamp onto my shin, which was how I understood it to be a lamp.

It hurt because it was unexpected, not because it hurt. She didn't have the strength to hit me hard enough, and the lamp was cheaply made, and she didn't have good leverage on the swing, throwing the end of it down from her chest like a hockey player slapping his stick against the ice. Which made me wonder, briefly, what had happened to all of the ice from the skating rink in the mall now that the mall had closed.

"What are you doing here?" she said again.

It had been a long time since I'd had to come up with anything substantial to say to anyone, and when she asked me the question, I didn't know how to answer.

She swung her lamp down at my shin again, though this time I was prepared for the attack and moved mostly out of the way.

"Wait," I said. "Wait."

And she paused, her lamp brandished higher, ready for another, stronger swing, and she waited for me to say something, but I didn't know what to say.

◇

Six or seven or eight years ago I worked a little job for a small zoo near where I lived with my parents, or not a zoo, more a nature trail, or a series of trails that had animals on it. I mean, the land had animals on it, wild animals: owls, bobcats, squirrels, snakes, rats, mice, hawks, buzzards, and other sorts of wild animals; but it also had a small area set aside for an odd assortment of caged animals. These consisted of two dik-diks, four ring-tailed lemurs and two brown lemurs, a porcupine, a pair of wallabies, a greenhouse-like structure full of butterflies, a capybara, and an African wild dog. It wasn't a good job. I was an office assistant and sometimes they would ask me to watch the ticket desk or to move furniture around in the small conference room they advertised for businesses that wanted to conduct meetings or ropes courses there. I didn't do anything interesting and I wasn't paid well and I didn't receive any benefits, but it was, out of all the jobs I held before leaving home, my favorite, mainly because very little was asked of me, the smallest amount of effort on my part warranted high praise, and when no one was paying careful attention, I could easily sneak away from my desk or whatever clerical task I had been assigned and spend half an hour, and sometimes up to an hour, wandering through the trails.

This was the last job I had before I left home to go out into the world and make something of my life, and my first thought, after living with my parents again, was that I should live there, that if I was really going to leave my parents' house, what better place to live than in the woods, among those trails and the animals that inhabited them. I pictured a small, mobile camp, somewhere in between the Hoot Owl Trail and the Woodduck Trail, or deep into the trees off the

Bluestem Trail. I pictured a minimal kind of life, a paring down, a small fire just after dark when the weather turned truly cold, nothing to signal that I was there, that anyone was there.

I pictured all of this so well that the next night I walked to the only bookstore left open in town, which happened to specialize in hunting and survival texts. For an hour or two, I browsed through various survival guides, including books that promised to show me how to survive in any climate and on any terrain, and books that instructed me on brain tanning and field dressing and head and leg removal and flint-knapping and on making primitive tools, like a primitive adze or a primitive vise, but ultimately I bought the book recommended to me by a man in his late twenties or early thirties, a pit bull of a man with a short, square haircut and tanned, rough-looking skin, who pulled a book off the shelf and handed it to me and told me if I was looking for a real and a really good survival book, the book I should use was this one, which he owned himself, and which he used when he air-dropped—I think he said air-dropped—himself into Southeast Asia with just a knife and some rope and a small pack and this book and spent six weeks living completely off the land before walking himself back out of the wilderness and into civilization.

He was an earnest-looking and trusting man, the kind of man who might have served several tours of duty in some part of the armed forces, eagerly, no doubt, and might be gearing up to serve yet another, and I felt a little guilty accepting his recommendation knowing what I had planned to use the book for, but not guilty enough to put the book back.

When I got back to my parents' house, I ate a quick dinner, spoke only briefly to my father, my mother having long before fallen asleep, and then hurried upstairs to start learning all I could learn about survival in the wilderness. I flipped to the contents page and glanced briefly at the headings, and then flipped to the section on how to build a hobo shelter, and then flipped to the sustenance chapter and read the section on procuring a snake using a forked stick, and then I closed the book and placed it on the nightstand, and then never opened it again.

◎

Which was what I told her, the girl with the lamp. Not the whole thing, but the bit about the zoo and the trails. I thought it might appeal to her, or to anyone, really, standing over me with a floor lamp in her hand. How dangerous is the guy who worked for a nature reserve? I told her this and then I began to tell her other things about myself, lying there on the ground, not sure what else to say or how, except to start from the beginning and as quickly as I could, until eventually I pulled us through the sludge of my recent past and into the mire of my present. I had come home again, I said, but I wasn't sure why, and I had plans for one of these empty houses, but I wasn't sure what plans. I said this one appealed to me, but I didn't know why about that, either.

Then she told me about herself, which wasn't much to tell. She had just finished school. She had left home when she was sixteen. She liked living in these old houses. She had stored some of her stuff in a few other old empties—she called them *empties* as if they were beer bottles—around town. She wanted to be a veterinarian. Her dad, before he died, had been a large-animal vet. It all seemed pleasantly run-of-the-mill, and so I stood up, finally, and lightly pushed aside the lamp, which had grown heavy in her arms and dragged along the floor, and leaned in to kiss her, and then a week later she made me leave the house, which I was afraid to leave, afraid I wouldn't be able to find it or her again, but she forced me to go. "It's been a week," she said. "Your parents must be worried sick. You need to go see them." And so I left.

I went back to their house and told them what had happened to me, and they were upset, my mother especially, though I can't say for sure what upset her most, that I had been gone so long without telling them where I was and that I was okay, or that I was still alive yet living so recklessly. When I told them about Wendy and about our plans, my mother locked herself into her bedroom and didn't come out again until after I left.

When I made it back to the house, I walked inside, afraid Wendy would have skipped out, that there'd be nothing left, no trace of her, and some small part of me worried I'd made her up entirely, but there she was, sitting cross-legged on the floor, and when she saw me, she jumped up and hugged me and then stepped back and looked at me and said, "I've missed you so much, I could just eat you up, like scrambled eggs." Then she mimed cracking eggs into a skillet and stirring them around with a spatula and then eating them up with a knife and fork, and I said, "Who eats scrambled eggs with a knife and fork?" and then she punched me in the shoulder and then she kissed me, and I knew I was home.

◇

We thought, Wendy and I, to make a home of the emptied house, mainly by rooting through the other houses on the same block, which I hadn't considered might be as stripped bare as our own. When, after hours and days of house-looting, we returned empty-handed, I figured we would give up on the idea of furnishings and homemaking of that sort and that we would settle into a less permanent lifestyle, our possessions carried with us on our backs. Wendy wouldn't have any of that, not since I first convinced her that I had serious plans to renovate and build in one of these houses. "We need something to sit on, at least," she said. And when I came home with seats I'd stripped out of one of the abandoned cars in a body repair shop nearby, she smiled and kissed me and said, "Now we just need something to sleep on."

What struck me now, though, about that first conversation, about our earliest confidences, and what worried me about this house full of animals she had claimed to have only just found, was that small detail of her life that I had at first thought pleasantly bland and unimportant. What girl, at one point in her life, doesn't want to become a veterinarian? It had seemed a safe assumption that she had long since given up on the idea of becoming a veterinarian. It had seemed a safe assumption that this feckless and transient lifestyle had precluded any faint desire to make something of herself. But then she showed me this house she had found, and I wondered if she had found it or if she had made it herself.

◎

The fact of the matter was: I didn't have any actual experience judging homes or estimating what it would take to fix one up, but it was something that came naturally to my father, who owned a now defunct and practically empty hardware store, and I had always assumed that if you were to toss me into a hardware-and-repair sort of situation, push come to shove, a store of knowledge, buried but innate, would bubble up, and I would be just as good at it as he was. And it occurred to me that Wendy had at some point in her life hit upon the same flawed philosophy, that a skill or talent would necessarily pass from father to child, except that she expected to know how to fix these animals because her father had known how to take care of horses and mules.

I can't say, then, that it surprised me too much when one night I woke up and turned to look at her and found that she had a bird. I asked her where she got that bird, and she said she couldn't sleep with all the racket the bird had been making outside and that she'd gone to investigate and that this is what she'd found. It had broken its wing somehow, and she had gathered it to her and tended to it. There was a gentle way to how she was holding that bird that made me certain she had done this before. "Are you going to maybe put that one with the rest of them?" I asked. She shook her head and said, "Not tonight," and then she put her lips to the bird's beak, though I couldn't tell if they touched, and then she said, "Tomorrow, you go into the house with the others, but tonight you sleep with us."

The whole night it didn't make a sound and she didn't let go of it, and when I woke up, she was asleep but still with that bird in her hand. I sat up and pulled my pants on and then poured some water into a cup for the bird, but the bird didn't stir, and I thought to myself, *I don't know you, bird, or how to fix what's wrong with you, but I don't doubt that you will soon be dead.* And for a minute or two, I considered lifting it gently from Wendy's hand and breaking its neck or smothering or suffocating it, though I didn't know the first thing about going about suffocating a bird. I thought I should do this for her, anyway, for her peace of mind, and for me, I'll be honest, for my own peace of mind. It would be harder on her when this frail creature died in a week or two weeks than if she woke up now to find it had died while she slept, but then Wendy began to shift and wake, and the bird lifted its beak and poked lightly at her finger, and my opportunity window had closed.

◈

For the next few weeks, I tried to ignore the toll that house full of animals took on us. But it wasn't easy. She was never home, it seemed. She was always at the other house, or she was out searching for other injured or sick or stray animals to ensnare. Our house, the house we were living in, had begun to take on the other house's smell. I don't know how this happened. Maybe that smell grabbed hold of her clothes and her hair and her skin and snuck in that way, or maybe it followed her home, some physical thing trailing behind her like a cartoonish wisp of smoke. Anyhow, I could smell it and I mentioned this to Wendy and she shook her head at me (scattering wisps of stink everywhere) and told me it was my imagination. And more than once, I woke up to find her asleep with another animal tucked under her arm like it was a stuffed animal she'd been sleeping with since she was a child. How she managed to coax these creatures into these docile positions, I never understood. Nor did I know where she found them in the first place, and when she wouldn't tell me—or told me only vaguely "Here and there" or "At the park" or "On the side of the road"—and when it appeared to me that some of them were less sick and more just stray, I began to suspect her of sneaking into people's homes, or into pet stores, or into the neglected city zoo, and stealing these creatures to bring back to our house. And if I hadn't become more and more engrossed in how angry this was all making me, I might have stopped to admire her way with animals, but in truth, I wanted desperately for them to die off or break free, but they didn't seem to want to do either. And after a month of this, and of living in a house that became increasingly dirtier and dingier, I decided I should leave Wendy and this house, that I should let her have her animals and this other house she had found herself and return to my parents' place before setting out in search of another abandoned shack where I could set up camp. Or maybe I would leave town altogether, start fresh again somewhere new.

Then, before I decided I would leave for good, she got sick. She was nauseated and throwing up, light-headed and weak and sweaty. I gave her some water. I stole into my parents' house and found her some variety of pills—for headache, for sinus, for cough—but none of them helped much. In the end, she asked me if I could go on my own to the house with the animals in it and change their cages and administer their medicines. I wanted to ask her, Is that really a thing we need to concern ourselves with? Is this an exercise we need to be devoting our time to? Instead, I asked her what she wanted me to do and then how to do it, and she explained, retching and looking green and unwell, and then I said, "Do you need anything while I'm out?" and she shook her head and lay down, and I left.

❀

It would be easy enough, I thought to myself, to show up at my parents' house. To show up and let myself in and climb upstairs to my old room and go to sleep, and then to wake up the next morning and act as if nothing had happened, as if nothing more than a long walk, one really long walk that I'd only just now returned from, had happened. My mother would act diffident toward me, would refuse to smile at me, and would tilt her head my way and say, "You think you're so funny, don't you?" but she would be happy to have me home. That much I knew.

And there would be no consequences, either, nothing that might damage me, anyway, in leaving Wendy and those sickly creatures, and there would be potentially bad conse-quences in returning to them. I thought of all of this as I walked, and I knew I should have turned around and gone somewhere else, anywhere else, but I didn't.

The house smelled, of course, as it was full of sick or dying animals, smelled of their fur, their hair, their feathers, of the mucous that dribbled from their noses or the pus-filled sores on their footpads or on their bellies, and it smelled of their piss and shit and of the disinfectant Wendy sprayed throughout the house to hide that smell, and of their breath, and of the animals themselves, whatever their smell was, a smell I associated with zoos and circuses, and, I supposed, this collection of monsters, ordinary monsters, was as close to a zoo as our small town was likely to see. But there was another smell, too. It was an overpowering and metallic smell that a part of me recognized at once as the smell of blood, but since there was no reason for there to be this smell in the house, I dismissed the idea.

Moving quickly through the house, hoping to root out the cause of the smell and get rid of it so that maybe the smell would have faded by the time I finished administering to the animals, I slid on something and fell forward, only barely throwing my hands out in front of me in time to break my fall. Turning to see what had tripped me up, I felt a wetness on my knees and saw a blooming red stain on my pants, and for a moment I was scared that I'd seriously hurt myself, hurt myself so badly that I couldn't even feel the pain of whatever wound resulted in so much blood, but then I realized I'd fallen into a pool or a smear of blood, and that what had tripped me in the first place had been the metal gate to one of the cages, pulled apart, twisted and mangled and tossed into the open doorway.

Eventually I found five more cages with their doors also torn from their hinges. Studying these cages, I couldn't remember what had once lived inside them, but they were empty now, the only sign that the cage was once home to some living thing being the trail of blood leading away from the bent or broken frame. The sight and the smell of all this carnage was upsetting enough that I quickly left that place without opening a single cage or refilling a single bottle of water, and when I finally walked back through our door, I found Wendy asleep on the floor, and, taking my pants and my shirt off, I went to lie on the floor next to her, but didn't fall asleep until just before morning.

⊛

I didn't tell Wendy what I had found. Instead I told her everything went fine, and then I asked her how she felt, and we went about our day, the secret of what was waiting for her at the animal house making me tense and nervous. I would act surprised, of course, shocked and devastated, would offer theories—It must have come in after me, whatever it

was, early this morning, maybe?—when she told me what
horrors she'd found, and then offer to help her clean the
mess up and console her as best I could. But when the time
came for her to go tend to her animals, she began to throw
up again, and I left in her place.

By the time I arrived at the house, I had prepared myself to find there nothing but death and decay and had presumed that whatever hadn't died naturally, or because of my
negligence, would have been taken by whatever had taken
the first five animals. But the animals weren't dead. They
seemed, in fact, energized by my arrival, as if they were hungry and thirsty and they knew that I was the one who had
made them so.

I searched the house first, ignoring the cries and caws
and barks of the animals waiting to be fed and watered, but
I didn't find any sign of a brutal struggle, and didn't count
any more among the missing. Feeling obligated to make up
for my poor showing the night before, I opened the windows
to air the house out and then began feeding the animals, giving them water to drink, and, one by one, cleaning their
cages. I cleaned the blood on the floor as best I could, and I
removed the empty cages, feeling that, had it been me, I
wouldn't want to live side by side with such a graphic
reminder of the fragile nature of life, the inevitability of
potentially violent death, and so on. I did all of this and felt
somewhat cheered by the work, which was methodical and
mechanical. Even handling the animals, which seemed to
have been tamed by Wendy or else were simply too sick and

weak to care who lifted them from their cages, calmed me. I enjoyed it, and while I didn't think it was necessarily the right thing to do or that it would help any of them, I gave the animals the medicines as Wendy had instructed—medicines of a questionable origin and usefulness, I would add—and when I finished it all, I left.

The next night, I did the same, and the night after that, and the night after that, and so on for a week, and then two weeks, and then a month, each night expecting to find them all dead in their cages, or half of them dead, and some number of them stolen away, but over the next month, they only seemed to grow stronger, and I wondered if maybe they were getting well and if one day they would be well enough that I could set them loose.

You could say, too, that over time I became attached to these animals. Not to all of them, but to enough of them that on occasion I had to stop myself from giving a certain squirrel or a certain pigeon a name, and that on other occasions, unable to stop myself from naming a raccoon, say, I had to stop from speaking that name aloud, from trying to scratch it behind its ears, had to stop myself from thinking of them as pets or friends.

You could also say that being in that house, spending time there, more time than was even necessary, was a release to me. That the house, despite the smell and despite the noise, or because of these things, became a place I often wanted to return to, became the place I thought of when I was at our home, when I was home with Wendy.

Wendy hadn't gotten better, or, rather, she would begin to feel better, gaining her strength and her color, and then fall back into whatever sickness had taken hold of her. For a time, I worried that she had contracted something chronic and incurable, potentially contagious, but then the idea that she wasn't sick, that she was pregnant, began to sprout between us, though this possibility was a thing we never directly spoke to. Instead we ruled out, over and over again, the things it couldn't be.

"Not syphilis," she said.

"Oh, no, certainly not that. I think the symptoms are all wrong."

"Heart palpitations, perhaps?"

"Let me check my *Physician's Desk Reference*," I said, and she smiled weakly.

"I don't suppose you've fallen prey to something so silly as the flu. Or mono?"

"If I have mono, it's certainly all your fault."

"Well, then, no, I suppose it must be malaria. Or diphtheria."

And after a while, this conversation, like the others before it, came to an uncomfortable, winded end, the two of us having painted ourselves into a corner, the fact that she must be pregnant soon the only idea left to us and still the only idea neither of us wanted to verbalize.

Unsettled by this and what to do about it, I often left our house and Wendy in it, after she had fallen into a restless sleep or shuffled herself quietly into a corner to let herself wallow in nausea. I walked up and down the streets of our neighborhood, wondering who if anyone lived in these houses around us, surprised sometimes to see a light on in a living room or a kitchen or on the porch, having forgotten that there were people around us who had their own lives, who lived in these run-down houses, but with furniture and appliances and families. Then, eventually, I would find myself back at the animal house, and there sit for hours with one or two of the animals set free from their cages and allowed to hesitantly sniff out a safe perimeter around the other cages. On occasion, I would lure one into my lap with a piece of food, some special treat, but mostly I just sat there alone and quiet and watched the animals sleep or turn about in their cages, or I would close my eyes and go to sleep myself, and soon I began to consider possible outcomes for us, the consequences of a pregnant Wendy, a new life brought into our routine, and I began to make plans, vague and potentially unworkable plans, but regardless, through this I came to feel certain about a burgeoning and sustainable new life for us, for our small piece of this world. *Look*, I would think to myself, *if you can take care of these animals— and not just you, but Wendy, too—if you and Wendy can take care of these animals, how much harder is a child?* And I would start to imagine this life, Wendy and myself and some faceless, sexless person bundled to one of our backs as we tended these animals and as we moved through our days together, but I never got very far with these images, and soon, no matter where I was, with Wendy at home, or wandering aimlessly through the streets, or at the animal house, I felt agitated and jittery and unhappy, so that when the thing came back, I at first welcomed the distraction.

⊚

Once it returned, though, the thing, which I only once saw the barest glimpse of, made short work of all I had done.

Feeling emboldened or strong or simply desperate, it went first for the dogs in the backyard. I like to think that I heard them howl that night they were killed. At some point in the night, I woke with a start, unsure of where I was or why I was there, and then turned to see Wendy next to me, and then slowly settled myself back into a tense and restless sleep, but it was just as likely a foul dream or thoughts of pregnancy that woke me. After I found the dogs, or, rather, their cages, mangled and empty, I knew it was back and I set to work on the house.

I boarded the windows. I boarded all but the front door. I stood on the roof and patched whatever holes I could find. I found steel wool under one of the bathroom sinks and began to stuff it into every open space. I searched the basement. I searched the attic. Closed every entry I could find. Still it found its way inside and stole next the nutrias and then the raccoon. Soon, I noticed a pattern—attack, rest two nights, attack, rest three nights, then attack again, and with each successive raid on our house, it would steal more. No amount of preparedness, it seemed, protected the house. The thing bored holes into the walls and dug underneath the house and found weak spots and exploited them. So I changed tactics and waited for it. There were days and nights I spent crouched outside the house, hiding, hoping to catch the monster in the act. I had found a knife, a kitchen knife, the blade dulled but its point still sharp, sharp enough. I waited and I consoled the animals it left behind and I cleaned up after it had done whatever damage it could attend to while I was gone or even as I sat outside waiting for it to arrive.

During that time, I dreamt about the animals in their cages, and sometimes I dreamt about the baby, and these were disturbing dreams, but not so disturbing as those nights my dreams bled one into the other and I dreamt that either the baby was the monster terrorizing Wendy's animals or that the baby was one of the animals, a weak and wasted thing living in one of those cages waiting for death—natural or violent—to come for it. And then there were times when I was inside the dreams, too, and these were the worst of them, though not when in the dream I was the monster or when I was my own child trapped inside that cage, or even when I was one of the other animals bearing witness to the massacre of my child, fearful of my own death, which was surely forthcoming, but when I was myself, when I wasn't anything or anyone more frightening or disturbing than myself, and it was me who unlocked the door to the house and ushered the beast inside.

And then all but the last of them was gone. I could tell even as I stepped inside. I walked through the house as quickly as I could and found it, the bird Wendy had rescued from our backyard what seemed so long ago. It looked sad, shivering from the cold or fear in its cage, which had been set atop the kitchen counter, which might have been why it had been spared. I went to it, kicking aside the mangled, empty cages littering the floor. I gently lifted it out of its cage and looked it in the eyes.

"Can you fly yet?" I asked. "Your wing all better yet?"

Then I put it back in its cage. I carried it to my father's hardware store and broke in through the back door. I grabbed some twine and some washers and a gas can and some scissors and a water hose and some rags, and then I walked all the way back to the animal house, stopping every so often to siphon off some gasoline from parked cars along the way.

When I got to the house, I set myself to work. I lined up a trip wire, tying off washers at the end of it to alert me when the trip wire had been tripped, and then I stacked the cages in a tight circle around the middle of the living room, into the center of which I placed that small bird in its small cage. I set the cage open just a crack, just enough so that if that bird got curious or scared, if it nudged that door, it would nudge the door open, and then I left.

I waited outside. Then I fell asleep. I dreamt the creature had followed me home. That it had waited for me, watched me enter the animal house, listened for my despairing cry, and then waited so it could follow me, thinking maybe I had another houseful of easily picked morsels for it to eat. It followed me, and as Wendy opened the door to greet me, the creature lunged at her, and in my dream, I pushed her aside and let the thing take hold of my arm, and for a moment, I was happy, or not happy, happy isn't the right word for what I felt, and not content, either, but I was satisfied, I was prepared, this was something I had prepared for, and even above the pain and the sight of my own blood and the sharpness of the monster's teeth, this fact stood out in my mind, and for the moment I was able to ignore the rest, ignore the rest just long enough to take that blade and shove it deep into that beast's head or through its neck, feeling like some modern Beowulf or knight, shoving it deep and then twisting it around and then slipping it out and pushing that knife back in, again and again and again until long past the point the animal had let go of my arm, had stopped moving entirely, and lay cradled in my bloodied lap, looking no more threatening than any other big dog or German shepherd. And then I woke up, and then I turned to Wendy only to realize I hadn't gone home yet. The dream was fresh in my mind, so fresh that I had to clench and unclench my fist to make sure I didn't have a knife with me, hadn't picked it up somehow while I slept. I tried to go back to sleep, and then the washers started rattling and jerking every which way. I jumped up and ran to the house carrying the gas can, and I did a quick sprint around the house, splashing gasoline around the front of the house and on the front porch and around the back and the sides and then to the front again. Then I soaked some rags, and I wondered why I hadn't prepared this stuff beforehand, but I heard a commotion going on inside still and hoped it would last. When the rags were soaked, I kicked open the door, and down the hall I could see the little bird flying and flapping like mad, a second or two above the wall of cages I'd built, and then it would tire, or be knocked from the tenuous perch it had found as that thing scrambled to get at it.

Then the wall of cages was knocked cleanly to the floor, and I saw a blur of dark reddish brown fur, and then it was gone after the bird again, and I stopped watching, cast that can stuffed with rags into the middle of that melee, and then closed the door and lit a match and then lit the trail of gasoline I'd laid on fire.

I watched everything burn. I stood there and watched. I wasn't sure what I was waiting for. For the fire to spread? I hadn't come prepared to do anything about stopping a spreading fire. For someone to call the fire or police department? If that's what I was hoping for or feared would happen, the neighbors disappointed me, for no one was called, or if called, no one came. For some signal of the beast, of its suffering, its death, its escape? After a while, as the flames consumed the house, I realized it was pointless and dangerous and foolish to stand there, and so I decided to walk back home, back to Wendy.

As I walked, all I could think of was my dream. All I could imagine was our front door torn open, the house wrecked beyond repair, and Wendy gone, stolen away, or maybe there, maybe the beast would have left her there, but only the ruined mess of her. And soon I wasn't walking. Soon I was running. I couldn't hear anything but my feet slapping against the sidewalk, couldn't feel anything but the blood pounding in my ears, and by the time I stopped, I was wheezing and weak-kneed and my head and my shoulders ached, and, light-headed, I doubled over. But the house was fine. The door was fine, and inside the house was normal. Everything was normal. Wendy was there sleeping, peaceful and quiet on our makeshift bed, and I watched her sleep for ten minutes, for thirty minutes. I watched her sleep and I thought about what I could do for her and what I could do for myself, and for the baby if there was a baby, and then I pulled the scissors out of my back pocket and held them clenched in my fist. I walked back outside and set myself up on the front steps with those scissors and I waited, and while I waited, I considered all the different, painful administrations I might perform with those scissors on any creature, man or beast, that might try to push past me.

All of Me

The zombie in me would like to make a few things clear.

The zombie in me would like to make it clear that there is no zombie in me, per se. Would like to make it known that there is only me, in fact, and that all of me is zombie.

That's what the zombie in me says every day, what he whispers in my ear every morning when I wake up, what he whispers as I apply the makeup I need to use every morning to bind my face-flesh together, what he whispers as I button my shirt and tie my tie. The zombie's voice in my head is a near constant.

The zombie in me says other things as well.

"Bite her face," for example, when I say hello to the receptionist, Barbara, as I walk past her desk on my way to my cubicle.

"Break his neck," also, is something the zombie in me

says, most often in reference to my boss, Keith, though in truth the zombie in me bears no ill will toward Keith. The comment, in other words, shouldn't be taken personally, shouldn't imply any personal animosity toward Keith.

Or Barbara, for that matter, with whom I eat lunch quite often, by which I mean, with whom I've sat in the cafeteria while she eats lunch, as I do not eat—at least, not what is served in the cafeteria.

For one, the food served in the cafeteria is very fatty and greasy and bland.

And secondly, none of it is human flesh.

⊛

As a matter of fact, I rather like Barbara. She smells like shampoo, even at the end of the day. And in the summer, when I walk past her desk on Mondays, I can always smell the lingering scent of suntan lotion coming off her skin, which reminds me of the beach, which is a place I haven't been to in quite some time. When I smell the suntan lotion on her or when I smell the shampoo on her, my impulses are torn, for the briefest of moments, between biting her face and kissing her neck. And then, before I can do either, I say, "Good morning, Barbara" or "Have a nice night, Barbara" and make quickly for my cubicle or the stairs.

Salt water being one of the bigger obstacles between me and visiting the beach. It stings, for one, and it's an abrasive, as is the sand.

Wearing a bathing suit being another sizable problem.

It would be much easier to take the elevator, of course, when running from my impulses or even at the end of an ordinary nine-hour day spent staring at spreadsheets and quarterly revenue reports. The stairs are bad on my knees, which, though you cannot tell through my suit pants, are held in place with a flesh-colored gauze. My knees aren't held together by much else. The mystical quality of my existence, perhaps, but that will take a person only so far. Not to mention that our offices are located on the twelfth floor. Twelve floors, even on a good pair of knees, can be a lot to take.

But the elevator is a dangerous place for someone like me. It is a place full of urges, of somewhat violent urges. There is this urge, for instance.

Well. On second thought, no.

In fact, I'd rather not go into detail. Let's leave it at this: It is a place for urges, which is why I take the stairs.

◈

I like Barbara, but she is married.

That she's married isn't the reason why I haven't asked her out on a date. A whole host of other problems stands in the way of my asking her out on a date, most of which I won't stoop to the discussion of as they seem fairly obvious.

The reason that it matters that she is married, the problem in the fact that she is married, why it's a problem at all, comes down to the simple fact that I am not that much more clever than the zombie in me.

By which I mean: "Eat his face" is what the zombie in me says when I am caught thinking about Barbara and the fact that she is married.

His face referring most obviously and unashamedly to her husband's face.

His name is Mark.

"Eat his face" is what the zombie tells me because the zombie knows that I am tempted. Knows that when it comes to eating someone's face when that someone's face is Barbara's husband's face, I am sorely tempted.

What troubles me more and more about the zombie is that he is, while not especially good with words, persistent. The zombie is persistent and also, only recently, only very recently, and much to my horror, very, very good at creating images, vivid, vivid images inside my head.

For instance . . . Let's not for instance. Let's simply say that these images are graphic and appealing and horrifying and leave me confounded and hungry and bloodthirsty.

Though there is one image, one the zombie has begun to lean heavily on.

It is an image of Barbara. It is a surprisingly calm and pretty image of Barbara.

She is with me and we are holding hands and we are near the beach, but not on the beach. We are on a boardwalk walking along the beach. I'm not in a bathing suit, but I'm not in my normal clothes, either. I'm wearing rags of my normal clothes, and it's clear in this beautiful, ridiculous image just who I am. Just what I am. And the image plays on and there is no sound, only the picture of us, the two of us, hand in hand, and it's lovely, and it plays on and it plays on and then Barbara leans her head on my shoulder and then she turns her face to me for a kiss, and that, right then, right before the kiss, that is when the zombie ends the image, and suddenly, in my head, I'm eating Mark's face off.

Don't think I don't understand the meaning of the zombie's play with images.

I've been introduced to Mark twice. The first time being on the day of their wedding anniversary, when Mark arrived at the office accompanied by a violinist and with a bouquet of roses. The other time being only recently, the time after she caught him with another woman, the day after that day, actually, which was the second day Barbara had called in sick to work and the phones were being covered by another woman, a temp, a temp who smelled like camphor, unpleasantly like camphor. Barbara had called in sick and hadn't come to work, but apparently she hadn't gone home, either, which was why he came looking for her at our office, which was when he found me.

"Nathan, right?" he said to me.

"Um, actually, no," I said.

And he said, "So, Nathan, has Barbara made it in to work, today?"

He said, "Is she here? Is she hiding in someone's cubicle?"

Then he said, contemplatively: "Cubicle."

Then he said, "There's something slightly sexual, isn't there, about that word, *cubicle*?"

To which I said, "No. I don't think so, no."

Mark is not a big man, but he acts disconcertingly bigger than he has any reason to act. He is somewhat threatening, in fact. Short as he is, small as he is.

He leaned in close to me, much closer to me than most people lean in, much closer than I am comfortable with, and said, not in a threatening way, not in a way that was particularly threatening, physically threatening, but threatening in a conspiratorial way, he said, "We'll get to the bottom of this."

"To the bottom of what?" I asked.

"This whole cubicle thing," he said, and then he laughed and clapped me hard—too hard—on the shoulder and said, "Okay, well, if you see her, let her know I came around, will you?"

Then he left.

His breath smelled like deli counter ham, I would like to point out.

The reasons why I don't feel comfortable with people leaning in close to me are many, of course, even aside from the deli counter ham smell. The main reason being that I've always felt discomfited by unnecessary intrusions into my personal space, though I don't think this is a zombie-based peculiarity, don't think it is out of the ordinary, that I am the only one who feels this protective of his personal space. The other reason being, of course, the fact that I am never fully certain how much scrutiny the makeup binding my face-flesh together can withstand.

Not very much scrutiny, if you ask me. Hardly any scrutiny at all, I'd say, but then I'm somewhat biased.

The zombie in me, of course, feels the exact opposite,

welcomes, in fact, the close scrutiny of others, welcomes even the soft stench of deli counter ham, welcomes all of this because, for one, the zombie is tired, is sorely tired of the charade, and secondly, because of all the pieces of human meat the zombie likes to eat, the face is perhaps the zombie's favorite.

◎

By necessity, I have established coping mechanisms.

For instance, I like to throw things. For instance, I sometimes feel a great and desperate urge to throw things.

Mechanisms, of course, by which I hope to cope with the painfully obvious.

The throwing of things being just one example of what I do in lieu of eating off the faces of my coworkers or snapping the necks of my bosses or breaking in half the spines of the husbands of certain women I feel an unfulfillable attraction to.

The throwing of things being, surprisingly, one of the more successful coping mechanisms I've devised, so successful that I have devoted an entire room of my home, which is not a very large home, which is not a home with a lot of rooms in it to spare, yet I have devoted an entire room for the sole purpose of throwing things in it, an entire room that was until just very recently ankle-deep in the various shards of the various breakables I have thrown, composed mostly of cheap glassware bought in secondhand stores, boxes and boxes of these glasses, which are stacked in my garage waiting to be thrown. This spare room, with the shards of glass covering the floor, this room is the same room I mentioned to Barbara, jokingly, or half-jokingly, after she finally came back to the office and took up answering the phones again, that if she wanted, of course, I had a spare room and she'd be more than welcome to use it. Mentioned all of this knowing, of course, that she would have other friends, that if not friends she would have other coworkers, and if not coworkers, family, she would certainly have family, not to mention any number of nicely outfitted hotels, with whom or at which she could stay. Mentioned all of this knowing, of course, that she would never take me up on the offer.

That she took me up on the offer, then, explains why I left work immediately after lunch, rushed to a nearby Salvation Army, bought what amounted to a poor representation of guest-bedroom furniture—a scratched, mirrorless vanity, a wrought-iron twin bed frame, a weak-looking sagging mattress, a large black beanbag chair—and then rushed back home to clear the room, to set it up, to make it look livable, to make it look lived-in, to make it look as if it had not recently been employed as a room in which I violently threw glasses and plates and other breakables as a means of curbing my hunger for human flesh.

Rushed being a relative term, of course.

The mystical quality of my existence notwithstanding, the fact that I am undead flesh moving around at all notwithstanding, I'm not generally a very fast mover.

The problem being, in the end, not the room or the furniture, which was cleared, which was set in place in time, but more my appearance, which was, let's say, somewhat bedraggled after all was said and done. Or not bedraggled, but ruinous, let's say. Let's say the pallor of my skin was a pale pea-green, for instance. Or, for instance, that the thumb on my left hand was set at an angle more pronouncedly right-angle-ish than usual, due in no small part to the accidental crushing of it between the wall and the bed frame. Or that the tip of my nose had sloughed off, I don't know how or why, and was held in place, I'm sure of it, by sheer will alone.

Let's just say this: When all was said and done, I looked more ghoulish than any reasonable person would hope for or expect to on the occasion of Barbara's appearance on my doorstep.

Or let's not say any of that. Let's not focus on the negative, but rather on the positive, on the fact that when she did arrive, she did so drunk and with fat tears in her eyes and hardly seemed to notice my somewhat skewed appearance. That when I left her to fix us a drink and took twenty minutes to patch myself back together, she hardly noticed that, either, or that I returned without any drinks, or that I confessed that, in fact, I didn't have anything to drink in the house at all. She only shrugged her shoulders, stood up, and then said, "Let's go out, then," grabbing me by the hand and leading me out the door, hardly noticing even then the queer texture of my skin.

Here's the thing about last night, about what happened last night.

Last night? Hands down, the best night of my life, or of this life, or of this nonlife.

Last night was such a good night that this morning, the morning after, when I came into work and Roger, who saw me shuffling out of the stairwell moving no slower than I normally move, looking no less meticulously arranged than I normally look, said, "Christ, Jonnie boy, you're a fucking zombie today," I exhibited Herculean restraint and said, simply, "Thanks, Roger. Nice to see you, too."

A restraint I can only credibly attribute to that night, to last night and this morning.

As to what might have happened between Barbara and myself last night, as to what might have happened when we were out together having drinks, if that's the first question on your mind, if, perhaps, a dimly lit, softly sweet scenario is the kind of scenario you envisioned for me:

Nothing happened.

Barbara's expectations of my role in last night's events didn't involve our engaging in any second wrongs in hopes of making the first wrong right. Rather, my role involved the buying of drinks, the watching of her purse and jacket, the finding of seats, the holding of a place for her in the bathroom line, for example. The holding of her hair as she threw up in my bathtub, as another example. And in between all of that, in between drinks, in those moments when she stumbled back to our table, tired of dancing, tired of being hit on, I was there to listen to her confess that she had suspected all along, had convinced herself it couldn't be true, that she felt so betrayed, not by Mark, not because she had a false understanding of Mark, who had been married when she'd first started sleeping with him and had only left his wife because his wife in fact left him when she caught him and Barbara in certain compromising positions, not wholly unlike the compromising positions she had only recently found Mark in with a younger woman from his office, but that really she felt betrayed by herself, by her complacency in the face of overwhelming evidence of her husband's indiscretions and underwhelming evidence of his love for her.

Such was the role I played that night.

But before it's concluded that I have no backbone, that I let myself, in that one night, become "the friend," before you decide that I can't "close the deal," let's disillusion ourselves of any Vaseline-blurred fantasies, let's throw some cold water over those most thrilling parts of our reptilian brains, let's discuss this gross misunderstanding of my existence, and let's take a closer look at my particular abilities in the realm of sexual fulfillment: I have no particular abilities in the realm of sexual fulfillment. I have no abilities in this realm whatsoever. The mystical quality of my existence does not account for such abilities or desires or needs.

Such is the life of a zombie, you might say.

Wouldn't it be better, simpler, if you were just actually dead? you might say, and on that point, I might not disagree.

Though last night, I didn't mind; with Barbara, I didn't

mind. I should have minded, but I didn't. When she woke up and when I saw her—and she looked bad, she looked awful, tired and rough, and she had large, dark circles under her eyes, and her hair was a tangled, ratty mess, and she looked like this but still somehow lovely, somehow absolutely lovely in a pair of matronly, flower-printed pajamas—standing there in my small kitchen, and when she asked weakly, hoarsely, for coffee and then for cereal and then rested her weary, matted head on my shoulder and then gave me a deep hug and whispered, "Thanks for this," I minded even less.

The point I'm trying to make here being this: I was in a fine mood when I left the house this morning. I was in a splendid mood this morning as I left my house.

Barbara left before me so she could go home and get a change of clothes, pack a bag so that the next morning and the morning after that and the morning after that she wouldn't have to leave again, and we could ride into work together, and "Wouldn't that be fun?"

After she left, I cleaned the kitchen some. I tried to whistle a tune. Failing that, I hummed.

As I drove, I hardly noticed the traffic boxing me at all times into the exit-only lanes.

If I could have skipped up the twelve flights of stairs from the lobby to our offices, I tell you now, I would have skipped.

And this was not because I was in love, or maybe it was. Maybe it was because I was in love. But this was not because I envisioned a happy and long-lasting life with Barbara at my side. This was not because we kissed, which we didn't, or because we made love, which I can't, but because she had been there with me in the morning, had come to me the night before and had stayed and had been there still when I woke up, that she had confided in me, that she had appreciated the fact that she could confide in me, and that for a small moment it seemed to me that I had achieved something undeniably human, had tapped into a sort of life I had for so long assumed unavailable to me.

So it should come as no surprise that when I stepped into the office and saw Mark at her desk, laughing loudly, jovially, standing there almost hidden by the overlarge vase of flowers, so large it could barely fit alongside her phone and computer, that when I came into the office and saw Mark there laughing and saw her laughing back, laughing and blushing and lively, saw them there together as if nothing had happened, it should come as no surprise that my first instinct then was a rageful one.

Should come as no surprise that I stopped in my tracks, blocking the door to the office, and that Roger crashed into the back of me.

Should come as no surprise, though I feel awful about it, that Roger became the outlet for this rage, and that before anyone could register that we were in the doorway or that Roger had said, "Hey, Jonnie, what's the holdup?" before Barbara had the chance to even notice I was there, I turned, grabbed Roger, poor Roger, grabbed him fiercely by the throat, my gray knuckles white from the force of my exertions on his windpipe, which was crushed almost immediately, grabbed hold of him, lifted him off his feet, marched him back toward the elevator, which hadn't closed yet, and threw him inside. Nobody noticed me do this at all. Except for maybe Roger, though by all rights he didn't feel this, didn't experience this or the tearing of limb from limb, didn't feel the bloody evisceration of himself, didn't feel anything at all, which is small comfort, I know, which is almost no comfort at all, not for Roger, certainly, and not for the part of me trying so desperately hard to be someone other than who I am.

⬡

It's a fine line. It's a tightrope. It's a balancing act. I'm perched atop a thin, wobbly fence.

Have I fallen off the fence? Have I stepped off the line, slipped from my rope? I could say I'm barely hanging on, that I'm holding on by a thread. I could say I'm hanging in there. But to look at Roger, or what's left of him, to look at what's left of Roger, I would say that I'm now, no matter your metaphor, no longer hanging or perched or balanced, but am standing firmly on solid ground.

Don't assume that I don't understand the difficulty inherent in trying to control what we cannot control or that I haven't considered the difficulties that everyday people face or that I haven't thought about the ways in which I am lucky, luckier than Barbara or Mark or Roger, that I haven't taken into account the fact that we are not really so different, or that I don't see Barbara's difficulties for what they are or how they compare to my own, that I don't understand how hard it can be to keep our baser selves in check or how much easier it is, ultimately, to go back to the evil we know and understand, the evil we have lived with for so long that it feels an inherent and important part of ourselves, to go back to this evil and tell ourselves that we had no other choice, that we didn't opt for this decision, but that really there were never any other options for us to take. I know about choices and about not having choices and how it feels when it seems you have no other choice. Don't assume that I wasn't sympathetic to Barbara, to the choices she was making with Mark.

I was. I am. Sympathetic, but also concerned. I'm concerned about the choices she's making and worried that she is blind to the host of other choices out there available to her. And it dawns on me as I am cleaning up the mess of Roger—the seventh floor is, serendipitously, for lease and occupantless—that I also have choices, that in this moment, I am faced with more options than I have felt faced with in too long of a time for me to remember. And it dawns on me, too, that for the first time there is a choice amid all of these other choices that is perfectly suited to me, to all of me, to the me that cares about Barbara and her well-being, and to the other me that cares about so very little.

Perfectly suited to both of us.

❁

As I survey the mess I made of Roger, there is a persistent voice in my head repeating, over and over again, "Let him rise, let him rise." The voice is saying, "Horde, an army horde of us," and it's saying, "Let him rise," and before that voice can take firm hold of me, I find a thin, sharp metal tray left here by the floor's last occupants and I press it hard against Roger's neck, hard and harder and harder still, until I sever through.

The point of this exercise being this: The mystical properties aside, our regenerative abilities and single-minded pursuit aside, zombies, even zombies, require heads.

There was a time, a long stretch of time, when it was all I wanted to do, create a horde, not an army horde, exactly, but a gathering, or not even that many, not even a gathering, but even just one, just one more. It was a trial and error process— more specifically, a process full of error. Not that the creation of other zombies is a complicated process, that process itself hinging almost entirely on biting, which is my most natural impulse. No, the actual creation of zombies worked once I got the hang of it, worked in the way that I understood how much damage the body could take and still become infected, be lifted back up, given breath, life, some semblance of cognition. But then, it never worked in that what I helped to create was never what I hoped to create.

What should I have expected, though? What was the best I could have hoped for, really? One monster bringing to life a second, a third, a tenth monster?

In hindsight, the endeavor was doomed to fail from the beginning.

Still, if I can be honest with you, if we can speak honestly about this, if I can tell you exactly what I felt during that long stretch of time, what I felt every time a new one came to life, lifted itself to uncertain feet, stumbled back a few steps, then saw me and then lunged for me, only to realize it would get nothing more from me, and then ignored me and everything I said to it, looked past me as if I didn't exist, as if I hadn't just that moment brought it to life, and then stumbled off into the night in search of some living morsel, what I felt was this: envy.

Envy and desire.

Envy and desire and power.

But never satisfaction. I never felt satisfaction, not even the satisfaction of a job well done, which is such a small kind of satisfaction that it's the kind of satisfaction that I get from submitting my salary sourcing reports on time.

But no matter. It's no matter to me at all. It's not a point I wish to belabor. I'm not the kind to dwell. I'm not the kind to say that things are unfair even when things are unfair. *We are dealt our hand in this life, and we can only do with it what we can* is more the kind of thing I'm known to say. *We are given opportunities, and we have to know when these opportunities come around so we can take advantage of them* is another.

And what I have now is an opportunity, what I have now is a chance. This is the thought on my mind, what's going through my head as I look at Roger and then leave him, or what's left of him. This is what's in my head as I make my way back to my office, back to the twelfth floor. And because opportunity is fleeting, because chances like this don't come around every day of your life, because when an opportunity such as this presents itself, you want to take advantage of it quickly, as quickly as possible, because of all of this, I take the elevator back to our offices, not the stairs.

It isn't large-scale change I'm hoping to effect. It isn't the grand course of human events that I want to influence, but just one person, just one woman, just the life of one woman. And as I wait outside our office, around the corner from our office, hidden by the potted ficus next to the elevators, it's her I am thinking of, her and her alone.

I wait for what seems an inconceivably long time. I wait for what feels like hours. I wait and wait and wait, but still, I am focused. My mind is focused on this new decision I've made, this new direction my life will take.

And when he finally turns the corner, I smile. For the first time in a long, long time, I smile in the way that someone who knows what he's doing smiles. I smile the way a man who knows what's going to happen next, who knows what his place in this life is meant to be, smiles. In that way, I smile.

But then I see her walking next to Mark. I see Barbara walking there at his side, and that's when things go dark.

◇

Barbara likes birds.

She watches them. She's a bird-watcher. She attends bird-watching events. She's rather devoted to them. She donates money and time to the Audubon Society. For a while, before Mark made her give them up, she owned parakeets, four or five of them. At one point, they had babies.

Once she told me she wanted to change her name to Bird, change her name to Barbara Bird. She told me that and then she laughed and then she blushed and then she said, "It's dumb, it's stupid. It's a stupid name," and I told her, "No, it sounds nice," and she said, "Mark says it's dumb." She said, "He's probably right."

I'm not fond of birds, personally. For what it's worth, they're not fond of me, either. Most animals aren't, but birds are at times aggressive in their dislike.

They have dead eyes, is the thing that bothers me most about birds. They have dead eyes and they seem to me life-like but lifeless, or maybe it's the other way around, or maybe it's nothing like that at all.

But still, her attraction to them gave me some amount of hope. Not a large amount of hope. Nothing has given me anything more than the smallest amount of hope. But still. The birds and their dead eyes: Are they so different from me?

Dead-eyed me.

Lifelike yet lifeless me.

I can tell you now, though, I can tell you now with confidence, with utmost confidence: It is not a hope worth hoping.

The thing is: Barbara likes birds, maybe she even loves birds, maybe she even likes me. But she cannot love me. She simply cannot.

I know this now. I can accept this now. This is a basic fact of life that I can now accept.

You could argue that her being twenty or thirty heartbeats away from death, you might argue that the broken form of her laid out awkwardly across my desk, you might argue that the misshapen state of her really leaves me little to no choice in the matter.

But that's not entirely true. It's not entirely true that I have no choice in this. It's not entirely true that there are no options left on the table for me.

There are steps, there are a number of steps I could take. At least let's recognize this: It's my choice not to take these steps.

Her husband is nowhere to be found. I can't see him, in any case, glancing briefly around my space, or in any of the cubicles near mine. Granted, there is a lot to see. Granted, there are a lot of bodies to see, and it's possible he's one of them. It's possible he's one of the many, covered, perhaps, by one of the others.

I am, admittedly, fuzzy on the details. Let's just say that my command of the details is not very commanding.

How about, let's say, of the details, what I know is this: Things did not go according to plan.

Or let's say that things did not go according to my plan.

Not that my plan was an especially good plan, not that my plan didn't have its own inherent flaws. Not that I don't know that my plan to help Barbara make sounder decisions in her life by taking care of Mark, by which I mean killing Mark, wasn't necessarily the best-laid plan.

But still, it was a plan. Still, it was a simple plan. It was a simple plan that did not, I know for a fact, include the slaughter of my office mates, least of all the slaughter of Barbara, who is even now making a soft gurgling sound as she's lying there across my desk.

The point I'm trying to make being: The zombie has plans of his own.

By which I mean: Some of the bodies are beginning to stir now.

What truly surprises me, though, what comes to me as completely unexpected is this moment right now, this very moment, this moment of wakefulness, of cognition.

I saw Barbara and things went dark, and things could have remained that way, could have been kept dark for an eternity, and what would I have known about any of it, what would I have been able to control of any of it? Yet here I am, things decidedly not dark, and I am not sure what to make of it, to make of any of it.

By which I mean: Is this a gesture of cruelty or generosity?

Is this the zombie laughing at me, laughing at my weak attempts to effect some change in me, in her, in the world? Or is this the zombie saying, "Here you go, one last look, one last look at least, a moment, at least, a reward for your efforts, doomed though we all knew them to be"?

Frankly, though, I don't care.

There is shuffling now going on behind me. There are groans, and there are things—picture frames, computers, file cabinets—crashing to the floor.

I don't care. I take my one last look.

As to the circumstances surrounding my arrival, I have no memory of this moment. I have no memory of who I was before, or what I was before. It's a blank. It's a pleasant and unassuming blank.

There was the one time. There was that one time with the memories, a slew of them. Relentless memories, a series of them, flashing through my head for fifteen, twenty, thirty minutes, one right after the other, nonstop, these memories, in no particular order, of no special significance, but personal, deeply personal, brief sensations, images, smells, sounds, forced out of hiding, maybe, by that darker part of me, forced out into the open to be devoured or simply to dissipate, those last remaining pieces of the me that was me before. A park bench, the quality of light in a dormitory cafeteria, the smell of lavender, the smell of cooking oil cooked too hot, a swimming pool, a bloodied knee, soft, soft lips, a blue couch, a dark room, a bright blue sky, a man's voice saying "Sometimes I just don't know about you, son," a flat tire, a long, hot stretch of road, mist rising off a small pond, a kite shaped like a swan overhead, the first cool day in October, on and on, these memories rose up from within me, traveled through me and then out. I staggered under the rush of them, and then they were gone, so quickly gone, I stumbled, grabbed for a chair, sat down hard on the floor, and that was it. I remember them still, but I remember them now as things I have seen in a movie or on the television, as disconnected sensations that don't touch me at all.

So let's not demean ourselves with talk of who I was and if this person still lives inside me. If my eyes are this person's eyes and if in them you can see remnants of who this person once was.

Let's not resort to this kind of nostalgic preening.

Let's not reduce my story to that kind of tragedy.

Instead, let's remark on how unsurprising this outcome really is, and then let's move on, inexorably, deliberately on.

To pick up where we left off: Her body bent awkwardly over the desk, the soft gurgle escaping her lips.

I want to tell her, *It wasn't supposed to happen like this, you know.*

I want to take her head in my lap. I want to smell her hair, smell her wrists. I want to kiss her neck.

I want to say to her soft, lovely things, whisper unyielding truths in her ear. I want to run my finger along the length of her nose, from the bridge to the tip, and then over and onto her lips.

I want to feel the warmth of her as her living body warms my thighs and my feet and the lower part of my stomach, makes my skin, which is cold and rubbery to touch, feel pliant and lifelike again.

These are the things that I want. These are the things I have wanted for some very long time now. I imagine that these are the things I have wanted since even before I became the kind of thing that could not have them.

But the zombie in me wants something else. The zombie in me wants to eat. The zombie wants to eat and he wants his horde, and as much as I try to deny it, there is no zombie in me, there is only me, and all of me is zombie.

Life on Capra II

Just as we bag that piece of shit swamp monster, the robots attack. Ricky goes down immediately, and that's a fucking shame because he was a good guy, and also he owes me— owed me—a pack of cigarettes and had promised to intro- duce me to the tomato who runs the commissary, a pretty little thing named Becky who he'd known back when he was in grade school. That lady has a fine ass and has expended more T&E avoiding me than I've spent trying to get her attention, and Ricky was my last chance, and maybe it's cold of me, but as I watch him fall face-first in the swamp muck, my first thought is how all those plans have just gone straight to hell.

Fucking robots, being my second thought.

I think about hoisting him up out of the muck and throw- ing him over my shoulder and hoofing him back to the con- voy, if only to have some good story to tell Becky once we get back to the barracks, maybe make like he wasn't killed with the first shot, that he was barely breathing but that I wouldn't leave my good friend Ricky behind, and that he expended his last breath to tell me to keep going, to never give up, that I would someday find true love in the sympathetic heart of a beautiful woman. But then I figure I don't actually have to go through all the trouble of carrying Ricky's deadweight body to be able to tell that same story, so I leave him where he is and start beating a hasty retreat.

That's one of the first lessons any new cadet learns here on Capra II: Simplify your life.

Twenty minutes later and five cadets lighter, we finally make it back to the convoy. Turns out we weren't the only battalion to be ambushed by the sonsabitches, and, unlikely as it seems, the piece of shit swamp monsters and the fucking robots made some sort of concerted play on us.

Five minutes later we're in the air on our way back to the barracks.

I look out the window down at the wreckage. Someone set fire to the swamp muck. I squint, wondering for a minute or two if I can see Ricky, but mostly all I can see are glints of light reflecting off the robot body parts and the last few of the swamp monsters writhing in flames. Then I put my head back and close my eyes and try to catch a little sleep.

◈

When the New Worlds Confederation started casting about for a planet to house the excess settlers, those who didn't exactly fit the profile of the young, able-bodied, handsome folk who settled Capra I, they took their money, shipped them off, deposited them on this piece of rock, and then forgot about them, that is, until the tithing stopped, which is why we're here.

It's a strange planet, Capra II. Or, hell, maybe it's not even a planet, just some rock floating through space the New Worlds Confederation decided to terraform. You can't tell these days, and, sure, maybe there was a briefing about it all when we shipped out, but I'll say right now, I'm not one for holding on to the finer details of an assignment. Either way, it's a strange fucking place. For one, the colors seem off. I can't explain how they seem off, only that when I'm looking around, the whole world looks like it's covered in some kind of filter, or like I'm wearing a yellow-tinted visor, even when I'm not. Blues look green. Reds look orange. Everything is covered in a haze. Something about the atmosphere makes us light-headed, too, and suppresses the smell of things, which, when you're living in a barracks with a hundred other grunts, isn't the worst thing you could ask for.

Still. It's a bit off-putting.

What worries me most is the emptiness of this place. Most of what we've got are those wild and unending swamplands, and whatever asshole decided to terraform a planet of swamps deserves a swift kick in the balls if you ask me. Practically uninhabitable, and even if you could devise some kind of structure that would survive the swamp muck, which seems to eat anything inorganic, one that could keep out the bugs and swamp rats and not allow the poisonous swamp gas to seep into your bedroom and kill you while you slept, you'd still have to contend with those piece of shit swamp monsters. You get pockets here and there, dry lands just above sea level that could pass for livable, and you'll see structures and the signs of society—a glass-cased infirmary, a one-room schoolhouse, carbide huts that make you wonder why the hell you'd take a material as formidable as carbide and build out of it a hut like you're part of some ancient civilization—and maybe if you squint and put your imagination to the test, you can picture how a life of sorts might've been obtained here, but the people are gone, and no one knows for sure why, though my money's on the swamp monsters or the robots having some hand in all of that. And whatever the case, it's a goddamn ghost planet out here, and to me it seems like we're just biding our time, giving whatever evil thing resides here a chance to size us up, find out that weakest part of us, and then do to us what was done to the colonists who first gave it a go here.

We are hunting swamp monsters, and part of me wants to say that we have done this before, wants to say we are in the swamps hunting swamp monsters again, but that can't be right, and so I shake the feeling off and do my best to keep myself steady, alert.

Ricky's on my right flank and, to release the tension building in the back of my neck and to give us something to do while we truck through this hellhole, I'm about to ask him about Becky, ask him about what she was like when they were in grade school together. He's made noise about how he can introduce me, make me seem like a decent enough sort of guy, that he and she go way back, and I want to know if he's bullshitting me or if he's serious. But then one of the swamp bastards rears up between the two of us, and it's a monster, all right, which I know. I know these things are real monsters, that what we're playing at here is no joke, but the sight of them, no matter how many surveillance videos I've watched, no matter how many pictures I've seen, no matter how many good men we've lost to these bastards, the sight of them does not fail to surprise me.

For one thing, they're *of* the swamp more than they are *from* the swamp. It's as if the swamp rises up, ten, fifteen feet up in the air, takes on a face with eyes and a mouth hole and swampy teeth of a sort, forms arms and clawed hands, a torso but no real legs, no legs to speak of, just a hovering jet of swamp muck that pushes these monsters up against gravity, against physics, against God. They make for a sick and unsettling sight, and this one's looking right down on me, and I've got a good shot, an opportunity to take this fucker out, but for some goddamn reason I'm holding the wrong gun. I've got a sniper rifle in my hands, and I feel like I'm in some kind of anxiety dream, where I come to school having forgotten a major test I have to take, or my clothes, because what the fuck is a sniper rifle going to do to this thing made of swamp shit and twigs?

◇

There's a moment when I feel like I know what's going to happen next.

A moment when everything is all at once familiar and uncanny—where Ricky is standing, the gassy smell of the swamp monster, the glint of sunlight glancing off the guns and armor of Johnson, Harald, and Spigs, the sound of the convoy in the distance, even these thoughts running through my mind—and in this moment, I'm struck suddenly by an all-consuming urge to shove Ricky down into the swamp, to heave myself at him with the whole of me, to shove the lot of us out of harm's way, and it's all I can do to stop myself, to curb this sudden and forceful urge, and then the robots attack—coming in out of nowhere—and I am surprised and I am not surprised.

◇

Just as we bag the swamp monster, the robots attack. It's a shock to see them there, the sun glinting off their metallic bodies, but it's almost more of a shock that I'm staring straight at the one about to laser Ricky's ass, as if I had some sixth sense telling me where it was going to rear up, my grenade launcher armed and ready. I blow the fucker's head off, and I'm about to look at Ricky and say "What the hell?" but he's off and running without even a "Thanks, dude," and I want to yell at him that he still owes me a pack of cigarettes, but what's the point because there are explosions all around me, all around us, and I bag another robot, and then a third, and I'm feeling pretty lucky to be carrying this grenade launcher when I could have sworn just a few minutes ago I had a sniper rifle in my hands, and before that, my service pistol.

I run through the swamps, first left and then right, looking for more swamp monsters or robots, or even anyone else from my squad, and then find myself looking at a wall of swamp trees with no way through or around. This sort of thing happens to me more frequently than I care to admit. I chalk it up to enthusiasm, the rush of adrenaline clouding my senses, so that I turn around and see that all the action is behind me, but by the time I run back to catch up to them, the swamp monsters have mostly dissolved back into the primordial muck, but I see one robot close enough that if I hustle I can tag him with my last grenade, but just as I'm honing in on him, I trip over something and land face-first in the swamp. I pull myself up. The slimy green water cascades down my helmet visor. The robot's gone—jet pack—and I look to see what I've tripped over, and it's Ricky, or the top half of him, anyway, and it's a fucking shame. He owes me—owed me—a pack of cigarettes and had promised to introduce me to a pretty young thing who runs the commissary who he'd known back in grade school. For a second, I consider reaching down and grabbing his dog tags, though what I would do with them—"Here you go, something to remember your old grade school chum by"—I don't have a damn clue, but then the comm in my helmet comes blaring into my ears, my commander yelling at me to hurry the fuck up unless I want to biv in the swamps tonight, and I leave Ricky, leave his tags, and hoof it to the rendezvous point.

Five minutes later we're in the air on our way back to the barracks.

I look out the window down at the wreckage. Someone set fire to the swamp muck. I squint, wondering for a minute or two if I can see Ricky, but mostly all I can see are glints of light reflecting off the robot body parts and the last few of the swamp monsters writhing in flames. Then I put my head back and close my eyes and try to catch a little sleep.

⚙

I'm in a warehouse. Above me and below me and on all sides of me are sounds of fighting. Robots. Again. When we arrived at this warehouse, I figured it would be the warehouse where the robots were holed up making more of themselves, as it seems that there is an almost endless supply of them swarming around us, and no one has the first god-damn idea where they came from or if there's someone behind them all. This is not the robot warehouse, however. It's one of our own. I didn't know we had a warehouse, and the fact that we do—and that it's full of crates of oranges and ammo and small wooden rocking horses—strikes me somehow as criminal.

"When the fuck did we build a warehouse?" I want to ask Ricky, but we never get any downtime, so I don't. The place is covered in dust and grime inches thick, and it's possible that the warehouse wasn't built by us at all, that it was part of the human settlement we came here to defend, only to discover we had come too late and it had already been overrun by swamp monsters and robots and other unmentionables.

It should seem odd, then, that somewhere holed up in this spooky warehouse is a device that, when you flip a switch and pull a lever, activates an electromagnetic pulse, but that's what I've been told, that and that it's my job to find it and activate it.

What I don't get, or, hell, one of the many, many things I no longer get, is why the fuck did we come to this warehouse in the first place? I can't tell you what we eat, but we don't eat or need oranges, nor do we suffer from a deficit of wooden rocking horses. We don't need ammo, either, which, if I'm to believe the stenciling on the sides of these crates, is the only other thing stored in this warehouse. For as long as I can remember, I have not one time run out of ammo, or, if I have run out of ammo in, say, my semiautomatic, or charge in my DevLazer Rifle 3000, I can simply toss it aside and pick up some other weapon, fully loaded, though I cannot tell you where these come from exactly. And if worst comes to worst, and even my service pistol runs out of bullets, I always have my knife, which is a wicked and jagged-looking thing, though what help it would be against swamp monsters or robots, I can't say. Still. It's there.

And the armory. Don't let's get started on how big our armory is.

So if we don't need oranges and we don't need rocking horses and we don't need ammo, there seems to be little good reason for us to be here except that there are robots roosting here—do robots roost?—and a switch somewhere in the middle of here to shut them all down. But if we hadn't come here in the first place, would they even have roused themselves, and even if they'd already been roused, they were roused here and we were safely somewhere else, and so it wouldn't have fucking mattered that the roosting robots had been roused.

I could go on, but what's the point? An order's an order, and the sooner I can find that electromagnetic pulse switch, the sooner I can get back to camp and head to the commissary to see if Becky's there behind the desk, see if she'll do more than roll her eyes at me when I tell her we should get together when she's free.

As I'm mulling over what else I might say to Becky, these three things happen all at once: I turn around yet another crate of wooden rocking horses, I see on the wall opposite me the electromagnetic pulse switch, and a robot crashes through the floor. Yet even as I'm fumbling for my weapon, even as that robot comes bearing down on me, I can't stop thinking of what I should say to Becky.

◈

The bunker's being attacked. This takes me by surprise, but by the looks of it, I'm the only one who didn't see this coming.

In truth, I don't remember being in the bunker. I don't remember suiting up or grabbing my rifle, either, but it's dark outside and none of us is wearing our sleep ordnance, and I've got a rifle in my hands—the sniper again—so it must have happened, and I must have been here when it did.

We're being set upon by robots and these monsters I've only read about: three-legged sonsabitches outfitted with some kind of grotesque and unsettling stereoscopic eye mounted on a long stalk branching out of its torso. Drool and all manner of particulate bungee in thick ropes from their gaping maws. Wiry tufts of hair sprout out of their knuckles. It's all pretty disgusting and stirs me up for a good fight.

Since all I have is a small knife and my sniper rifle, though, I figure the most I can do is aim for that eye and hope for the best.

And I figure I should move cautiously. I'm navigating down one hallway and up the next, swiveling left and right, surveying the landscape of dead soldiers and broken robot parts and the blown-to-bits alien monsters, when, streaking past me on my right, Ricky runs pell-mell into the thick of the fight, and seeing him run by like that, I'm thrown for a wild loop.

I can't say why, but something about seeing Ricky, seeing him running, seeing him with his head on his shoulders and not blown the fuck off, seeing him at all, feels wrong. My head swims. I career into the wall. Something in the distance in front of me explodes, and hairy, tufted hands fly past me, and bits of gore squish against my helmet visor, and then Ricky's head tumbles down the hall, as if it's beating a hasty retreat and it couldn't wait on the rest of him, which is only seconds behind, or is holding the bastards off while the head makes its escape, and I should be horrified by this, but there's something comforting about the sight of his head rolling to a stop at my feet, as if before some piece of the world had been out of true, and now things have leveled out again.

Whatever exploded ahead of me has set off a chain reaction, and the walls ahead of me blow out as smaller explosions rocket in my direction. It's as if the entire bunker has been layered with minicharges and the entire structure is buckling, and I wonder at the shoddiness of our base camp.

Regardless, I turn tail and run.

Left and then right and then right again and then left again. Rooms and control panels and doorways blur past as I run toward the exit. A part of me, though, feels as if I'm in a maze, as if I've never seen this place before, as if I don't know where I'm going or which way is the way out. All the while, I'm keeping my eye out for Becky. I don't know why. A fine ass is a fine ass, but nothing is worth being blown up for, and what with Ricky being headless and all, and Becky's natural inclination to ignore my every pass at her, there's nothing in it for me.

I know I'm a fool for looking for her, and I will be a fool if I stop for her, yet I can't help myself. And then I see her.

I run past a doorway, and I catch sight of her out of the corner of my eye. She's still sitting primly, beautifully, behind her desk, oblivious to the shitstorm raging around us, and I try to stop. I throw on the brakes. I reach out for the doorjamb. But nothing happens. I don't stop. I can't stop.

I'm pushed forward. Some force—gravity, momentum, an unexpected planetary shift?—is pushing me forward. And for the first time, or maybe not the first time, maybe this isn't the first time at all that this thought has come into my head but is only the first time I've considered it seriously, I wonder who is in control of me, of my legs, my eyes, my choices.

And with more effort than I have ever known myself to exert, I turn myself around.

I can't say that it is painful, the feeling I get when I perform this trick. In truth, the word itself—*painful*—means jack shit to me, and if you were to ask me to describe what pain was, I couldn't. But the sensation—stopping in place, standing still, turning myself around—is a queer one, for damn sure. And while I can't say whether it hurts or not, what I can say is that when I take a step, I feel less like myself than I can begin to explain. What I can say is that I can't help but turn my head to look at where I had been standing just to make sure that I'm not still standing there. But I'm not there. I'm here. I'm moving back to where Becky was, but it's slow, it's slow going and difficult, and with every step I feel like I'm leaving a piece of myself behind.

I make it, finally, to the next doorway—to what kind of room, I don't know—and lean heavily against it, still fighting against the powerful, undeniable urge to go back to running for the exit.

But then as I try to push myself off and stand up straight again, I push myself through the door and the doorway—I don't know how; the door doesn't open—and my foot catches on something and I trip and I fall, and maybe it's the sense of free fall, but even as I am falling, faster and faster, I feel light as air.

Here is what I don't understand. Here is that question that bothers me in the swamps, in our barracks, while at the warehouse, whether fighting swamp monsters or hairy-knuckled beasts or those fucking robots, the question that burns in the back of my mind during every waking moment, and it is this: When have I ever seen Becky's ass?

I'm not going on about her clad in her unmentionables, or even bare, at the risk of sounding crude and ungentlemanly. I'm talking about nothing more than just her backside in a pair of shorts or her commissary uniform. I'm talking about seeing her standing up or walking around or doing anything anywhere that isn't behind that commissary desk. And I have to admit that the answer to that question is never. And yet the compulsion to say her backside is fine, the need to make her love me based on my idea of it, is so strongly felt that it will sometimes seem more real to me than anything else I have seen or done here on Capra II. I have never caught even a glimpse of it, yet I will find myself, even in the heat of battle, pining keenly for it and, by extension, her.

That fall must have addled my brain some, because when I stand up, I'm in the swamps again. Then the swamps begin to flicker, and I close my eyes and give my head a gentle shake and when I open them up, I'm in the warehouse, and then this flickers and I'm back in the bunker, surrounded by noise and fire and explosions and a bloody fucking mess of monster bits and robot pieces and the disjointed remains of my squad landing all around me as if some huge explosion just blew everything to hell.

I don't know where I am or what the hell is going on, and so there's no good reason left for pushing forward, but I lash myself to the idea that I still need to find Becky, and with that occupying my mind, I trudge on as best I can. Debris is still raining down on me, and the landscape is still shifting around me and under my feet. I'll find myself at one moment turning down a corridor in the bunker and the next blocked by a copse of swamp trees. At one point, I come to an intersection—some piece of the warehouse by the looks of it—under heavy fire, and I wait until the shooting stops, and then I make a run for it, but I trip halfway across when the scene shifts first to the swamp and then quickly back to the bunker, and I land hard on my arms and elbows. The wind is knocked out of me, and I huff myself back onto my feet when I see a man standing in front of me, looking back at me, who I'm about to ask for help when I realize it's me. I'm looking at me, at my reflection, and it's an unsettling sight. It's not that I see myself for the first time in a long time and hardly recognize the man in the reflection— created by a windowpane all but completely shattered by shrapnel and the fighting. It's not like that at all. It's like I've never seen my own self reflected before, like I never knew what I looked like at all, and so who I'm looking at is a stranger.

I lift my hand up to wave to make sure I'm looking at me when the rest of the glass is broken out by Ricky, who is thrown headfirst through it by one of the fucking robots, who then turns its red mechanical eye at me, and then I start to run again.

I don't remember the last time I took a shower. I don't remember waking up in the mornings or putting myself down to sleep. I don't remember the last time I took a drink of water or drank down a beer or ate a good breakfast or ate any goddamn thing or the last time I fucked. A man can't live without these things, or without most of them, yet here I am, trudging along, first in this bunker and then in the swamps and back to the bunker again.

To me it seems that the basic and necessary parts of my life aren't being lived, or not by me, or not so I can remember them, and as if I'm pulled out of whatever black hole I reside in only to navigate through these maze-like halls and among the crates of some damn warehouse, through the muck of a swamp that should smell like death but that I can't recall smelling like anything.

I've seen Ricky's head blown off or his leg torn off or his guts spilled out more times than I can count now, and I'm beginning to hit on an idea about what's going on here, but it's an idea just out of reach, or it's like it's the idea of an idea, or the idea of an idea of an idea, and the harder I try to suss that idea out, the further away from it I'm pushed, or not pushed, not really that, but more like the idea itself, more and more versions of this same idea, stand in the way of my understanding it. Or it's like I have a map that leads me to another map that turns out to be the same exact map as before with instructions that will lead me, I know, to another damn map, over and over, again and again. Or it's like none of those things at all, and I'm just wasting my time trying to figure it all out, and so finally, in the end, what I decide is, *Fuck it*, and I close my eyes and blindly start shooting and blindly start running, and when my Gatling gun runs out of ammo, I toss it aside, and when my semiautomatic and my automatic rifles run out of ammo, I toss them aside, too, and this continues, on and on, I'm tossing shit behind me until, my eyes still shut, my legs still pushing me forward, I have tossed off every weapon in my personal arsenal but my knife.

And through all of this, I have been touched not one single time.

No stray bullets, no robotic arms grabbing at me, no swamp muck splashing my legs as I run, not even a shoulder of bunker wall knocking me off course. I must have run through hell and back, run in the swamps and through the warehouse and up and down one bunker corridor after another, stepped on the various pieces of my comrades in arms, and nothing has touched me, not once, and so I stop and I open my eyes, and I look around me at a world that has gone inside out.

◇

I keep expecting something to come back to me, memories, or a deeper sense of myself, my past, those relationships I've had and that I left behind when I joined up with the New Worlds Army to come fight here on Capra II, but for a long time, the oldest memory I could hold on to was the memory of the moment before, and even now, when it seems as if something has shifted inside me and I'm able to hold on to things, I can only really remember back to the beginning of the attack on the bunker and nothing at all before that.

So when I look at what I'm looking at, hoping some mechanism of memory might kick into gear to give me a clue as to what the fuck this thing in front of me is and what the hell I'm supposed to do to get around it, I'm not surprised, though I'm a little disappointed, when nothing inside my ragged brain magically comes to order.

Whatever it is, it stands nearly three stories high, and the high-pitched angry drone of it drowns out every other sound. The longer I look at it, the more details come into focus, and it begins to look like some bastard monster, the likes of which I've never seen, and comprising all the monsters this furious planet, Capra II, has seen fit to throw at us. It rises up on the jets of the swamp muck, even though we are clearly in the bunker, and out of its undulating torso sprout robot manacles and the hairy-tufted arms of the bunker beasts. Where there should be a head there's that stereoscopic stalk, and in the center of that pulses the cold, red eye of a robot.

Any minute now I expect to see Ricky come running past me only to get his damn fool head lasered off by that red eye and then the rest of him shoved into the open, swampy craw of that thing, but it doesn't happen. There's no one else around. There's only it and only me.

I stand in front of it waiting for something to happen because I'm sure as hell not going to be the jackass who makes the first move against this thing, but all it does is pulse and undulate and sway, and after a while I get the sense that we're two players playing at the same game. That it can wait as long as I can wait, and that nothing will happen for an eternity until one of us makes something happen. I also get the sense—or not even the sense, but the clear and certain knowledge—that on the other side of this is Becky and her fine ass and her commissary uniform and her sweet smile and a life of goodness without reproach. And while I can stand here as solid and still as stone and never risk inevitable death and dismemberment, I know, too, that in this eternity of stillness never will I find true love in the sympathetic heart of a beautiful woman, and when it comes down to it, that's the only thing I want.

◈

Here is the future I see for us. Here is how things are going to go from this moment forward:

Things are going to go south. Between me and whatever that thing is that is between me and Becky, things will definitely go south, but not so far south as to go hopeless. I'm a trained soldier in the New Worlds Army, after all, and resourceful, and strong, and if there's one thing I know now, it's this: The love of a good woman will change a man, and the faintly attainable nature of that love will make him capable of implausible, death-defying acts.

Then—big bad beastie dispatched of—I will find my lovely lady, will stumble blindly toward her desk in the commissary, will crash unceremoniously, yet bravely, into the doorway, will slump down but not quite all the way down to the floor, will softly call her name, will close my eyes, will wait for her tentative, gentle touch. When she holds me in her arms and lowers me to the floor, I will open my eyes and look deep into her own and smile a rakish smile. She will say something along the lines of "You came" or "I didn't think you'd come." I will open my mouth to say something along the lines of "I could never leave you behind" or "I'll always come for you," but before I can say anything, she'll silence me with the soft pressure of her finger against my lips, and I will pull her down to me and push her finger aside for her lips, which will crush against my own. And in that moment, nothing else will matter in even the slightest way. Then I will pull myself to my feet, buoyed by that kiss and her true love and her sympathetic heart. I will stand and pull her close to me and I will hold her in my arms and we will gaze at the unforgiving landscape laid out before us and I will say, "Let them do their worst," and we'll laugh and pull each other closer, and together we will root out what is evil about this place, root it out and cast it aside, and unearth that small something of goodness that must exist in every new planet, and by the power of our love, this tiny rock will flourish.

But even I know what really lies in store for us. Even I know I won't get that far. Won't make it five steps before that thing grabs me by my nethers and tears me in two and stuffs me down its craw and seeks out every last one of us and sunders the planet itself, but what do I care? With Becky on the other side of it, what other choice do I have but to close my eyes, throw down my knife, and make my run for it?

Juan Refugio Rocha:
A Meritorious Life

R OCHA, JUAN REFUGIO (b. 1957). Zookeeper, animal trainer. Place of birth: Antigua, Guatemala. Very little is known about the 1979 Fuego del Zoológico Público, only that the grounds caught fire in the early morning of October 18, 1979, that the fire consumed the entire grounds and all its structures by daybreak, and that, in the fire, only four animals perished—one howler monkey, one chimpanzee, and two gorillas, one male and one female. The man who freed the animals from their cages and herded them out of their habitats was Juan Refugio Rocha, a twenty-two-year-old Guatemalan who had been working at the zoo for six months, during which time he had been trying to teach the gorillas to speak.

As a child, Rocha had been adept at communicating with animals through clicks, whistles, taps, nudges, snaps, and squeezes. His father had owned donkeys, which Rocha had cared for and which the family had used to earn money for food and clothing, renting the beasts out as transportation and pack animals. Rocha had trained each animal, and in all his years as keeper of the donkeys, no one was thrown, no packs were lost.

In 1974, Rocha left his parents' house and moved to Mexico City. From there, he moved to the state of Chihuahua, where he worked intermittently for carnival acts, training dogs and elephants and jungle cats. In the late spring of 1979, he got word of a public zoo in need of a keeper whose duties also involved light veterinarian work. By May, Rocha had taken the position, and in a few days found himself obsessed with the gorillas.

Rocha, having never seen a gorilla before, knew little of their behaviors and nothing about their habitats. Through study of their personalities and through close observation of their physical characteristics, Rocha determined that the zoo owned one male western lowland gorilla and one female western lowland gorilla. He spent his days at the zoo caring for the animals, and the nights he spent in his room or at the library, studying their behavior. He went to great lengths to acquire the bamboo shoots, thistles, wild celery, and tubers that they ate. He constructed a realistic environment similar to the western African lowlands in design and humidity and greenery, and he gave them grasses and branches with which to build nests.

Once the two gorillas were settled, he made his first steps toward establishing a line of communication. Witnesses reported that when Rocha entered the habitat screeching and hooting and clicking to get the animals' attention, the gorillas began to squawk and let out a high piercing keen. The animals charged at him, running on their hind legs, "like people," with surprising dexterity and swiftness. They worked as a team, flanking and herding Rocha into a corner, and once he was trapped between the two, they began to kick and punch him in the back and in the head. Three men, groundskeepers who had been standing by to watch the animal trainer, finally managed to pull him out of the habitat, by which time Rocha had suffered a minor concussion and two broken ribs.

Rocha did not give up. Over the next six months, he entered the gorilla habitat no fewer than ten times, and the animals continued to greet him with the same volatility and aggression. The gorillas took the food he offered them, lived in the habitat he created for them, and in that habitat they were peaceful. Once he entered their world, however, as if they had been trained for it, the gorillas circled him, trapped him, ignored him as he spoke, and then beat him. After five or ten minutes, Rocha needed to be pulled from the cage, with a broken arm, broken fingers, broken ribs, badly bruised skin, cuts, contusions, abrasions, or minor concussions.

When the fire started, Rocha was with the gorillas, standing outside their habitat talking to them, as he often did, from a safe distance. He hooted and chirped and howled at them for a full fifteen minutes before leaving to attend to the other animals in the park. By the time help had arrived and the other animals had been freed from their cages and environments, the fire raged out of control, burning until dawn, when the last embers snuffed out and all that was left—the zoo, the howler monkey, the chimp, and the gorillas—was ash.

The Disappearance of
the Sebali Tribe

I.

In the summer of 1974, two young anthropologists, Joseph Hammond and Marcus Alexander Grant, published, to very high praise, an article in the journal *Dialectic Studies in Anthropology* entitled "The Drameção Ritual: Silent Conflicts of the Sebali Prepubescent Male." Through the success of this article, and based on proposals for continued research on the Sebali tribe, Hammond and Grant received research funding from the National Science Foundation and the Sloan Foundation, and the two young men were each offered positions teaching anthropology and sociology, Grant at Yale University, and Hammond at his alma mater, Harvard University. The article and their subsequent findings were then published as a book, *The Sebali Continuum*, which included color and black-and-white photographs of the tribe as well as detailed observations and analyses of the tribe's history, its health and system of caring for the sick and the old, religious beliefs, mating rituals, community mores and taboos, agricultural practices, the birth and death rates of the tribe, the passage of the tribe's collective memory (through oral history, storytelling, and pictographs), and the rituals for burying tribal leaders once they have died. The book became an immediate success. Grant was thirty-two years old and Hammond was thirty-four, and together they had been studying the Sebali tribe for five and a half years.

One year later, they both disappeared.

At the time, the two young men had been planning a last extended visit to the small South Pacific island where the members of the Sebali tribe lived. After their departure date came and went, it was assumed that the two—commonly absentminded—had left without saying good-bye. When, after some months had passed, no one had yet heard from them, friends and colleagues began to worry that something might have happened to them both. A year passed without word, and many speculated that the two had been killed, either en route to or while with the Sebali tribe.

Their disappearance caused a furor, and search committees were formed and papers were published, and a rift formed between those who, as delicately as they could, implied that Hammond and Grant got no less than they deserved and that there had been a long line of anthropologists who had meddled or "gone native" to bad and sometimes fatal effect, and those who argued that Hammond and Grant died honorably in the service of their science and for the betterment of our understanding of our place in this world and its history.

Such arguments and speculations continued for another three years until it was proven almost single-handedly by a twenty-four-year-old actor turned anthropologist, Denise Gibson, that Hammond and Grant were fakes, that the Sebali tribe did not exist and had never existed other than in the minds of its creators. This discovery left suspicions that linger in the anthropology community even today, and raised questions, for those close to Hammond and Grant, for their friends and colleagues, as to who Hammond and Grant really were and what they had hoped to gain.

II.

Denise Gibson has lived in Boston for the past five years. She is now a graduate student in the Boston University anthropology department, although when she first heard about Hammond and Grant, their work on the Sebali tribe, their book, and their disappearance, she was an undergraduate student. She is small and attractive, with a soft voice and blue eyes that often look, during the overcast months of a New England fall or winter, gray. She has short brown hair, and though I only saw her wearing them once, she sometimes wears glasses, and when I picture her, I picture her in those glasses. Born in Texas (when I asked her if she thought it odd that she and Grant hail from the same state, she smirked at me in a way I have found particular to Texans and said, "It is a big state, you know"), Denise had plans of becoming an actress, attending, for the first two years of college, the University of Texas at Austin, where she studied theater. After two years, however, she applied to be and was accepted as a transfer student at BU, where she began her career as a student of anthropology. When pressed, she will admit that there are universities and colleges in Texas that have decent anthropology programs, but that she left because she felt, after a lifetime spent in Texas, the place had become suddenly small, and that she needed a change.

Though a keen observer of people, a skill I am sure good actors should possess, she has a studious, shy, quiet quality about her, and an ability to focus her attention that seems better suited to scholarly work. The first time we met, I found her sitting at a table reading an issue of the *Annual Review of Anthropology*, so enrapt in her article that I had sat down with my coffee and cake, and cleared my throat, only to go unnoticed by her. Unwilling to interrupt someone quite so deeply involved in anything, I waited a few more moments until, as I watched as the hour we had arranged for the interview slipped effortlessly by, I scraped my chair against the floor, banged my coffee mug onto the table, and said, rather too loudly, "So you must be Denise." At which point she looked up from her journal, smiled at me, and said, "I was beginning to worry you weren't going to show." Many people, when they find out Denise once aspired to be an actor, will ask her to perform impressions, which, she informed me early into our interview, are the domain not of actors but of stand-up comedians. "I will give you the benefit of the doubt," she told me, "and assume you weren't going to ask me to do my best Katharine Hepburn."

If you were to ask her, as I did, how it felt knowing that she had helped uncover the Sebali tribe hoax, she might shake her head and smile, somewhat ruefully, and say, "I hardly did a thing about it, really." She might then ask you where you're from, if you'd had a nice trip, if you needed another cup of coffee, if you'd ever been to Boston before, if you'd made a visit to the Common yet, "which is really much nicer in the spring and early summer," she might go on to say, "but we just had a good snow, and you should really go see the park before too many other people go tramping through it." And then she might mention Frederick Law Olmsted, who, she will explain, is best known for his design of Central Park in Manhattan, but who also designed a series of parks joining the Boston Common to its outlying neighbors, which is called the Emerald Necklace, and then she might suggest that you visit Jamaica Pond, a component of the Emerald Necklace, located in Jamaica Plain, "which hardly anyone ever goes to anymore," she will continue, "because the neighborhood's been run down a bit, but it's a nice park, really, and if you go at the right time, it's quiet and empty, and you can sit on a bench and look out over the pond that is there and sometimes see a goose or a swan or a cormorant, even. But if you go there, then you've got to visit El Oriental for lunch, and since the thought of anyone else going to El Oriental only makes *me* want to go there, too, then I just might have to join you," which is how I eventually found myself sitting with her, one recent afternoon, in a small Cuban restaurant (El Oriental de Cuba) in Jamaica Plain, a Puerto Rican, Dominican, and Cuban neighborhood located on the south side of Boston. While she finished with great relish her lunch and I sipped on a small, Styrofoam cup of café con leche, I tried my best to figure out how this small, unassuming young woman from Abilene, Texas, uncovered the truth behind one of the largest anthropological scams of the past fifty years.

III.

Joseph Hammond was born in 1942, the third of eight children. He was born Joseph Farrow. The name Hammond was his mother's maiden name. The family lived in Salina, Kansas, where Joseph's father worked as a salesman, trading in brushes, shaving kits, aftershave lotions, makeup, hair dyes, and other such items. His mother worked as an occasional housekeeper, but spent the majority of her time at home, raising her children. Most of his family members—those few

I could track down—refused to return my phone calls. And when they did agree to speak to me, they would not comment further than to reaffirm certain biographical information already publicly known and now assumed mostly false.

The only information I was able to confirm was that Joseph left home at the age of fifteen and that he was not heard from again for almost three years. Little is known about what actually happened during those years. According to Hammond's own account, he spent them traveling by railroad from Dallas through the Southwestern states until he reached California, where he spent one year at the Anthropology Library on the UC Berkeley campus. There he read such works as Liden's *The Living Earth* and Kelley's *Studies in Javanese Paganisms*. After a year, he left California, again by railway, and traveled to Alaska, where he worked for two years on a fishing boat, netting Alaskan king salmon. Within days of his arrival in Alaska, Hammond met an Inuit couple with whom he quickly became friends. Most of his time was spent on the fishing boats, and any time off the boats Hammond then spent with the Inuit at their home, among their neighbors, observing their daily lives and learning their customs. In a short, unpublished essay— what some believe to have been the beginnings of a memoir— Hammond recounts the times that he went "in the icy, choppy waters, using only handmade canoes . . . fishing with Prepayit for seal and walrus, with sharp and hardened spears, tipped, sometimes, with our own blood for good luck."

It was during this time, again according to his own

accounts of his life, that Hammond decided to pursue full-time studies in the fields of anthropology and sociology. It was also during this time, according to an interview with *LIFE* magazine, that Hammond decided to apply to Harvard University:

And you were accepted?

Yes. They accepted me, but I didn't know about it for almost three months. I had left for another fishing trip, my last one, and the acceptance letter arrived on the day after I left. It was quite a shock coming home to that letter.

Why was that?

Well, on that trip, I almost didn't come home at all.

Because you almost drowned?

Right. A buckle or a clasp from my overalls caught on the net as it was dropped into the water, but nobody—not even me—noticed it until it was too late. It was June, but even then, the water doesn't get much over forty, and there I was in the water. I couldn't breathe, couldn't swim, couldn't see, and I didn't know what was holding me down. Fishing expeditions are dangerous all over, but I think they're worst in Alaska. The water's rough, and it's always cold, and someone was always losing a finger or a hand or was knocked overboard. I was lucky, though. One of the new guys, someone I'd only talked to once or twice, he jumped into the water and he had the sense of mind to bring a knife with him, and he swam down in there and just cut me out of the net. Now he's my best friend. In the end, I was able to go to Harvard all thanks to Marcus.

The 1975 November–December issue of *Harvard Magazine* contains a photograph of two men standing side by side on a boat at sea. One of the men is holding in his hands what could be a salmon. The photograph is cropped in such a way that one can tell that the two men are on a boat, and that the boat is at sea, or, at the very least, on water, but little else. The men in the photograph are said to be Hammond and Grant, in Alaska on a fishing boat, some time during the last trip Hammond took before leaving Alaska for Cambridge. The photo, submitted to the magazine by Hammond shortly after he and Grant had accepted their respective teaching positions, is accompanied by a short paragraph, titled HAR-VARD AND YALE TO CALL TRUCE AT LAST?, about the two good friends who had found themselves teaching at rival schools, in which Hammond is quoted: "Whether he saved my life or not, come football season, all manner of friendship between Marcus and me will have to end."

The second time we met, I showed Denise a copy of the magazine and the photograph. She shook her head and said,

"Who has time for this kind of thing? Who has the time or the energy to rent a boat, and, apparently, a fish, because, frankly, at this point, I doubt that's even their fish, and who knows if they even left the dock? The frame's so tight, you can't tell how far out they are, or where they are. All to take a fake photograph to submit to the Harvard alumni magazine, just to corroborate a fake story of how they met. And for what? Why go to the trouble?"

In 1869, a farmer, William "Stubb" Newell, digging a well on his land in upstate New York, unearthed what appeared to be a petrified giant, at least ten feet tall, proving the biblical claim (Genesis 6:4) that giants once walked the earth. In 1912, an amateur archaeologist, Charles Dawson, uncovered the remains of a man whose skull was distinctly humanoid and whose jawbone was distinctly simian, a discovery that would have provided the missing link in Darwin's theory of evolution. In 1953, on a highway in rural Georgia, three young men claimed to have nearly careened into a flying saucer, and had hit one of the aliens left behind with their car, the body of which, two feet tall, hairless, and alien in appearance, they turned in to the authorities. The jawbone turned out to be nothing more than the jaw of a modern orangutan, antiqued for effect, and the petrified giant was quickly found out to be a hastily carved statue—fresh chisel marks were a dead giveaway—buried by a tobacconist and atheist, George Hull, who hoped to make a mockery of a Methodist reverend who had argued in favor of a literal reading of the Bible. And the space alien? A store-bought capuchin monkey, lethally drugged, shaved, and de-tailed, over a drunken bet made by one of the young men, a barber named Edward Watters, that he could get himself featured in the local news within a week. It seems that men and women, though mostly men, have engaged in such hoaxes—scientific, historic, literary, political, mathematical—from time immemorial, whether for fame, notoriety, money, to bolster a deeply felt belief, or as nothing more than an elaborate joke. As to what personally drove Hammond and Grant to construct this particular, elaborate, and exhaustive hoax, it is uncertain whether anyone will ever know, though it sometimes seems to be one of the only questions left that Denise still wants answered.

IV.

When he was six years old, Marcus Alexander Grant began painting murals on the walls of his parents' house. These were, judging by the photographs that I've seen, childish images, but of vibrant color and surprisingly mature technique. When he was nine, he began making and then mixing his own paints. As he grew older, he demonstrated a good eye for color and a talent for the older arts—frescoes, mosaics, designing and firing and painting pottery. With his blue-black hair, dimples, and soft black eyes framed by simple, steel-rimmed glasses, Grant was often remembered as everyone's favorite of the two anthropologists. Relaxed and nonchalant, he dressed in jeans, work pants, old pullovers, workman's boots. His was a wardrobe suited for fieldwork, for the outdoors. While teaching at Yale, he refused to wear a necktie and drove to and from campus in a battered orange Chevrolet C-10 Fleetside pickup truck. From the ceiling of the truck hung a bent straw cowboy hat, which he claimed had been given to him by a migrant worker he had met while picking avocados in upstate California.

Grant spent the first ten years of his life in Chihuahua, Mexico. His grandfather had owned acreage in Texas, ranchland used for raising longhorn cattle, but when the cattle had to be put down and the ranch sold, Grant's father, Alexander, left home for northern Mexico, where he worked as a ranch hand and became enchanted with the country, the countryside, and its people. He met and married Maria Martinez in 1942, and two years later, Marcus was born. In 1954, with the death of Marcus's grandfather, the family moved back to Texas, where they settled in Lubbock and where Grant's father found work as an electrician repairing radio sets and television sets, and Grant's mother earned money cleaning houses and occasionally waiting tables.

Grant's father, who hated working with electronics, hated the small, crowded workshop covered with wires and transistors and cathode-ray receivers, had, for twelve years, been pulling together his and Maria's earnings in order to place money on a piece of land, with any luck the same land originally owned by his father. Whether Maria convinced him otherwise or whether Grant's father came to the decision himself, land was never purchased and the money was used instead to send Marcus to Texas Tech University, where he studied the visual arts. According to school records, his first two years were abysmal, and in his third year Grant left the visual arts department and changed his major to anthropology.

V.

Excerpted from "The DramEção Ritual: Silent Conflicts of the Sebali Prepubescent Male":

> After a Sebali boy completes his tenth year, his life becomes quiet, for between his eleventh and thirteenth years he is, according to tribal tradition, no longer permitted the use of language. Or rather, language is taken from him. It is done so bodily, in the ritual of dramEção.
>
> Symbolic in nature, the ritual involves the "removal" of the boy's tongue. The symbol of the boy's tongue—oftentimes the tongue of a wild boar tied once around with a lock of the boy's hair—is then placed in the center of a bonfire, which is kept constantly ablaze. The tongue is placed next to other tongues symbolizing the language and manhood of other boys of the tribe, and each tongue will remain inside the ring of fire until its respective owner, through meditation, study, and prayer, retrieves it, thereby retrieving the tribe's lan-

guage. During drameção, the boys are not permitted to speak with anyone else of the tribe. Nor is any member of the tribe—elder, mother, father—allowed to speak to any boys in the midst of drameção.

The ritual, however, extends beyond the symbolic. After speaking with the elders of the tribe, and after lengthy discussions of drameção with boys of the tribe who had just completed the ritual and retrieved their "tongues," we came to understand that the tribe's language is not merely prohibited, but that literally the tribe's language is, for a time period ranging from two to three years, forgotten.

The article goes on to explain the existence of marleh root, a soft root similar in shape to a carrot but the color of dried parchment. According to ritual, marleh root is boiled for two days before the beginning of the ritual, just long enough for the marleh root, which is tough and fibrous, to disintegrate, and the entire concoction is reduced to a syrupy stock which is then presented to the boy just before the "removal" of his tongue. Each boy is required to drink the same amount of the marleh stock, just under one cup, every seven days "for a time period equal to one month," and, according to the findings of Hammond and Grant, it is this juice that, when drunk, causes a temporary loss of language memory, and "the juice's potency is increased exponentially with each subsequent ingestion."

Furthermore, the root itself is inconsistently potent, though Hammond and Grant speculate that the greener roots are the more potent roots. This inconsistency isn't accounted for in the somewhat arbitrary recipe, so that it is possible that by the time the boy drinks his fourth cup of the syrup, he will be drinking a potion nearly twenty times as potent as that drunk by his brethren, a potency strong enough to make him lose memory "not just of his language, but of himself and who he is supposed to be."

VI.

Denise began her studies at Boston University in 1978, the year people first began to suspect that some dark fate had, perhaps, driven Hammond and Grant off course, and, like most other anthropologists and ethnologists at the time, Denise became swept up in the fervor and the lingering buzz surrounding *The Sebali Continuum* and the Sebali tribe, only made more interesting by early speculations of the disappearance and possible deaths of Hammond and Grant. Then, almost two years after the disappearance, a modest group of friends and colleagues, five of them in all, left for the small Pacific island where the Sebali lived in hopes of finding the lost anthropologists, or, if not the two of them, at least a sign of what had happened to them. The company was made up of two Yale professors, a language specialist (who had learned the language of the Sebali people from Hammond himself), and two good friends. They returned, months later, empty-handed but for a shocking report that the entire Sebali people had disappeared, apparently and inexplicably wiped out.

As far as I can understand it, as it was explained to me by Denise and a few others in the field, the phenomenon surrounding the Sebali tribe stemmed not from the extensive and comprehensive documentation of the tribe by Hammond and Grant, which was remarkable, but from the purity of the tribe, which had survived, unmarred by anything outside of its very small chain of islands, longer than any other group of people. "The Sebali people," Denise told me, with a hushed urgency that bordered on wistfulness, "were aboriginal in the truest sense of the word. Untouched. For a millennium, maybe longer. Consider," she then went on to explain, "a group of people removed to an island and that island placed inside a box and that box sealed off from the rest of the world for one thousand years. Remove that island from its box, and what you have then is Hammond and Grant's Sebali people. That the tribe even existed—had not been wiped off the face of the earth through starvation or by disease or by too much inbreeding—overshadowed the fact that they were discovered by two unheard-of amateurs, barely out of school, who had recorded faithfully their daily routines and rituals down to the tiniest detail, and had managed to do so without disrupting the tribe's social structure." She paused, a look of disbelief on her face, and then continued: "I mean, how could we have believed that they ate and slept and hunted with these people, wholly foreign people, without once tarnishing their society?"

Before the truth about the tribe had been revealed, a few scientists had originally conjectured that, perhaps inadvertently, Hammond and Grant had caused not only their own disappearance, but the disappearance of the Sebali people as well, which led to a minor resurgence of an ongoing debate in anthropology and sociology concerning the ethics of fieldwork. Not a few cultures have been irrevocably altered through the intrusion of science and anthropologists, and there have been some cases of anthropologists tampering with small tribal communities—falsifying observations or, worse yet, guiding tribal thought toward more and more exotic rituals and ways of life—in order to achieve the kind of shocking evidence that most people have come to expect of a relatively untouched tribe of aboriginals such as the Sebali. Most, however, considered these accusations, at least at the time and in light of the disappearance and possible deaths of Hammond and Grant, unfounded and somewhat inappropriate.

"There have been times," Denise explained to me, "when it seemed that a people have disappeared, vanished, as if the earth had opened up, swallowed them whole, but once research is done, a good explanation, nine times out of ten, clarifies what happened." Like everyone else studying or working in anthropology at the time, Denise wanted to figure out what happened to Hammond and Grant with the hope that this might help her understand what had happened to the Sebali.

The scouting party, while searching the remains of the

Sebali tribe for signs of Hammond and Grant, took a number of photographs but did not bring home physical samples, leaving the site untouched, instead, for a future, more extensive research party. Denise was able to study reprints and enlargements of the photographs, consisting mainly of pictures of emptied-out huts, littered with broken pieces of pottery, dried pieces of meats and fruits scattered on the dirt floors, as well as huts that appeared untouched, the rooms clean and appearing like a home just recently vacated by a family that planned to return in a matter of moments, but she found the photographic evidence difficult to work with. Photographs, though they are indispensable to sharing discoveries, testing theories, and publishing articles, cannot, according to Denise, replace firsthand observation, fieldwork, or simple legwork and research.

Boston University, in collaboration with Tufts University and the University of Wisconsin–Madison, received funding to begin a summer program that would allow students of anthropology to work together with professors and field specialists in cataloging the remains of the Sebali tribe and looking for clues as to what caused the tribe's disappearance. Denise, however, was then only a first-year graduate student and was not chosen to participate in the program. Instead, after examining the photographs brought back by the original scouting party, she contented herself with spending her time researching a paper she planned to write, a biographical piece on the lives of Hammond and Grant and their contributions to the science of anthropology, which, she hoped, would provide her with some clues as to what had happened.

Denise began her research close to home, at Harvard University, where Joseph Hammond taught a course on untouched civilizations, and where he himself had gone to school from 1960 until 1964. While involved with her research, however, she struck a wall.

She had no problem finding information on Hammond after 1975. "I had interviews, articles published by him and about him, his course work, his lecture notes, his slide presentations, his test papers. But when I wanted to go back as far as his years as a student, I couldn't find anything." Denise checked official school records through the Registrar's Office and then through the office of Alumni Affairs and Development, but was unable to locate student records, grades, class schedules, thesis papers, immunization records, financial statements, or anything else that would connect Hammond to Harvard.

"At first," she explained, "we thought that maybe his files had been misplaced, or that maybe some fanatic had somehow gotten his hands on these records, but we couldn't believe that anyone could be so thorough. Most of these records are kept in separate files, such as his immunization records, which would have been kept in the Health Services office, and his high school transcripts, kept with the Registrar's Office."

Frustrated, Denise went in search of professors in anthropology or sociology who had been with the college long enough to have perhaps taught Hammond and who might remember him.

"That's how I found Dr. Stephens," she said. An associate professor in 1962, Dr. Stephens taught in the Department of Anthropology for four years before leaving to teach in Chicago, but who had just recently returned to Harvard. "I asked him about Hammond, but he had no idea, didn't remember him at all, not from back then, couldn't remember ever meeting him." Stephens went on to explain to Denise that he had come back to Harvard, in fact, to take over the one or two classes Hammond usually taught, but Hammond left before Dr. Stephens's arrival, and so the two had, to Stephens's knowledge, never met. Denise left Dr. Stephens's office more confused and frustrated than before. Unsure of how to continue her research, she took a long walk, walking from Harvard Square across the Charles River into Boston proper, and from there continued walking until she finally reached her apartment, a walk of nearly five miles, and by which time the sky was dark and her feet a little sore. "Exhausted and cold and uncomfortable," she told me, "I considered on my walk home dropping the project, leaving the Sebali tribe, Hammond, and Grant to someone else, moving into an area more interesting, more generous, and I cannot say that, if I had not found the message stuck to the refrigerator that Dr. Stephens had called and that I should call him back as soon as I could, I would not have given up, but the message was there, and so I called him."

After Denise left his office, Dr. Stephens, himself intrigued by the mystery of Joseph Hammond, found an old photo album that contained photographs taken at a 1963 department mixer, one of which captured the entire department, department head, professors, associate professors, and students—graduate and undergraduate—their wineglasses raised, the kind of photo taken toward the end of a party in which everyone is leaning against everyone else in order to remain standing up. Joseph Hammond, Stephens told her, was not in that photograph, nor any of the other photographs, which, by itself, wasn't damning or interesting evidence, but then Hammond wasn't in the mixer photographs for 1962, either, or 1961, or 1964, which Stephens found altogether a little too strange. It was this final bump in the road that caused Denise Gibson to change course.

Regardless of the frustrations and obstacles concerning her research on Hammond, Denise still felt that by looking into the two anthropologists' histories, she would find the solution to the puzzle of their disappearance. "I brought a healthy amount of suspicion with me when I looked to Grant, but then Grant's life fell into place like dominoes, and then Grant led me right to Hammond."

The now commonly held belief regarding Grant is that he merely wanted a chance to paint frescoes and make pottery and reinvent old techniques for creating art. Hammond, however, when compared to Grant, who could not bring himself to lie even about where he was from, who did not have the foresight to doctor school records or change his name, who just barely corroborated the story about saving Hammond from the icy depths off the coast of Alaska, Hammond is now considered nothing less than a highly skilled con artist whose main goal in the creation of the Sebali tribe was economic. Marcus Alexander Grant, as everyone now knows, never saved Joseph Hammond's life off the coast of Alaska, but then again, no one believes that Hammond was ever in Alaska to begin with. While no one knows exactly what he did between the years he left home and the years he entered college, what we do know is that at the age of eighteen, Joseph Farrow enrolled at Oklahoma State University, in Stillwater, Oklahoma. He spent two years in Oklahoma before he left OSU (or was dismissed; no one is quite sure), after which he moved to Lubbock, Texas, where he enrolled into Texas Tech University as a transfer student. Originally a student of business administration, he changed his major to anthropology. Neither he nor Marcus Grant, however, completed their studies at Texas Tech, nor at any other American university. Farrow flunked out of school by the end of the fall semester of his senior year, and it was around this time, too, that he began calling himself by his mother's maiden name. And when Hammond left, Marcus Grant left with him. Once Denise figured out the connection between Hammond and Farrow, it was not long before she came to the conclusion that the photographs, the artifacts, the rituals, and the degrees were fakes.

"Well," she corrected me, "not fake. The artwork is real artwork, but the work is Marcus Grant, not Sebali."

As soon as she felt she'd gathered enough evidence to

explain the riddle of Hammond and Grant and the disappearance of the Sebali tribe, she called Dr. Stephens. "I told him that I thought the Sebali tribe never existed—that they were made up—and he was very quiet on the phone for a minute, and then asked, 'What makes you say that?' So I told him what I'd found out about Hammond, and then, once I'd finished, he told me that he'd get in contact with his colleagues on the island and tell them what I'd found out and that he'd make sure that, if I were right in this, that I'd receive full credit for my research here." A few days later, Stephens called Denise. "They're good forgeries," he told her. "Damn good." When she asked him what would happen next, he told her that everyone was coming home and that, once they'd returned, they'd put all of the pieces together and figure out exactly what happened.

VII.

To this day, however, nobody knows exactly what happened. The riddle of the Sebali tribe has been solved, but no one is sure why Hammond and Grant did what they did or, more importantly, what happened to them when they left the United States in 1977. In truth, no one knows if they even left. Their apartments, which have been searched more than once, failed to reveal any clues as to their whereabouts, and their things, left behind these many years, have since been confiscated by the FBI, and their old apartments cleaned out and rented. (Once it was revealed that the two had misused funds awarded them by federal agencies, the FBI joined the investigation, as did the Treasury Department.) Hammond and Grant have disappeared as cleanly as, so it would seem, the tribe they invented. There have been rumored sightings of Hammond, and Denise still finds herself looking closely at any old Chevy Fleetside pickup if she sees one at a rest stop along the New Jersey Turnpike, or parked behind Fenway, whether orange or green or blue. A few months before we met, Denise flew out to Akron, Ohio, after someone had sent her a clipping of an art sale advertisement that mentioned pieces of primitive pottery and stonework of the Sebali tribe for sale, but the works, ironically, turned out to be forgeries. Otherwise, aside from the interviews she has given me, Denise claims that she has done her best to put the mystery behind her, though even about this she seems at least faintly unsure.

I conducted one of our last interviews at her apartment. We had planned to meet at a local bar, but she had left a message for me with the bartender, who then gave me directions to her apartment, which was only three blocks away. She apologized when she answered the door. "I'm afraid I'm feeling a little fluish," she told me, and I offered to reschedule, but she invited me inside instead. She offered me a drink, and we sat and we spoke about Hammond and Grant and about Texas and the anthropology program. I asked if she had continued to look for or wonder about the final whereabouts of the two men, and she was quick to say no. I was surprised by the swiftness of her reply, and perhaps the surprise, if not a measure of disbelief, registered on my face, because she then told me that a number of people, professors and colleagues and family, had expected her to continue to explore and then write about the Hammond and Grant episode, and had urged her to do so for some time. "It's been kind of hard," she said, "to get them all to drop the matter." And then, for no other reason than that the question appeared fully formed in my head, I asked Denise if either of them—Hammond or Grant—had ever tried to contact her. "Not even a phone call," she said with a bright and unaffected laugh. "Can you believe it? The nerve of those two." And it was then that the phone on the table next to the sofa rang loudly, filling the apartment, and a startled look passed over her face before she smiled at me and quickly reached for the phone, and it was in that moment that I suspected that Denise was not quite free of Hammond and Grant, and that she might never be. It was her mother calling, and I sat quietly, waiting as she chatted amiably about her brother's newborn baby girl, and after a few minutes, she said her good-byes and hung up and turned back to me. "Have you ever cooked a really big meal?" she asked. "Four or five courses? For a big party of people? You spend all day shopping for ingredients and then chopping and sautéing and roasting, and you're excited about the meal, taking a bite here and there as you cook, and it smells great, and you finish it all and bring it all out to the table, and you're proud of it, and everybody digs in, and they all love it. But you just spent all day cooking and running around and your back is sore from standing in a cramped kitchen for the entire afternoon, and you find that, all of a sudden, you just don't have the appetite for anything you cooked. It looks good and smells good and you're sure it tastes good, but you're just not hungry anymore. That's more or less how I feel about Hammond and Grant. No more appetite."

"But sooner or later, you're bound to get hungry again," I said.

She laughed again and said, "Maybe some day."

In May, Denise will graduate. When I last spoke to her, however, she was not yet certain what she would do after graduation. Princeton has offered her a postdoctoral position, and she has had two interviews with the Smithsonian Institution's National Museum of Natural History in Washington, D.C. "I'm not sure, though," she told me on my last day in Boston. We were walking along the Cambridge side of the Charles River. It was a bright, cold day. She stood staring quietly at the water as it moved sluggishly past. "I'm not sure what I want to do. Both of them—they're both good opportunities, and my parents were happy to hear about them because, I think, in their minds, anthropology, when it comes to having a job or a career, isn't any more promising than theater. But the academic world, it's just . . . it's so small, and now when people meet me, and at job interviews and job fairs, all they want to talk about is the Sebali thing. The more people talk about it, the more I think about what they did—Hammond and Grant—and what they're doing now, whatever new con they're playing now, and I find myself almost admiring what they did, the fact that they, by their own sheer force of will, invented a new life for themselves. And I'm beginning to think that, if there's some way for me to do the same thing, I should maybe start working to find it."

"Do you think they're happy, whatever they're doing now?" I asked her.

She was quiet for a moment before she looked at me and said, "If I ever find them, I'll let you know."

One-Horned & Wild-Eyed

A Chinaman sold it to me," Ralph told me as he led me through his garage toward the side yard. I thought about telling him that whoever sold him whatever it was he was going to show me probably wasn't a Chinaman—most likely, considering Houston, some Vietnamese guy or maybe a Filipino—but I figured it didn't matter really, that it would only upset him, make him think I wasn't taking him or what he was going to show me seriously, which, in all honesty, I wasn't. "You're not going to believe this shit," he said. "You're not going to fucking believe it."

Considering all the shit I was never supposed to fucking believe from our past—schemes, foolproof business ideas, or just the crap he'd bought or found or built—my expectations were pretty low, but I smiled at him encouragingly because we'd been friends so long.

We stepped out of his hot garage and into the even hotter

morning, humid and suffocating, and we walked into the side yard. When he and Melissa first moved into the house, he set to work on this yard with considerable intent, building a small coop and clearing the brush and weeds that had grown there and setting it up for a half-dozen chicks he bought, telling me he planned to raise chickens. "Fresh eggs, man," he told me, as if that alone were all the explanation anyone would need, but in a matter of days, a pack of wild dogs ran through his fencing and broke through his coop and slaughtered those chicks. A month or so later, he tore everything down and threw up an uneven chain-link fence, which had since rusted and half fallen over. It wasn't much space, really, a dog run and nothing else, and he'd done little with it since except plant patches of sod there a couple of springs back, which had browned and died. The rest of the ground was made up of weeds or loosely packed reddish sand, and I figured he'd left it to the wild, but now in the middle of it there was a good-sized shed, which he must have only recently built.

"You're right," I told him. "That shed is, um, a pretty nice piece of construction."

He shook his head. "Not the shed, jackass. What's inside it," he said. Then he smiled and looked at the shed and then back at me and said, "You don't want to guess? Give you a hundred guesses and you'll never get it."

"Yeah," I said. "I don't care. Just open the shed. I got to get back home."

"Suit yourself," he said. Then he pretended to fuss over the lock and the door, stalling to build suspense and whatnot, until finally he opened the shed and then, with a sweeping wave, he stepped aside to allow me a good look, and for a moment all I could see was a bright white light, ethereal and ghostly and frightening.

Ralph then reached his hand right into that light, and I wanted to grab him, jerk him back from it, sure if he dipped any part of himself in there it would be melted right off, but then I heard him grab hold of some jingling contraption, and what he pulled out wasn't like anything I'd ever seen, and certainly wasn't what I expected to see. It looked like some kind of pearlescent undersized horse or overlarge goat or some bastardization of the two, with maybe something else—moose? sea lion?—thrown in for good measure. It stood just a head or so taller than Ralph, who wasn't too tall to start with, and it was thin and sleek and strong-looking, with something rounded and unhorselike about its face. In truth, though, these observations came to me much later. At first, I found I couldn't look right at it, like I was looking right into a flashlight or like I was driving into a rising sun, but judging by what I could see of it, it was an unsettling thing to look at, not ugly, but not pretty, either.

"What the hell is it?" I asked.

"Are you fucking kidding me?" he said, and then he grabbed it roughly by the top of its head where there was a nearly translucent and wicked-looking horn growing there or planted there or something. "It's a goddamn unicorn, Mano. Can you fucking believe it? I bought a goddamn unicorn off a goddamn Chinaman. And for cheap, too," he said.

◇

I was late getting home. The house was a minor disaster, as was Victor, our boy, who was wandering around the house in just his diaper, something—mac and cheese? whipped cream?—stuck to his chest. I found Sheila in our bathroom, half-dressed and half–made up.

"Jesus," she said when she saw me. "You're an hour late."

"Sorry," I said, and I picked up Victor, who'd grabbed me by the pants and then held his arms out to be lifted up. "You know Ralph. It's hard to break away when he gets going," I said. I played with Victor, peekaboo mostly, and I watched Sheila finish dressing, and then I asked, "You ready for this?"

She stopped fussing in the mirror and turned and smiled and posed, her hands thrown up and out, her hip thrust to the side, more like she was a cheerleader or some Hooters waitress than a real estate agent. "What do you think?" she asked.

She looked lovely, and for the first time I could remember, the sight of her made me sad.

"You look great," I said.

"It's my first open house, you know," she said.

"I know."

"I need more than 'You look great,' " she said.

"You look so good, honey, I could take you and throw you on that bed right now—"

"Fine," she said, interrupting me before I could finish my thought. "On the bed, okay. But would you buy a house from me?"

I laughed. "I would buy a house from you, and I already have a house."

"You couldn't afford it. You can't afford the house you already have," she said, but she smiled and kissed me on the cheek. "Next time, try not to spend so much time over at Rafael's."

"He hates it when you call him that," I said.

"It's his name. He should be used to it by now."

"He goes by Ralph."

She shrugged. "Ralph's a boy's name. What about Ralphie? Should I call him Ralphie?" She said this and went back to our room, and I would have had to holler to defend him, to remind her he hadn't gone by Ralphie since we left middle school, and in the end decided it wasn't worth the effort. Then she came out, an inch or two taller in her heels. She took Victor from me and kissed him, and then she kissed me, a long, deep kiss, and then she wiped the lipstick off my lips.

"Ralph's got this new thing," I said, taking Victor back from her.

"I'm sure he does," she said. She found her purse and then her keys.

"This is," I said. "Different."

She was holding Victor again, giving him more kisses. "I shouldn't be too late," she said, "but if he gets hungry, there's food for him in the fridge."

"I mean, really, pretty different," I said.

Then she handed me Victor again and said, "You can tell me about it when I get home. I have to go."

"You won't believe it," I said.

"I'm sure I won't," she said, and then she opened the door and waved and said, "Love you two." And then she was gone, and then Victor, who didn't want her to be gone, started to cry.

◈

I sat Victor on my knee and tried to distract him, tried to console him, but my heart wasn't in it, and it wasn't like crying was bad for him, and so I let him go at it for a little while. *After a while, he'll stop,* I thought, but he didn't, and then I got tired of the crying, but still had no idea what to do right then to stop it. I lifted him off my knee and held him so that his eyes met my eyes, though his were scrunched and wet and unseeing, and I said, "You want to go see something different?" I grabbed a cloth and wiped his chest and put a shirt on him and some shoes, then grabbed a couple of diapers to throw into the car and walked outside only to remember Sheila had taken the car. So I went back inside and grabbed the stroller, and twenty minutes and a few more crying jags later, we were back at Ralph's house.

I walked us back around to the side yard and Ralph was there, and as far as I could tell, he hadn't moved, not to go inside, not to go take a piss, nothing. That morning we had stood there looking at his unicorn for a good half hour not really saying much of anything, and then he had gone into the garage and had come back out again with two lawn chairs and a small cooler full of ice and beer. He was still sitting in his chair and the cooler was there, the lid open, the ice melted, the empty beer cans floating in the warm, dirty water.

He saw me and said, "You think I need to build a fence, like a real fence here?"

The sun was beating down on his high forehead, and he was sweaty and red. "I don't know, Ralph," I said.

"I think I need a fence," he said.

I lifted Victor out of the stroller and set him on his unsteady feet and then opened the gate to the fence and nudged Victor into the yard. For the first time, Ralph noticed Victor was with me, and this brought him out of whatever state he'd fallen into, and he grabbed Victor, a little too roughly as far as I was concerned, as far as Victor was concerned, too, the suddenness of Ralph's grab, how tightly he held Victor's arm making Victor start crying all over again.

"What the hell is wrong with you?" I said.

"Sorry, Mano," he said. "Just. I don't know what she's like around really little ones, you know? I don't want to spook her."

What about spooking my boy? I wanted to say, but instead I just took Victor from him and sat him in my lap and tried again to calm him down, and then he must have seen Ralph's unicorn because all of a sudden he became quiet and still, and all three of us sat there looking at it.

✧

After he first told me it was a unicorn, and after I got over the initial shock of the thing, and when I was still just playing along, I asked him, "Does it have a name?" ignoring for the moment the unreality of the thing he was showing me, or, rather, the unreality of his belief in it.

"Yeah," he said. "The Chinaman told me her name was Fable, but that name's for crap if you ask me. So I'm thinking of changing it to Sabre Bitch," and then he laughed, and then, slightly more seriously, he said, "Or maybe just Sabre, you know, 'cause of the kids."

Then he pulled up a canvas bag, like a bag you might see in a cartoon expecting it to be full of oats or something, and he opened it and started rooting around in it with a scoop. I asked him what he was doing, and he told me he needed to feed it soon, and I asked him what you were supposed to feed a thing like this, and he told me fairy dust, and I laughed and he said, "That's no joke." Then he opened the bag wide and showed me the fine, phosphorescent powder inside it. "The Chinaman threw it in as part of the package."

"Fairy dust," I said, my skepticism not even thinly veiled. "It looks like play sand you can buy at Walmart." Then I spat on the ground and said, "Fairy dust" again.

Ralph laughed a nervous, unfamiliar laugh. "That's what I thought, too, so I told him no thanks," Ralph said. "But then he grabbed my arm, grabbed me by the wrist, and he shook his head real serious, and I asked, 'What is it?' And I don't know, he could've been lying, but. You know what he said?" I shook my head and rolled my eyes. "I shit you not, he told me it was ground-up fairies, and that I had to feed the unicorn half a cup of this stuff four times a day." He laughed that nervous laugh again. I scoffed. "That's what he told me, Mano. And I believe him."

I looked inside the bag again, trying to picture that fine powder as something other than pink and blue play sand. "How do you feed it this crap, anyway?" I asked.

"You mix it," he said. "With water or whiskey or beer, but that shit will get expensive, so I figure water will do."

That was this morning, and something in the way he sat there in his chair gazing at the unicorn made me think something subtle had changed, and when I asked him how Sabre Bitch was doing, he snapped at me. "Watch your language," he said, and I said, "Sorry, I didn't mean to—" and then I stopped, and then I said, "Sure thing, Ralph, won't happen again," feeling contrite and like I needed to apologize some more, though I couldn't have said why.

I dipped my hand into the cooler and pulled out an empty can and crushed it and then said, "Jesus, man, it's not even one."

He looked at me and then at what was in my hand and then he said, "Not me. For her. She got hungry, so I mixed her up something to eat."

"What happened to water?"

"She didn't like it with water, so I mixed some of the beer in there, too."

And then we didn't say much else to each other, and we sat there looking at his unicorn until Melissa came home and started hollering at Ralph because he had apparently forgotten to pick the kids up from her mother's, and then, distractedly, he said, "Hey, man, I have to go, okay? I'll see you later," and then he stood up and he looked down at me and Victor, who was still quiet in my lap, who had been there so quiet and so still for so long that in retrospect I should have been worried about him, about what might have come over him, and Ralph waited until, grudgingly, I stood up, too, and then placed Victor back in his stroller, and he stood there, Ralph did, watching us until we were out of sight and almost halfway home.

◈

"It's not real," Sheila said as she stood pressed up to the kitchen counter. She was cutting up a cucumber, cutting one slice at a time, sprinkling that slice with salt, and then eating it. Watching her, I felt impatient, like I should grab the knife and cut the whole cucumber and put it all on a plate and set her down somewhere so she could give my story the attention it deserved.

"I think it is," I said.

"It's a goat," she said. "One of those poor little goats with its horns twisted together."

"It's real," I said.

"It can't be," she said.

"Sheila," I said.

"Meme," she said. She called me Meme when she didn't know what else to say to me, when she couldn't refute the logic of my argument because there wasn't any, when she wondered, not for the first or last time, I'm sure, who this man was she married.

"I think you should see it," I said.

"Fine," she said. "We're going there Monday for dinner. I can see it then."

I had already grabbed my shoes and socks and her shoes and Victor's shoes, and I was looking for Victor. "You don't want to go now?" I asked.

She sighed and moved from the kitchen counter and sat heavily on the couch. "I'm tired, honey."

There was something shaky in her voice by this point, which I chose to ignore. "Oh. Okay," I said. Then I said, "Well, since you're back, you mind staying with Victor while I go?"

She took one of the pillows off the couch and threw it at me, not at all playfully, and said, "Jesus Christ, Meme, I just got home and you haven't even once asked me how the open house went, and all you've done since I got here is talk about Ralph's stupid goat."

"It's not a goat," I said before I could think better of it.

"Fuck," she cried, and picked up another pillow, but kept it squeezed tight against her chest. "Fine," she said. "Go, I don't care. Go to Rafael's and look at his fucking goat," she said.

I knew that if I left to go see that animal that the trouble I would come back to would be far greater than any trouble I'd come home to before in the four years we'd been married, that the trouble would involve an anger I couldn't rightly imagine, a different kind of anger, I could tell, which had already begun to brew inside her, and still, for a moment, for the smallest of moments, I considered going anyway.

"I'm sorry," I said. "I got so caught up, is all. I'm sorry." Then I said, "How did the open house go?"

But she didn't give in that easily, and so I opened up a beer for her and poured it into a glass like she liked it and then sat next to her on the couch and picked up one of her feet and began to give her a clumsy massage and then asked her again how it had gone. And then she told me that it went awfully and she started crying, and then Victor toddled into the room, and I sat down on the couch next to her and picked Victor up so he wouldn't bother his mother, but she took him and hugged him and I made a joke, I don't remember it now, but she laughed. Then Victor made a sound, one of his weird little squeaks, and this made her laugh, too, and then we were fine, or close to it. Close enough that she could tell me about the open house, and I could tell her it wasn't as bad as she thought it was—though maybe it was, and maybe it was worse than that, even—and then we talked about other things, and then it was time for dinner and I took us all out for hamburgers, and when we came back, I gave Victor a bath and read him his stories and put him to bed so Sheila could rest. And when I came out of his room, I found her in the living room wearing this pair of old, faded maroon workout shorts that, as dumb as it sounds, never failed to rile me up when she was wearing them, and she reached out her hand to me and I grabbed it thinking she wanted me to help her off the couch, but instead she pulled me down onto it, and we had a nice little romp there, and then we watched some TV, and then we went to bed where we had a second go at it, and finally she fell asleep, and as she slept, I crept out of the house and hoofed it over to Ralph's place.

When I got there, I found Ralph sitting in his chair dressed in his robe, and by the drape of it and by a flap of it that hung open at the top of his thigh, I could tell he wasn't wearing anything underneath. Worried I might have intruded on some private and disturbing moment, I stopped and was about to turn back around, but then saw the heavy rise and fall of his chest and realized he had fallen asleep. I was quiet then as I opened the gate and took my seat next to him, gently flipping the robe back into place to cover his nethers. The unicorn hardly noticed me or my quiet administrations. As far as I could tell from watching it, the unicorn hardly noticed anyone. It was generally quite still, or not still, not exactly still. It seemed to have a way of standing still that made it look like it was in constant motion, or as if it existed in another place at the same moment it existed in our place, a shimmering, jittery, vibrating kind of stillness.

I didn't know how long I had been sitting there until Ralph stirred in his chair, coughed or sneezed or groaned, I don't remember, and this broke my concentration, and I looked up from watching the unicorn, took notice of the early morning light cresting over the horizon, and then, checking my watch, realized it was nearly seven in the morning, and that surely by now Sheila was awake and aware of my absence.

◇

I smoothed things over by coming home with coffee and breakfast and acting like I woke up earlier than normal, a fire in my belly, full of energy and a need to get outside and greet this day, and by the looks of the expression she threw me, Sheila didn't buy one word of it, but she didn't say anything about it, either, and the morning proceeded. Just before lunch, Ralph called to tell me that dinner was a no-go, and he gave some excuse about Melissa and a sensitive stomach, but I could tell by the sound of him it was something else, which I didn't push to find out about. I called Sheila's office and left her the message, and then I grabbed Victor and his things, and then I walked him over to my mom's house and left him with her, and about five minutes after that, I showed up unannounced at Ralph's house.

I was hoping at worst to find him sitting outside the shed looking at the unicorn, and, at best, that no one would be home at all, or that Melissa would have him holed up inside so they could finish their fight or whatever had changed their plans, and that way I could sit there all by myself. Instead, I found Melissa sitting in one of the lawn chairs, a *People* magazine spread out across her thighs, a cigarette dangling from her lips. She heard me coming and saw me before I could turn around and sneak back home.

"Hi there," she said.

"Hey," I said. "Ralph around?"

She lowered her sunglasses and looked at me over their

rim. "No," she said, dragging out the o. "Was he expecting you?"

"I guess not," I said. "I was around, and, you know," I began to explain, trailing off as she moved a stack of magazines out of the second lawn chair. Then I said, "Where is he?"

She looked at me again and smiled a secretive, mean-spirited kind of smile and asked, "Don't you know?" Then she said, "Mr. Industrious got himself a job."

"You mean work?" I asked.

"A job," she said. And for a moment that hung in the air between us. For as long as I had known him, Ralph had only ever had one job, which he'd quit after less than a year. Instead of a job, he'd find work, he'd make money, just enough, enough to get by, and when he needed more, he'd find more work and make more money. I didn't know what he did. He fixed roofs sometimes, and he sold products sometimes, and he made phone calls of some kind or other from his home sometimes. He must have done other things, too, because sometimes he would be gone for a week, for two weeks, for a month, and then he'd be home again, flush with cash, which would last him another week, a week and a half at most. For a time, I remember, he was buying cars and motorcycles around town and driving them up to Massachusetts and New York and Chicago, where he'd try to sell them, and then, once he was there, he would wait around until he could find someone who needed a car or a truck driven back down to Texas. It was a strange and not altogether enviable life that he'd cobbled together, but through this he'd managed to avoid finding full-time work since those months right out of high school he spent working as a stock boy at the Fiesta.

The morning was quiet between us as we both tried to operate under this new set of circumstances, and then the unicorn made a sound. Not a whinny, exactly, and not like it was saying something, exactly, not like it was trying to speak to us, but not like it wasn't, either. Saying something or trying to say something, maybe, something melodic and interesting and worth paying attention to. Melissa opened her magazine back up and then closed it again and looked up at the unicorn and then slapped at a mosquito that had landed on her leg.

"Growing up," she said, "I was dolphins."

"Dolphins?" I asked.

"My sister, she was unicorns. Christ. Unicorn everything. Unicorn stickers, unicorn posters, unicorn folders and book covers, and a unicorn backpack. Unicorn shirts, and this unicorn figurine she kept with her even after high school. Every goddamn thing in her room, covered with unicorns." She took a drag off her cigarette. "Hell, I should get her out here to see this. That'll screw her over."

From what Ralph had told me, Melissa and her sister didn't get on too well. She was younger and not prettier than Melissa, but pretty in a way, this according to Ralph, that made everyone act like she was prettier than Melissa, which was a serious blow to Melissa's ego and had been eating at her for some long time now. Then a year ago she moved up to Wisconsin and found work in television broadcasting for a local news station, which wasn't why there was bad blood between them, but the move and her success had only seemed to make the bad blood worse.

"How would that screw her over if she likes unicorns?" I asked.

She laughed and said, "This? This thing is not a unicorn. I mean, fuck, maybe it is, with that horn, and it looks kind of like a horse, I guess, and it does something, anyway," she said. "It's done something to Ralph, at least," she said. She turned and looked at me over her sunglasses again. "To you, too." She sighed. "But my sister, if I convinced my sister that this was what a unicorn really was, she'd hate it." She took one last drag off her cigarette and then stubbed it out and then pulled out another one and lit it, and then she said, "God, she'd hate it. Course, she wouldn't believe it. Nothing I could say or do would make her believe it, so I guess it wouldn't matter."

"Sheila doesn't believe it," I said. "Or maybe she does. I don't know." Then I said, "What about you? Do you believe it?"

"It's because of that thing, you know," she said, ignoring my question, waving her cigarette at the unicorn. "The job." She slapped at her leg again. "He didn't even tell me he got a job," she said. "I wake up and it's still dark out and I hear him rustling around the room, and I find the light and turn it on, and there he is, his hair smoothed back, and his face shaved clean, and he's wearing pants and a shirt and a tie." Then she said, "I don't even know where it is he's working."

I didn't know what to say to any of this, or that I should say anything, so I kept my mouth shut and let her speak her mind as long as she wanted, so long as she didn't decide it was too hot outside or that she was tired of sitting out there with the unicorn, because I had this feeling that if she left, she'd make me leave, too.

"And you know," she said, "two days ago I would've given anything to get him out of this chair and into the house, to help me with the kids, to do any goddamn thing that wasn't to do with this unicorn. And now this. I know what he wants to do," she said. "Build a fence, maybe buy the lot next to us, make it into a pasture or some shit." She slapped her leg again, and I started to get the feeling that when she did that she was, in her mind anyway, slapping the unicorn, or maybe she was slapping Ralph. "Six years, I've been with this man for six years, and I never told him he had to get a job, I never pushed him, though I sure as hell wouldn't have minded. Six years, I've done without and I've held on, because I figure, give him space, let him find his own way, and then, boy, things will turn around. He's a man of special talents, I thought, and he can't be locked into a job that doesn't let him use those talents, that doesn't appreciate them." Then she said, "Ha. Ha, ha, joke's on me." She looked at me and smiled and said, "Less than a week with this thing and he's already found a job to take care of it."

She looked, then, back at that creature standing in her side yard, and she stared at it with a trying-to-move-it-with-her-mind kind of intensity, and this went on for an uncomfortably long time, and I wondered if she was trying to move it with her mind, or wish it out of existence, or look into its heart to see if she could figure out what it was about this animal that had inspired in her layabout husband the sudden urge to clean up and work and provide. Then she shook her head at it, giving up on whatever she was trying to do. It pawed its hooves against the ground and shook its mane and dipped its horn. Then she took a long drag off her cigarette and, coughing as she exhaled, she said to me, "Don't you worry, though. One of these days, while Ralph's at work, I aim to make a pair of pants out of that animal." She winked and took another drag, a shorter one. "Maybe a jacket, too." Then she was quiet, smoking her cigarette, and it was right about then, I think, that I got the notion that I should steal this creature from them.

My mom called then and told me I had to come pick up Victor or have Sheila come get him because she had to get to a doctor's appointment. She didn't seem too generous about the situation, but really she'd already called a few times, and since I'd blithely ignored these calls, she had every right to her indignation. There was a moment, just after I hung up the phone, when I considered calling Sheila and feeding her some story, asking her to swing by and pick up Victor, but I didn't, only because Melissa was sitting right there, listening intently to what I said, and the idea of letting her overhear me lie so easily to my wife made me feel guilty and at the same time thrilled in a way that made me uncomfortable.

Reluctantly, I left.

By the time I got to my mom's again, she was carrying Victor out to her car, and when she saw me, she looked ready to start hollering at me, but she just handed me, without word or fanfare, my son, and then she gave me a cursory peck on my cheek before loading herself into her car and driving off without so much as an offer to give us a ride.

◈

When I got home, the car was in the driveway, and I braced myself for a hellish fight. I figured she would tear into me about lying to my mother and about leaving Victor with her to begin with and then about forgetting about him, and that this would lead to some shouting, some storming around, some random household objects thrown about, most of them aimed at my head, my chest, and as I stood there on the front sidewalk, I wondered what made us fight like some 1970s sitcom couple, and then I wondered if it was worth going inside at all, if maybe Victor and me, we could keep walking, and maybe I could take him to a bar and set him up with some pretzels and let him look at one of those Trivial Pursuit video games and then take in a couple of beers myself, though I couldn't imagine further than finishing that second beer, couldn't imagine what would happen after that. I shrugged my shoulders, bent down and pulled Victor out of his stroller, was struck briefly by the image of me walking into the house with Victor held up in front of me like a shield, and then I walked inside with him clinging to my side.

She was there looking exasperated and wild and disheveled and, honestly, pretty sexy, though I'm sure that last part wasn't intentional, was more to do with the weird, unsettling pleasure I took from working myself into trouble with her. I felt my body tense, waiting for that first wave, but all she did was take Victor from me and take him into our bedroom and then close the door behind her. At first, I figured I'd performed some sort of voodoo, or maybe Victor had, but then I thought about Sheila in our bedroom, in the dark, holding that boy tightly, and I pictured everything that normally would've come out of her, and how instead it was building up inside of her, and I started to imagine what might come next. This upset me enough that I had little choice but to sneak off into the kitchen, where I grabbed a six-pack of beer and an unopened bag of chips, which I took with me into the backyard and proceeded to finish, the chips crushed one fistful after another into my mouth.

Five beers and an empty bag of chips later, I felt sick and sweaty and overcome with guilt, which I blamed on the chips.

Back inside, the house was still and quiet and the bedroom door was still closed. I considered risking opening the door, but thought better of it. This was uncharted territory for me, and something about the way this had played out, something about our situation, or my own distractions, made this new development feel dire and irrevocable and exhausting. I sensed something large on the horizon, large and charging toward us, and this feeling that I should flee urged me out of the house and into the car and kept me driving until long after night had settled over Houston, and then farther still, until the engine stopped dead as I was pulling off the highway, leaving me only enough momentum to coast to a stop on the shoulder.

◈

When we were kids in high school, Ralph and I bonded over the fact that we thought we were outcasts, even if we weren't, and that we lived a reckless life, when in fact we were safely ensconced in our families' suburban homes. We snuck out of the house not to drink or smoke or fuck, but to drive around back roads and listen to music and to pretend to race other cars in the lanes next to us whose drivers were oblivious to whatever games we were playing, which made it easy for us to win every time off the starting line. We would visit cemeteries, and we would tromp through creeks and what passed for woods. We perceived life and our movement through it as if we were still eleven or twelve and not sixteen or seventeen, but we reveled in this as if we had made a conscious decision to do this and hadn't been somehow left behind.

One time we found ourselves moving slowly across an unexpected clearing, a patch of dirt and flattened grass and weeds we'd not come across before, which turned out to be a private landing strip. We found this out when a small airplane—a Cessna, maybe, or a Super Cub, neither of us knew, though we speculated for hours on it afterward—began its descent nearly on top of us, or so it seemed at the time, when in truth the plane was probably half a mile away and no real danger to us, and we ran screaming and hollering across that flat expanse as fast as we could and holding hands, as if this would protect us from being inevitably caught up in the plane's propeller. When we cleared the landing strip, we fell and laughed and told each other how awesome we were, and afterward, for a week or two weeks, we retold that story, embellishing it to ridiculous and impractical heights.

We did things back then, is the point I'm trying to make. Not huge things, not important things, not life-changers, nothing so serious as that, but still. We had an impression of ourselves, of who we were, right or wrong, and we acted out our lives accordingly, and as I sat in my car I wondered when we had come to some reckoning of ourselves, some reappraisal of our personal narrative, when we had stopped thinking of ourselves as guys who did exciting, adventurous, childish things, and then through the basic laws of cause and effect stopped doing those things, or, rather, when I stopped doing those things, when I stopped believing in that story we told about ourselves, because, miserable or not, married to Melissa or not, Ralph was still doing things. Things, for the most part, I wouldn't do. Things I had no interest in doing, but things, nonetheless, and he had eked out a life for himself that, though just a shadow of the lives we had imagined for ourselves, was at least closer to those lives than anything I had made for myself, and that had now brought him to a Chinaman with a unicorn to sell for cheap.

Without thinking or looking, I threw my car door open and pulled myself out of the driver's seat, only to be honked at as another exiting car swerved around me. Then I slammed the car door, and then I opened it and slammed it again. Then I walked down the exit ramp and across the access road, and then I looked around to see where I was, which was less than an hour's walk from Ralph's house.

Ralph was there as he had been the night before, asleep and barely covered by his bathrobe. The unicorn turned to glance at me, but regarded me only a second before it turned its gaze back inward, or so I assumed, back to whatever it was unicorns thought of when trying to ignore their surroundings, the fact that they were trapped in a shed in a suburban hellhole outside of Houston.

Quietly, I opened the gate and I checked Ralph to make sure he was fully asleep. A bruise had begun to purple on his lips, which were beginning to swell, and one of his eyes looked like it would be seriously blackened by morning, and I wondered at what kind of marital strife had caused this, though I was pretty certain it had something to do with the unicorn. Then I checked the house to see if any windows were lit up, and satisfied that no one was awake and spying on me, I quietly, slowly, gently moved close to her, held my hand out to her, not sure if that's what you were supposed to do, but figured it couldn't hurt. She ignored my upturned palm, and feeling hesitant but desperate to touch her, I reached my fingers out to her pearlescent skin, to run my finger down the length of her throat and neck, which looked cool to the touch and soft.

I don't know what I was expecting to happen when I touched her. An electric shock, maybe, or to feel an incredible warmth or stunning coldness, or to be flooded with memories, of the girls I'd loved, of their perfect faces, their soft lips, of my son's birth, of my wife's long, bony fingers, of the first time I'd had sex, or images of the future, my own or the world's. But nothing happened. Nothing, that is, so drastic or dramatic as any of that. I raised my hand to her head and touched her lightly and then drew back, in anticipation of something, but then gently ran my fingers in a soft line down the length of her neck, the feel of which sent a shiver through me, and she shook her mane, and she made a sound or I made a sound, but whoever made the sound, it was loud enough to wake Ralph, or maybe he had been awake that whole time, awake and standing behind me, waiting for the perfect moment to interject, to say, "What have we got here, Mano?"

It was a strange and violent fight that followed. Strange because, in hindsight, it's possible Ralph had had no intentions to fight when he saw me standing there, and strange, too, because we weren't, neither of us, much for fighting. Ralph was short and overweight and strong but clumsy, and I had a suspicion he needed glasses but wouldn't ever own up to it, a suspicion only cemented by how wildly he swung at me, how long it took for him to catch sight of me out of the corner of his eye whenever I moved to the left or the right of him. He said, "What have we got here, Mano?" and I wasted no time, swinging wildly around even before he hit the M of *Mano*. I hit him hard on the neck, though I'd been aiming for his face. This threw him off a bit and made him start coughing, made him grab his neck with both hands, and for a moment, I stopped, not a little upset to see him there in pain like that because of me. He took this opportunity to throw himself into me and slam me into the corner of the shed, hard, so that I felt the pain of that corner digging into my back all the way down to my feet. Then we proceeded to punch and kick at each other, to grapple and push, grunting and swearing, and at least once I landed a lucky punch right on his swelling lips, splitting the top lip open so that now we had some blood in the mix.

When I had imagined this fight between Ralph and me, and I had imagined it a number of times before, though I had never tried to imagine the circumstances that led to it, it was me, always me, who got the upper hand of it, quickly straddling a prone and defeated Ralph. I was the more athletic, the more cunning, I had always assumed, and maybe that's true, but at the moment, it didn't matter, and soon enough I found myself flat on my back, Ralph pressing down on me, his red, swollen, sweaty face hanging heavily over my own. Then he spit on me, and then he said, "What the hell, Mano?" Then he spit again, but this time into the dirt. Then he said, "Jesus Christ, what the hell?" And then for a moment I felt like a fool and an idiot and an asshole. Then I heard a hoof paw in the dirt, and I tilted my head back so that I could see the unicorn, upside down and behind us, and then I tilted my head forward again and saw Ralph, his lip bleeding still, his mouth moving, though I didn't hear or understand what he was saying, and then I tilted my head farther forward and saw that his bathrobe had twisted open so that, except for the corduroy belt still tied around his belly, he was bare and vulnerable from his chest on down, and seizing my opportunity, I jerked my knee up into that softest part of him with as much force as I could muster, which made him pitch forward and land heavily on my face before I could roll him off of me. Then I stood and kicked him once more for good measure, hard enough to stop him swearing and hollering for a moment at least.

I took a moment to catch my breath and then saw that a light had come on in one of the upstairs windows, and then I thought I saw the silhouette of Melissa move away from the lit window, and then other lights started to come on in the house, and so as quickly as I could, I grabbed at the harness Ralph had tucked over the unicorn's head and I pulled, firm but gentle, not sure what I would do if the unicorn decided not to go with me. It didn't take any coaxing at all, though, and I had her out of the shed, and then I kicked open the gate, and then pulled her into the alley, which dead-ended, and then led her around the side of Ralph's house and into the front yard. Then as soon as we'd cleared Ralph's property and were moving into the street, that unicorn stopped and abruptly and smoothly tossed her head, and with a subtle flick put a gash in my chest the length of my arm and then swept my legs out from under me, and the last I saw of her she was trotting down the street, spearing that horn through every mailbox she saw; I watched that unicorn lower her head and spear through first one mailbox and then another and then another, and before long I lost sight of her, but I could hear her still, her hooves against the pavement, her horn tearing through the aluminum boxes, the crash of them hitting the street. Then I laid my head back against the street and I closed my eyes and I listened for as long as I could, and I waited. I waited for something else, anything else, to happen.

"Wolf!"

My father didn't become violent until, one night while camping outside of Nacogdoches in the East Texas Pineywoods, he was bitten by a stray and sickly wolf.

Perhaps it was a dog.

⊛

Before I continue I would like to put to rest some of the myths concerning werewolves, reveal truths that, had I known them before, might have saved more of us:

The Full Moon

Father's changes were not restricted by the light of the full moon. The changes, in fact, began even before he returned from his trip, rushed home by his fellow bird-watchers.

His beard had filled out, climbing up his face, covering his cheekbones, and reaching up to the lower lids of his eyes.

His nails had grown longer, sharper, and seemed, at the end, to be made of something harder than metal.

His snout had grown, too, allowing for an enhanced sense of smell.

In fact, all of him, by the end, had grown large, and at times I wondered at the deep reach of his long arms, at his hands and how vast they had become.

Silver Bullets

No matter how many I fired—

into his chest (near his heart),

into his side (piercing, so I discovered after the autopsy, his kidney),

through the thickest part of his neck,

into his soft underbelly,

and into his skull—

no matter how many silver bullets, he refused to quietly lie down, fall into a peaceful, interminable sleep, refused to keel over dead, refused, even, to turn from my youngest sister, whom he slaughtered before I could fire even my last shot.

Sunlight

When we captured him, my mother and I, finally, after two weeks of hiding and foraging and planning, after having buried the rest of his "brood" as Father liked to call us, or, rather, after we buried what was left of them, most of them being—well, let's not go into that just yet—but finally capturing him with a net knotted together by my mother's thick, supple fingers, Father was sleeping on his back in a wide strip of sunlight that poured into the living room and spilled across the rug and across his favorite chair.

❀

Father had gone to the Pineywoods (more specifically, into the Angelina National Forest)—that year as he had every year since my birth and most likely before—in search of Henslow's sparrow.

Not that the sparrow in question is particularly difficult to spot, though it is listed as an uncommon and inconspicuous bird. Not that he hadn't observed and recorded his observations of Henslow's sparrow numerous times in the past.

More that this particular sparrow was an obsession of his, one none of us outside of Noah quite understood, and we had our doubts about Noah, too.

Still, despite the yearly trips and frequent sightings, I could only find this blurred photograph of the bird in his office, in a box that contained other ornithological trappings (some ten notebooks describing sightings, habitats, movements, dates, times, etc.; some twenty ornithological texts, including *The Audubon Guide to the Birds and Waterfowl of East Texas*; two pairs of binoculars; and a small box of photographs [all of them as unfocused as this one, for though he was a fine observer and though he could sight birds quicker than his bird-watching fellows, he never had the steady hand necessary for photography]).

What I am trying to say is: My father was a patient man, an observant man.

The point I'm trying to make perfectly clear is: My father was a man who liked birds, and that men who like birds are, on average, men of a peaceful nature.

⬡

My youngest brother, Noah, who had, more than any of us, inherited Father's ability to sit and wait and record, sat at our father's bedside for two days after he was returned to us from his camping expedition. The doctor had been summoned, had arrived, had administered medicines, and had proclaimed him (our father) in no real danger.

"But what about the hair on his face?" Noah asked. "What about his fingernails?" he said.

The doctor laughed and said, more to Mother than to any of us children, "Your father merely needs a good shave and some super-sturdy nail clippers. Certainly nothing to worry about."

"And his nose?" Noah asked. "What do you make of his nose?" he said.

But the doctor had a ready answer for that as well: "It's only made to look bigger by the hair on his face. See if he doesn't look as normal as Sunday once you've given him a good shave."

Or maybe he had said, "As right as rain."

In any case: Mother had my sisters shave him.

They used clippers first and then shaving cream and a

fresh razor and then more cream and a new razor, as the other had been dulled by the bristles of his beard.

Two hours later, Noah, who had sat silently by throughout the entire process, came to us, Mother and I, and told us that Father's beard had grown back again.

"Just as full?" I asked.

"More so," he said. "And, also, I'd like to take a moment to point out that against a clean-shaven face, his nose looked even larger still." That is how Noah spoke. Very much like our father.

"Must you watch him like that?" Mother asked. "Haven't you homework or housework to finish?"

"I've done it all," he said.

"Fine, then," I said. "Keep us informed. Tell us what you find out."

To that effect, Noah kept notes. But his notebook is incomplete.

What I can read of my brother's notes reads much like Father's bird-watching notes. It is amazing how even his handwriting looks so similar to Father's. Father, it seems, taught Noah well. None of the rest of us cared so much for birds or for sitting quite so still. The date, a brief description of the weather, small descriptions of the length and growth of Father's hair, the hardness of Father's nails, how they grew now to sharp tips, the low guttural, mewling coughs rising up from Father's throat that gave Noah chills—such were Noah's final observations before Father woke, newly and fully transformed, and filled with what I can only imagine was a terrible hunger.

◈

Mother fashioned the net out of raw silk and numerous thin bands of copper wire.

◈

I don't know why Mother and I were spared for so long or how we survived while the others, one by one, were hunted, slaughtered.

Noah first, but quickly followed by Josephine, who had been sleeping poorly, waking early in the mornings (had, in fact, been awake and watching Father the morning he left for his trip, watching him as he packed the last of his things, long before the sun had risen, before any of the rest of us had woken), who had, in the middle of the night, stumbled to the kitchen for water and then to the guest room, where we kept Father while he lay unconscious, drawn there, I suspect, by the light beneath the door, hoping, perhaps, that Noah was still awake and watchful, or that Father had finally woken.

Then there was William, who might not have been third, but who—

But wait. I'd rather not go on in this manner. I'm not yet prepared to rattle off their names, the gruesome manner in which Father took them.

I would like you to understand something.

I would like you to recognize that I am trying my best to get through this.

I'm trying to be straightforward, honest, earnest.

To present facts, and only facts.

To paint a picture.

But.

What if I were to say I have nothing left to give?

What if I were to confess that I loved my mother dearly but that I am happy the rest of them are gone, eaten, disposed of? Noah, Josephine, William, Richard, Sarah, Rebecca, and Ruth? Even Father?

What then? Am I a bad son, a bad brother, a bad person, if I tell you that I liked that it was just Mother and me and no one else? Does that make me a monster, too?

⬦

We found him sleeping.

The plan, originally: to use Mother as bait (by then, who else was left?).

While he chased her, I would, with our newly fashioned net, trap him, and with any luck, would do so before he caught Mother.

But. He was snoring. His legs twitched. There were flies circling his head, every so often landing on his teeth or his tongue, which lolled out of the side of his mouth.

I could see lodged in his gut the soft end of a silver bullet.

We were covered, my mother and I, in two and sometimes three layers of clothes. I was wearing my hiking boots and Mother was wearing Noah's, and we had gloves on. We were suited up and hidden beneath the scent of the already dead.

We were stopped short by the sight of him lying on the floor in the middle of a patch of sunlight. We had expected him awake and waiting. We had prepared ourselves for running and screaming, had prepared for one of us to fall, a sacrifice for the other.

We stopped when we saw him sleeping there, unsure of how to proceed, and then we moved, very quickly. We threw the net, caught him by surprise, pushed him over, and, swiftly, Mother tied the ends together, and then, with Mother's yarn, we cinched him tightly into the net.

Father thrashed and growled and yelped. I kicked him once, twice, three times in his stomach, aiming for the silver bullet. Then it was Mother's turn, and she aimed her kick for his head, his snout, but as she pulled her leg back for a second go, her pants cuff, which she had forgotten to tuck into her boot, rose up, exposing for the briefest moment her pale, bared calf, and he nicked her once with a slick and sharp canine, leaving a long gash across the back of her leg.

Why didn't I kill him immediately, when I had him trussed up, had him ready to be spit over a fire? He who devoured my brothers and sisters? Who ruined my mother?

I could have rushed in. I could have harnessed the mentality of the countless torch-bearing mobs who had come before me, who once stormed castles and murdered monsters. Would anyone have blamed me? Would anyone have stopped me, or would they instead have lifted up pitchfork and ax, screamed "Kill the beast!" and pushed me forward?

I could have killed him without reproach. But he was, remember, at one time, my father.

Don't get me wrong. I had no doubts. I did not try to bring forth the kind, gentle, patient soul of the man he once was. I did not say things like, "Dad, it's me, your son Henry." Did not say, "I know you're in there, somewhere." Did not ask him to remember the good times. Fishing up in Kansas. The small perch I caught with my Snoopy fishing pole. Early mornings driving through our small town to buy donuts, leaving before everyone else had woken up, the car radio turned off, the two of us quiet, listening to the sounds of the tires rolling over cracks in the road.

Did not say, "Remember how we loved you?"

I did not once say anything of the sort. Father would have had to turn to Josephine or perhaps William for such overdrawn displays of sentimental histrionics, and little good it would have done him, or them.

He was what he was, and I understood this, and understood, too, that I would kill him eventually. In the end, I suppose, I did not kill him, did not, as you would say, end it there because I, too, like my father, was once patient, observant, curious.

◊

Mother was very good about handling herself. We had made plans, contingency plans, in case one of us were bitten but not devoured. But I can only imagine how I would have reacted had I been in her position. Would I have been able to bind my own mouth shut? Lock myself in the basement, where we had already buried the remains of my brothers and sisters, her children? Would I have been able to resist the smell of my own son's living flesh, the sound of his footsteps above me as I lay waiting for starvation finally to be done with me? Resist the knowledge that he was vulnerable, available, raw, and unsuspecting? Would I have been strong enough—finally so hungry for meat that I would have begun feasting on my own flesh—to wait patiently and alone for death to come for me?

No. I don't think so. I don't think I would have been strong enough at all.

❀

We found William, who most resembled Father, faceless, as if the wolf within Father, no longer satisfied with devouring Father from within, took a certain untoward pleasure in eating away at Father's image as reflected in my brother's face. In fact, they were, almost all of them, disfigured—not that their disfigurement much mattered, not by the time we found them.

Rebecca's nose (a perfect match for my father's) had been slipped easily from its dock; Richard's eyes, sucked (I can only imagine) from their sockets; Noah, whose shaggy head of tight curls not only matched Father's in color and texture but covered as well a perfectly matching mind, both of which were removed, taken in—Noah looked as if he had been scalped.

From Josephine, Father took her cheeks; Ruth was missing her chin and her left ear; and Sarah, who bore no resemblance to Father at all, who was, in fact, the spitting image of our mother, Sarah's face was untouched, completely smooth and untouched, and when we found her, she appeared to be sleeping, to be sleeping peacefully, if awkwardly, her neck bruised and broken.

The rest, of course, was a matter of the strength of Father's hunger.

Father became, so it seemed, quickly bored with meat not freshly killed, and for Sarah he had had no appetite at all.

❁

It was Mother's idea that we should hide ourselves beneath the scent of my brothers and sisters. By her thinking, if we smelled like those bits of flesh that he had already finished with, nudged at and gnawed away but ultimately ignored, then he would pass us by, disinterested.

❁

I did not build a cage for my father.

Nor did I knock him unconscious, secure him, with rope and tape, to the kitchen table in order to slice him open, figure him out.

I did not drag him by chains from town to town, calling

out, "Come, see the eighth natural wonder! Come, look upon the horror that is my father, the Wolfman!"

I did not charge for admission, did not benefit by his capture in any way whatsoever.

What I mean to say is: I was not cruel. Not at first.

⟡

I heard Mother in the basement below, thrashing and growling, and at night, for the first two or three nights, I heard her howling as well, her throaty expulsions growing weaker with each successive night.

It was she who dug up my brothers' and sisters' bodies, to finish off in her desperate hunger what my father had left untouched.

Don't think that I did not consider, at least once every night, opening the door just enough to fit through the crack raw meats, bloody strips, or even small birds or mice, fresh kills to ease Mother's hunger, quiet her down, and toward the end, I dreamt of lacing slabs of beef with rat poison, in hopes that I might quickly end her pain and my suffering. But I have to admit that I let her die a slow and empty death, and I did so for selfish reasons, did so because I did not want it to be me who finished her off.

⟡

I only lost my temper, truly lost my temper, once. Displayed concerted cruelty only the one time. When he refused to eat. When I tried to feed him a starling that I had found, that I had caught for him, and he refused it. I held it by its feet with tongs and dangled it so close to his craw that as I tried to tempt him with it, it would bump into his snout, a feather would catch on one of his teeth. But he ignored it, or tried to, couldn't prevent his nostrils from flaring at the smell of it, the small bird full of fear and unable to fly away no matter how furiously it shook.

He wouldn't eat it, and so I threw it at him, broke its neck, I believe, on his chest, and then I gathered it up, took it away, roasted it in the oven, and showed it to Father once more, showed him that I would eat it if he would not, but I couldn't suffer the smell of it, began to retch even as I drew it to my face, and so I threw it away.

His claws fell away almost immediately upon his death, his snout shrank back to a reasonable size, his body returned to its previous near-bald state, and the madness leaked from his eyes, leaving small orange tracks, like painted tears, down his cheek, his innocent brown pupils surrounded once more by a pure white sclera. The lycanthropic demon had, of course, left its vessel once the vessel could no longer sustain life. His teeth, the canines, are not *missing*, no, but are in my possession. I removed them shortly before he died, and when removed, they were three inches long, could have been, perhaps, longer as I was unable to remove them from the root, broke them, by accident, at the gums.

Would you or anyone else deny me the symbol of my mother's ruination?

I do not claim to understand the physics, or, rather, the biology behind the process of my father's transformation, first into a wolf and then, once dead, back into himself, and while it defies explanation that his teeth have also reverted back to the shape and size they were before he changed, this change, in light of all of the other changes performed after his death, seems only fitting, does it not?

◈

When I finally unlocked the basement door, almost two weeks after she had walked herself down there, I had covered my face in a thick, wet towel. I carried with me two large boxes of baking soda and the shovel.

No weapon of any kind? you might ask. No form of protection?

Discounting the shovel, no, no weapon. She was dead, I was sure of it, and if not dead, so close to death that she would have posed no threat. As for protection, my best protection would have been earplugs. I had prepared myself for the sight of my brothers and sisters, exhumed, eviscerated, had even prepared myself for the sight of Mother, wasted and ruined, the sight of her splayed out across the floor, facedown, her back rising in quick, shallow breaths, had prepared for all of that, but could not suffer the bald and angry mewling noises escaping with each exhalation.

Mother's hair I collected in bags, swept up piles of her

fur, bagged the bunch of it, and set the bags in my closet. She was, I'm certain, once as covered in fur as my father, but her hair grew coarse and then fell out in clumps as her food sup- ply dwindled, as her body lost the strength to maintain even the simplest functions. The bags are still there, I'm sure, in the closet, as innocuous as those bags ready to be delivered to Goodwill, but I am not sure what use I or anyone else might find for them.

⊛

I secured him to the ceiling with strong bolts and thick chains that made him hang, uncomfortably, I hoped, so that his feet could touch the ground, but only if his long arms were stretched to their limit.

Then I went into the woods. I had to drive there, as all the woods around our house had been replaced by houses and stores and roads. I went into the woods and I found a good, clean perch next to a small but loud enough waterfall, and that's where I sat. I had my father's notebooks with me to use as a guide, and I had my rifle, and I waited for my father's favorites to fly into view, to stop at a nearby tree, or even glide lazily overhead, and I shot them, as many as I could, which were very few considering how long I sat, how many shots I fired, but enough for me to bring back to the house a box heavy with them. He had not eaten for four or five days, and I knew that despite their now cooling bodies, despite his love for their blank and uncomprehending eyes, Father would have made short work of them. I laid them out in a wide circle just out of his reach, and then I hung from the ceiling with a bit of fishing wire one of Henslow's sparrows, hung it just in front of his snout. I laid them out and sat against the opposite wall and watched him squirm, lick his chops, stretch his neck out to the sparrow, almost, almost, as far as he could stretch, and then, exhausted, his head would fall back. He would whimper and whine.

It wasn't until after the end, once starvation, not me but starvation, had finished him off that I pulled him down from the ceiling, laid him out, lifeless, across the kitchen table, and, using the bread knife, opened him up and went digging for my father.

Farewell, Africa

I.

No one, apparently, had thought to test the pool before the party to see that it worked. The pool, which was the size of a comfortable Brooklyn or Queens apartment, had been designed by Harold Cornish and had been commissioned as a memorial installation for the Memorial Museum of Continents Lost. It was the centerpiece of the museum as well as the party celebrating the museum's opening. In the center of the long, wide pool was a large, detailed model of the African continent. According to Cornish, the pool, an infinity pool, would be able to re-create the event of Africa sinking into the sea. "Not entirely accurately," he told me early into the party, before anyone knew the installation wouldn't work. "But enough to give a good idea of how it might have looked when it happened."

Harold Cornish is the artist responsible for *The Cube* as well as *The Barge*, both of which are larger installation pieces—respectively, an overlarge cube perched, by some mysterious mechanism, on top of a cube not much larger than an end table and which has been set on its side, and a brushed-steel barge city that floats in the middle of Lake Erie that, for a year, was Cornish's home and studio and that can easily accommodate, according to Cornish's estimates, a population of a hundred thousand people. The pool, which he has named *The Pool of African Despair Pool*, is his first commissioned work and is the first work he has constructed as a memorial. It is also the smallest work he has designed since leaving art school, and it is the first piece of his to utilize hydraulics.

The walls of the pool, which stop at just below the water's level, are retractable and are set on hydraulic lifts, and should have slowly begun to creep upward so that less and less water could escape over the pool's edge. The walls would continue to rise, then, until no water could escape, so that soon the pool would fill up and the water level would rise and then cover the sculpture of Africa completely. This was all supposed to happen quite gradually over the course of the entire evening, leading up to the time Owen Mitchell would deliver his speech.

As I made my way through the party, though, I walked by the pool on occasion to check its progress, but couldn't tell that anything was happening, which I at first attributed to my own ignorance of the mechanism of memorial installations or of art itself. But when I mentioned this to Mitchell, who seemed to be paying as much attention as I was to the pool and then to his watch, he shook his head, sighed, and said, whispering, "The damn thing's not working." Then he took a sip of champagne and said, "Too bad this didn't happen with the real Africa."

II.

If you were to ask Owen Mitchell about his speech, his most famous speech, the speech often referred to as the Farewell, Africa speech, he would tell you that it was a full fifteen minutes too long.

"You look at that speech," he told me shortly after I met him in his hotel room as he was preparing for the party. "You read the whole thing; I think you'll agree with me. You can say about twenty minutes, about twenty minutes' worth of words, real and good words about the sinking of the African continent, and the rest is fluff, is posturing, or you start to see the speech repeat itself or traffic in generalities, which, fine, which, okay, that's standard practice, that's not great, but it's acceptable, for another ten minutes, that's acceptable, and another ten minutes puts you up to a thirty-minute speech." Mitchell shook his head and then sighed and said, "The president, however. The president had a time block. Forty-five minutes, he told me. 'It's up to you to write me that speech,' he said. And frankly, forty-five minutes? At least fifteen minutes too long."

Mitchell has been known to edit the speech down. Whenever he would come across the speech in a bookstore or when he was at someone's house and saw that they owned a copy of the speech, which was, for a long time, being reprinted in textbooks and on its own, he would pull it off the shelf and turn to the beginning of the speech and then start to cross out words and sentences and, sometimes, entire sections.

"Once," he told me, "I got carried away and accidentally edited a friend's copy of the speech down to a five-minute affair. Ten minutes if you read it really slowly." He laughed and said, "I saw what I'd done and quietly put the book back on the shelf and then, later in the evening, made a show of finding it on the shelf again and pulling it down and then pretended to be shocked at what someone had done to it. My friend was so embarrassed and upset that for a moment I almost told him the truth, but I never did."

I asked him what he cut out when he edited these, if he had specific passages he always cut out, or if his edits were subject to some kind of whim.

"Whim, mostly," he said, wrestling with the bow tie that went with his tuxedo. "But there are parts that I will always edit out."

"Like what?" I asked him.

"The very beginning, those first lines," he said. "Every time. Those are the worst. No matter what, I always cross out that first part."

When he told me this, I was surprised and not a little disheartened, for while I am not a huge fan of the Farewell, Africa speech—I find his first inauguration speech and the speech he wrote for Jameson when Jameson first proposed the creation of the office of world governor to be both more eloquent and full of more promise and sturdier judgment than the Farewell, Africa speech—what I liked most about the speech were its beginning lines, which, with their oddly syncopated repetitions, create a verbal space, in my opinion, anyway, of unsettled comfort or discomfiting calm, the only kind of space, in any case, that might prepare the public for the announcement that the African continent was sinking inexorably, inevitably into the sea.

"Must we say"—the speech begins—"have we come to that moment when we must finally say, are we now at that final moment when we must say, with sadness in our hearts but determination in our hearts, too."

"That part?" I asked him. "That's the part you will cut out no matter what?"

"Every time," he told me. Then he checked himself and his tie in the mirror, and then he checked his profile, and then he shook his head and looked at me and smiled, and then he said to me, "Tonight, the speech I'm reading tonight? I've knocked it down to twenty-five minutes. And that's without trying to rush through it."

When the museum's board of directors first approached Mitchell about the museum opening, he politely declined. He left the administration shortly after the Farewell, Africa speech to run for office himself, hoping the speech would thrust him onto the political stage, but he was handily defeated in an ugly, vicious campaign, and since then, he has done his best to distance himself from his failed foray into politics and the speech. Not because he dislikes the speech, so he explained to me, but because for so long he found himself defined by that speech and that speech alone.

At first, then, he had little interest in resurfacing at a party celebrating the opening of a museum commemorating the sinking of Africa. When the board of directors contacted him again and asked him to reconsider, however, he had a change of heart.

In the past ten years, Owen Mitchell has published a novel to little acclaim and designed various portable housing models, which he has submitted to competitions and to the World Disaster Relief Organization, but, for his troubles, has so far only received letters thanking him for his interest in world disaster relief. He worked briefly as a lobbyist and then as a lawyer. He has taught both graduate students and high school students, and once he was the host of the Academy Awards—"the technical stuff, you know, the part they film and record and show clips of during the real thing," he told me—but he has yet to rediscover the success or pleasure he had achieved while working as a speechwriter.

"So, after thinking about it for a while," he told me as we spoke in the museum courtyard, when I asked him what had changed his mind, "I realized, sadly, that this speech was the last good thing I'd done." He shrugged his shoulders, popped an hors d'oeuvre into his mouth, and looked like he was about to say something else, then thought better of it, and then looked over and past my shoulder and said, "Uh-oh. Looks like they're draining the pool now."

III.

When I first met Karen Long, two days before the museum opening party, she had an easy and relaxed air about her. Karen is the events planner for the museum, and she was giving me a tour of the exhibits and party space and laying out for me the itinerary for the opening night celebration. She walked slowly and talked very quickly, and for a while I worried that she would finish telling me about the exhibits long before she had finished showing them to me, and I wondered if she was perhaps more nervous than she had been letting on.

"This is my first big event for the museum," she told me when she met me in the front hall. Then she laughed and said, "Not that I haven't done a ton of other big events." And then, a few minutes later, as she was demonstrating an interactive world model for me ("For the kids, you know, who love this kind of hands-on stuff. See? Here? If you push Japan down with your foot, how it stays down? But if you push Spain down, it pops right back up? We'll provide galoshes, of course."), she interrupted herself: "Not that there could be another event I could have planned for the museum, since this is the opening night, right?" Then she slapped me playfully on my shoulder.

"Now I'll take you to see our exhibit of relief trailers. I think you'll like it. It's quite impressive."

Before she took her current position with the museum, Karen worked in publicity and events planning for the Walt

Disney Company, and before that she worked as an intern in the administration's communications office, where, briefly, she worked for Owen Mitchell before Mitchell left.

She deftly led me through the museum and its exhibits and answered almost all of my questions, knowledgeably and smoothly, but would not confirm or deny the rumor that the museum wasn't able to find anyone from Old Africa to attend or speak at the opening. Instead she said, smiling her wide and toothy smile, "We're very excited, you know, about the delegation from Old Japan. And of course the representatives from Costa Rica. Or maybe it's Honduras. I'll have to check my notes."

The first time I saw Karen the night of the opening, she was standing over the pool next to Cornish, watching as the water drained out of it. I walked over to her, not sure exactly how I would phrase the question I wanted to ask her, namely, *How's it going?* Or, for that matter, any other question I might ask her, since the answer to those questions—*Is the pool working all right?*, *Is it true that the waitstaff is almost out of champagne?*, and *Is it true that a number of the bottles of champagne have gone missing?*—seemed either obvious or, in light of the situation, mean-spirited. Not to mention that she would, in each case, I was certain of it, decline to comment.

It didn't matter as she saw me coming toward her, and before I could even say hello, she asked me, "Do you know anything about fixing hydraulics?" I said no. "Then I can't use you right now, but thanks for your kind effort to be helpful."

I smiled at this and then asked her if it would be okay if I shadowed her for a few minutes.

"Really?" she asked. "Watching me watch this pool drain is newsworthy?" That was all she said before she turned back to look at the pool, which had almost completely drained, and so I took her nonanswer as a yes, and for five more minutes, the three of us—Karen, Cornish, and myself—stood there and waited as the pool dried up. Then Cornish stepped over the wall and got on his hands and knees, the wet spots at the bottom of the pool turning his gray wool trousers black, and he opened a gear box, or something like a gear box, and after another few minutes, he said, "Oh. Okay. I think I've got it."

"You sure?"

"Oh, yeah. Won't be but another ten or fifteen minutes."

"Fine," Karen said. "I'll leave you to it." Then she looked at me and shook her head, with disgust or anger or frustration, I couldn't tell, just as I couldn't tell if this was directed at me or at the situation or at Cornish or at the world at large. Then she walked past me quickly enough to make me hurry behind her, but not so fast that I couldn't have kept up.

Over her shoulder, she said, "I'm sure you've heard about the champagne by now."

I feigned ignorance, and she stopped, and I nearly ran into her. She looked me square in the eyes, and the beginnings of a smirk or grin made one side of her mouth twist up. Karen Long has piercing blue eyes and pale, pale blond hair that she often uses to cover her face, which is a soft, oval face brought into sharp relief by a long, not unattractive, angular nose. It seemed for a second, as she stared at me, that she might punch me in the face. That, or lean in to kiss me on the mouth. It was an unsettling look, and then it passed, and then she said, "And you no doubt know that ten bottles of champagne went missing entirely?"

I nodded, afraid of what she might do if I tried lying again.

"Well. That's what I'm doing right now," she said, "looking for those bottles or the people who took them. If you're going to follow me around, you might as well know what I'm doing so you don't think I'm just wandering aimlessly."

I nodded again and said, "Sure thing," and said, "After you," which was when the commotion started, and the three men with the water hose showed up.

"Never mind," she said. "I think maybe we found our guys."

IV.

The general consensus, for a long time, was that Africa was too big to sink. By the time Africa sank, we had already lost Central America and some of Australia and all of Japan. I had been in the city only a few months after we lost Japan, and I had started working my first job as a reporter around that time, too. In my office, a few of the reporters and editors started a betting pool, and to make me feel more at home, I suppose, they invited me to join the pool, and before I fully understood what we were betting on, I said okay. Then they asked me what I thought would go next and how much money I wanted to bet on that. It was fairly crass. I thought so at the time, and I think so now, but at the time, thinking so, I still placed a bet. Most people figured somewhere in Europe. Spain, maybe, or Portugal, or the British Isles. Especially the British Isles, as those seemed ripe for sinking. A couple of people figured Greenland would go next, and one guy put a couple of dollars on North America, or maybe just on any part of North America, Nova Scotia, maybe, or Alaska, because he said the odds were too good to pass up, but even he didn't put any money on Africa. In fact, when they were making the pool sheet, no one even thought to include Africa on it, not the whole continent, anyway, because everyone knew. To be safe, then, I told them to add Africa and that I'd put money on Africa. They told me I should just bet on South Africa, maybe, or Egypt, or Madagascar, which, at least, was an island. I made them give me odds on Africa, on the whole thing, and then I put down a quarter and that was the only thing I bet, and they rolled their eyes at me, the rest of the reporters and editors in on this pool, and they acted like I was the biggest jackass they had seen, and this made me defensive, and so I said to them, hardly serious at all, "If you think I'm an asshole now, you just wait until after it sinks and I win."

Sometimes when I think about this, I can't help but laugh. I want to laugh at the situation and at what I said, which was stupid, and the ridiculous and horrible nature of the thing we were betting on itself, and then at the fact that out of everyone, I won, but it's not really something to laugh about, is it?

I didn't think I'd win, of course. Nobody thought I'd win.

It's a silly thing to think sometimes, but there are times, there are a lot of times when I think about that bet, when I think about the bet and about how Africa sank, how quickly Africa sank after I made that bet. There are times, late at night or if I wake up early in the morning, if a trash truck or my neighbors, the ones above me, who often fight and scream late into the night, if something wakes me up and I find myself lying alone in my bed in the dark, I will remember that bet I made, and I will blame myself for what happened, blame that quarter bet for the way Africa sank right into the sea, and though I know it's a foolish way to think and to act, I will look back on that bet with great and shuddering regret.

V.

There were screams at first, but only from those few men and women closest to the action, the people, in other words, who had gathered around the now empty pool to see what Harold Cornish was doing to it. Otherwise, the rest of the party seemed oblivious to what was going on by the pool. If you knew him or if you'd heard him speak, you could maybe pick out the brittle, nasal sound of Harold Cornish among those first voices, but maybe not. Apparently, the guys— three of them, all drunk on stolen champagne and holding, as if they were firemen, an average-sized water hose—didn't know that Cornish was inside the pool working on fixing the hydraulics, and when he lifted his head up to see what the hell was going on, he received a faceful of water. This struck the gentlemen with the hose as extremely funny. One or all of them then doubled over in laughter, sending, for a brief moment, a spray of water up and out over the crowd, so that soon those who had had no idea that anything was happening were quite focused on the pool and the men and the hose.

I turned to Karen to see what, if anything, might be playing across her face as this all transpired, but she had left my side, and after quickly scanning the courtyard, I spotted her kneeling down and leaning into a row of shrubs planted against one of the far walls. She had hiked her black, sparkling dress up over her knees, and her left hand dug into the bushes in search of the water spigot, which she found, and, after briefly turning the nozzle hard to the left and jetting more water into the crowd, she managed to shut the hose down. By the time I turned back to look at the men with the hose, security had confiscated the water hose, and the three drunks—who later turned out to be interns with the bright idea of speeding along the process of sinking the model of the African continent—were being escorted into the museum proper.

Then Karen was at my side again and she said, shaking her head, "You're taking me out for a drink after all of this." I looked at her, not a little surprised, and she said, "I deserve a drink after all of this, and so someone's taking me out for one, and it might as well be you."

Before I could say anything to this, the speakers let out a high-pitched whine that hurt our ears, and everyone in the courtyard turned to the stage, where Owen Mitchell was now standing, his finger tapping against the microphone. At the time, I thought that someone had made a mistake and told him it was now time for him to speak, that he had quietly protested, the commotion only just ending, that an overeager employee of Karen Long's or someone from the board, nervous about the way this party had begun spiraling out of control, had practically shoved him onto that stage to give his speech, whether we were ready to hear it or not. Later, I found out this was not the case. Mitchell stepped up to the microphone of his own accord, he told me. "Things had gotten out of hand," he said, smiling. "No one seemed to remember why we were there."

He cleared his throat. The whining stopped. He tapped the microphone again and cleared his throat again. The crowd, those of us still left in the courtyard, fell silent. I turned to look at Karen again, and she was looking up at the stage. Mitchell looked out at us and he shaded his eyes, and then he looked down at the notes in his hand, and he folded them and stuffed them inside his jacket pocket, and we waited for him to begin his speech.

It was a short speech, shorter, maybe, than even he had planned. It was not the speech we knew. Mitchell had managed somehow to boil it down to its essence, or maybe he made it into something entirely new. I can't remember it now, not its specifics, not past those first few words, and Mitchell hadn't written it down, had abandoned, at the last moment, his own notes, and cannot remember it himself. It spoke of tragedy, I think. I think, too, that it spoke to the enormous loss of life, to the sense that this world had been pushed to the brink, but in truth, the speech might not have been about any of that. It was not the speech we knew, yet by the end of the speech, I felt as if I weren't listening to Mitchell as he spoke in front of us, as if the words weren't coming from him, but had been borne inside my own head, had always been part of my own thoughts, that Mitchell was simply reminding me of something I already knew and had somehow forgotten. Judging by the soft sighs escaping Karen's lips as she stood to my right, the way her lips moved as if she were reciting the speech along with Mitchell, I was not alone in this.

"They told us the center will not hold," he began, and there seemed to be no other sound but the sound of his voice. "If we lose this, they said, the center will not hold and we will not survive, yet here we are." He smiled. "Here we are."

Juan Manuel Gonzales:
A Meritorious Life

GONZALES, JUAN MANUEL (1804–1848). Innkeeper, forger. Place of birth: Delicias, Mexico. Don Rafael, who owned land in what is now the Rio Grande Valley of Texas, had a son, Hernando. As the story goes, Hernando was in love, but his love, for Gabriela, the daughter of his wet nurse, was forbidden by his father. When Don Rafael discovered that Hernando and Gabriela were still meeting, in secret, and that their affections had only grown stronger despite his wishes, he sent Gabriela to Mexico City, where he enrolled her in a school for nurses, and in exchange for her agreement to end her foolish affair with his son, Don Rafael agreed to pay for her schooling as well as a room he acquired for her at an all-girls' boardinghouse. In addition to this, Don Rafael provided Gabriela with a stipend equal to fifty dollars a week.

Hernando, struck dumb by how quickly Gabriela acqui-esced, refused to leave his father's house for two weeks after Gabriela went away. He canceled all appointments with his friends and instructed the house staff not to allow anyone, but for the unlikely Gabriela, entrance onto the large estate.

Then, one hot summer afternoon, Hernando, who had that day moved no farther a distance than that between his bed and the chaise lounge set beneath his bedroom window, was surprised to see in that bedroom window the face of a faithful servant and friend. At first startled and then quickly angered (for had he not given specific instructions?), Her-nando at once decided to shove the intruder, push him out of the window and off the wall, so that he would fall and perhaps break his legs. As he grabbed the man's shirt, ready to give him a strong shove, the servant pulled from his per-son a carefully folded letter and shook it in Hernando's face, saying, "Please, Don Hernando, please, I have instructions from Gabriela." Quickly, then, Hernando pulled the young man inside, grabbed the letter, and read it and read it again and read it for a third time before once looking up at the ser-vant who had delivered it, at which point he said, "You may leave."

As per the letter's instructions, Hernando approached the innkeeper, Señor Juan Gonzales, hired by Don Rafael to run the inn in order to pay off a debt, and informed him that letters would soon arrive, sometimes many in just one day. Gonzales was to keep these letters, and every Sunday after the eight o'clock Mass, he, Don Hernando, would come to the inn for breakfast and Señor Gonzales would slip the letters to him, hidden wrapped with the tortillas. Señor Gonzales was not, under any circumstances, to hand the letters to anyone else.

For three months, Gabriela mailed all letters for Hernando to the innkeeper. Don Rafael, at first glad to see his son had finally given up his foolishness, quickly grew suspicious of Hernando's Sunday visits to his innkeeper, Señor Gonzales. When confronted, Señor Gonzales, easily intimidated, told Don Rafael that, yes, Hernando received letters, though Señor Gonzales claimed not to know from whom. Don Rafael instructed Señor Gonzales to set aside one of the letters to be handed over after Hernando had retrieved the others. Unable to disobey Don Rafael, yet unwilling to betray the young Hernando, Señor Gonzales took the first letter to arrive on Monday, hesitated only a moment before opening it, and set himself the task of copying it over and over again, doing so for the full week, meticulously tracing each letter until he had finally mastered Gabriela's hand. And then, Saturday night, Gonzales forged a letter from Gabriela, claiming that she no longer loved Hernando, that she had met another man, a doctor, and that she wished to never see him again. He sealed this fake letter into an envelope and marked the envelope with a small X in the top right hand corner.

Anxious about the deception, however, Señor Gonzales, by mistake, gave the forged letter to Hernando, and accidentally passed one of the real letters, one that had arrived just the day before, to Don Rafael, only realizing his mistake as

Don Rafael, after opening the letter, handed the unmarked envelope back to Señor Gonzales.

"Aha!" exclaimed Don Rafael. "It is just as I suspected. It is a letter from Gabriela. And also as I suspected, she has finally broken his heart, has left him for another man, a doctor."

Escape from the Mall

I have only known Roger for a couple of hours now, but when he comes over to me, he's got a look on his face that tells me he's got something on his mind.

He's wrapping a strip of tattered cloth around the palm of his hand. It's a serious venture, this wrapping of the cloth around the palm of his hand. As he walks over to me, he seems to be considering this process more than he's considering me, more than he's considering the act of walking, which is why, even though we are all huddled here—the seven of us—here in this janitor's supply closet, which cannot be much larger than a decently sized public toilet, why it takes a good minute or two for him to reach me. Why it takes him long enough that for a moment I consider meeting him halfway, if only to quickly get over with whatever it is he is going to propose to me.

Instead, I try to think back over the past couple of hours

to see if I can remember what he might have done to the palm of his hand, but I can't remember anything in particular. Granted, there is a lot to remember. Granted, there is a lot I'd rather not remember.

The way Jennifer slipped on the wet tile in the middle of the food court just as the hordes rushed over her, for example. The way she screamed for our help. The way they slurped as they slurped her up. I could stand to forget that.

Not to mention the way that black guy, that black guy with the kid, the kid who's now sulking, red-eyed and snotty and blotchy-faced in the corner, the way that guy turned around at the last minute, at the very last minute, right before Roger jimmied the closet door open, turned around and charged into the throng of them, wielding Roger's Louisville Slugger and yelling over his shoulder, "I'll always love you, Tyrone," the way they kind of just parted for him, like the Red Sea for Moses, stepped aside and let him charge right into the heart of them before the mass of them swallowed him whole.

That.

I'm pretty certain I'm not the only one who'd rather forget that.

But as for Roger and his palm and what might have happened to his palm that might now require such deliberate attention, I can't say as I remember.

He hasn't stopped moving toward me even as he's come close enough to me that he could probably whisper whatever it is he's going to say and I'd still be able to hear it, and for a moment I think to myself, *Maybe he's going to kiss me.* And then I think, *That'd be unexpected.*

But he doesn't kiss me, which is fine, as I think it might hurt Mary's feelings, Mary who's been looking at him doe-eyed since he decapitated the one that was about to rip her skull off and eat her brains out.

He doesn't kiss me, but he leans in close enough that I could bite his nose if I wanted to. I guess he could bite my nose if he wanted to, too.

Neither of us bites the other one's nose.

"How you holding up?" he says, whispering hoarsely.

"Great," I say. "What happened to your hand?" I ask.

He lifts it up and points it palm forward at my face and says, "This? Nothing. This ain't nothing. I'm good, man. I'm good."

I don't get much of a look at it before he drops it quickly back down to his side, but the smell of it that lingers in the air where his hand was just a second ago smells rotten and earthy. But before I can force the issue, he tells me he has a plan.

"A plan?" I ask. "A plan to do what?"

"We've been sitting here almost an hour now," he says. "We're starting to get restless. We're starting to panic."

I shift my eyes to get a look around the room, and no one looks restless or panicked. Everyone looks tired and sad and sweaty. No one looks restless or panicked at all, except for Roger, I realize, once I shift my eyes back to him.

"Sure," I say. "What's your plan?"

⊙

This story has nothing to do with me. I know this, even as I am in the middle of it. This story has everything to do with Roger and Mary and Tyrone and the security guard. I don't know the security guard's name, but he's got a look about him, a look that makes me think that this story is his story, too, more his story, anyway, than my own. He's got that reformed-addict-turned-security-guard-waiting-to-make-the-ultimate-sacrifice-for-people-he-doesn't-even-know-in-an-attempt-to-atone-for-the-misery-he-caused-in-his-youth kind of look. That, or maybe it's just that he looks bigger than the rest of us. Bigger and unhurried, too, as if he has seen all this before, or as if just this sort of situation—a zombie attack, an alien invasion, a giant, ferocious lizard, mutated by the nuclear annihilation of Hiroshima, rampaging through Houston—was what he had been planning for, what he had expected when he signed up for the job as a security guard for this mall in the suburbs. But when I mention this to Mary, who, every time I speak to her, looks surprised to see me there with the rest of them, she tells me he's stoned.

⊙

I've got a story for Mary, too.

Recently divorced, mother of two.

Not the prom queen from high school, maybe a late

bloomer, but when she bloomed, pretty enough that she married that prom-king type.

Maybe an actual prom king from the rival high school, or not a prom king at all, but a quarterback, or point guard.

All in all, a miserable affair: You're married to an unappreciative man mired in the glory of his past, supportive of him but lonely, too, until one day, you come home to hear him tell you that he doesn't love you anymore, that instead he loves Missy, a saleswoman at the Toyota dealership where he works, not as a salesman himself, or even as a mechanic, but as the guy who cheats car buyers into buying extra care insurance packages for things that will never break. Now she's juggling kids, two part-time jobs, attorney fees to wrest alimony and child support from her ex-husband, inappropriate advances from her much older bosses at both of her jobs, and today. Her day off of all days, the day she has set aside for herself, not even the whole day, but the few measly hours her mother agreed to watch the kids, a couple of hell-raisers made only worse by the divorce, the one day she picked to come to the mall, not even to buy anything, not that she even had the money to buy anything, but just to look around, just to have a few moments to herself, just to revisit the world she thought was going to be her world, today is the day the mall is overrun by the evil undead.

Of course it is.

She is surprised not in the least by this.

And maybe she didn't trip in the sporting goods store by the exercise equipment. Maybe she didn't trip at all, but gave herself up, handed herself over, because could it be worse, really, than how she felt now?

All of this, though, all of this speculation I keep to myself. And I've decided to speak to Mary as little as possible in case she makes any more stray comments that might unhinge the fragile framework of my coping mechanism, as she's already done with the security guard.

⚬

Roger's plan might just be the dumbest plan I have ever heard ever, but I go along with it anyway. Why not, right? What have I got to lose, right?

Or, rather, other than my life, what have I got to lose?

I go along with it because I know the others will go along with it, too. They've followed Roger's lead since the moment the screaming began, way on the other side of the mall, somewhere near the food court, the screaming loud enough that we could hear it from so far away. They followed his lead into that fray even when, in the opposite direction and only a hundred yards away, there were doors leading outside, leading to our escape. Even then, they followed him.

By *they*, of course, I mean, *we*.

We followed him into the fray.

We watched him save first Tyrone and then his father, and then, at the end, right before we shuffled into this janitor's closet, Mary in the sporting goods store.

And then into this broom closet: We followed him here, too.

Now he wants us to go up into the ceiling.

"The ceiling," he tells me, whispering still. "That's our ticket out of here."

I look up. He slaps me quickly and lightly on the face. "Don't look up," he says. "You'll give it away."

I shift my eyes around the room a) to see if anyone just saw Roger slap me and b) to see whom I might give this precious and vital information away to.

"To whom?" I ask.

Roger leans in closer and I wish he wouldn't. There's a smell to him that's ripe and uncomfortable. Maybe it's the adrenaline in his blood, or maybe he lets off a funky kind of sweat when fighting the evil undead. Whatever it is, I'm doing my best to breathe it in through my mouth.

"Don't say anything," he says. "Don't react to what I'm about to say."

"Okay."

"We don't want to freak anyone out."

"Sure. No. No problem."

Now his voice drops to an actual whisper, and I can't hear him, and for a moment, I wonder if he's saying something and I just can't hear him or if he's decided now is the time to pull that trick where you move your mouth like you're talking when really you're not saying anything at all.

"I can't, I can't hear you," I tell him.

He doesn't like to repeat things, I can tell by the look on his face, but before I can apologize for something that wasn't my fault, he says, again, "One among us has been infected."

◈

This news takes me by surprise, but only slightly, and only in that it was Roger who figured this out and not me.

I figured that if anyone were to discover that one of us was infected, it would be me or one of the other unnamed peripheral characters, and only moments too late.

For instance, say one of us would be crying in the corner, hunched over and sobbing and rocking, and another one of us would see this person in pain, and we would sigh in disgust at Roger and Mary and the security guard and Tyrone, all too caught up in their own drama to notice the rest of us, and we would walk over, gently place our hand on his shoulder, sit down softly next to him, and say something like, "It's okay, it's going to be okay, we're going to make it out of this, I swear, I promise, we will," and we would place our other hand on his knee, a sign of friendship, a sign of "You are not alone," and he would place his own hand over ours, and we would say, "That's right, it's going to be just fine, don't you worry," but it would come out a little hesitantly, or distractedly, as we would be distracted by the queer texture of the hand on top of our hand, cold and wet and a little sticky, but we wouldn't look down, not yet. We wouldn't look down because we would feel guilty for thinking poorly of our comrade in arms, our newfound friend, desperately sad and in need of comfort.

"Do you have a family?" we might ask. "Do you have someone waiting for you?"

And he would nod, a gentle but increasingly vigorous nod.

"Oh yeah?" we might say. "Where? Where are they? Tell me, just tell me about them," we would say, knowing that sometimes talking about something else, anything else, might distract us, if only temporarily, from the fear and the pain and the sorrow.

Then would come that too-late moment when we look down at the hand covering ours and discover it to be a rotting mass of flesh, at which point we freak out and the creature whips its head around and bites our face off, or when, pivoting off our question about his family, he whips his head quickly around and says something to the effect of "My family? They're waiting just outside that door" before biting our face off.

Though, truth be told, zombie-like creatures aren't known for their ability to speak.

Nor for their understanding of ironic timing.

Or even their understanding of delayed gratification.

So, really the surprising thing about Roger coming to me with information about one of us being infected is that there is one of us infected and we are not yet all dead.

Still, it's a little disappointing to find this out from Roger, who has discovered it all on his own and in enough time to try to think of what to do about it.

"Really?" I say. "Who?"

"Not yet," he says. "We screw this up, we're cooked," he says.

Then he nods seriously and gravely. Then he puts his hand heavily on my shoulder and nods again, and so I smile back at him, which I guess is all he needed from me, because then he moves on to the next person he's going to tell about his plan.

For my money, I peg Tyrone as the one among us who is infected. Not that I've got anything against the kid. He seems like a nice enough kid, or did before he was turned into a mindless and brutal killing machine. He seems nice enough, but he's also the one we might all least suspect, which is why I suspect him most.

There's a small, bloody mass on the side of his head, which I originally figured for random brain matter or organ matter splattered there during the run through the maze of maternity clothes after we ducked into the department store. Now I am beginning to wonder if it's not his actual brain I'm looking at. If that's maybe where they got him, in his actual brain, not enough to kill him, not enough to really slow him down. But to make him one of their own, how much brain would a zombie need to eat?

Not much, by my reckoning.

The longer I stare at that piece of Tyrone's brain sticking out of his skull, the more I wonder why no one else but Roger has noticed it, and then what I might be able to do to preemptively disable the thing that once was Tyrone. I scan the room for a piece of equipment that might quietly and quickly be transformed into some kind of specialized weapon, but the most threatening thing I see is the mop and mop handle, or the broom, or the disinfectant spray, none of which seem all that promising. As I'm trying to figure out if there's some way I can take a roll or two of toilet paper, light them on fire, and turn them into some kind of something, though, Mary crosses over to Tyrone and pulls his head to her chest, to comfort him, maybe, or to comfort herself, or maybe both, and he hiccups one time and then sobs heavily into her, and I see the piece of brain matter slip off his head and fall into her lap.

❁

When I first heard the screams, I was walking into the mall, and Roger, who had just passed me going the other way, was walking out of the mall. Then the screams happened and then we both turned around, and maybe he gave me the benefit of the doubt, maybe he saw in me what we all hope to see in ourselves—selflessness, bravery, willingness— because when he saw me turn around so I could walk back out of the mall, having decided that the new pair of shoes I hoped to buy wasn't worth dealing with the kind of hysterical, pained, violence-ridden screaming coming from the far part of the mall, he grabbed me by the shoulder, a strange glint in his eye, and said, "Are you thinking what I'm thinking?"

Perhaps it was the tone of his voice, the surety of it, the assumption that I was like him, that everyone was like him, and how little room for argument there was in what he said and how he looked at me. Whatever it was, like an idiot, I followed after him.

Regardless, Roger is a guy I can't make up my mind on. A guy I can't get a good read on.

He's a mystery, and that makes me nervous.

Take, for instance, that action he played with the Louisville Slugger. I didn't see where he got it from, but I saw him wielding it with a fierce determination, watched him knock the head off one about to eat Mary's brains out, saw him pose after the swing, as if for *Sports Illustrated*, as if he'd hit a home run, heard him, as he helped Mary to her feet, say, "That's a stand-up double if I ever saw one," and I'll admit, since I saw him perform that nifty little trick, I've wanted to give it a go myself, except that, thanks to Tyrone's dad, the bat's gone.

Which was cool and all, what Roger did with the baseball bat, but then he's earnest to the point of embarrassment. Like after Tyrone's dad lost that bat, and we were all quiet and uncertain as to what to say to Tyrone, except for maybe "That was some kind of stupid, what your dad just did," all of us quiet, that is, until Roger sat on his haunches and held Tyrone by the shoulders and looked deep into his eyes and told him, "That makes you the man of the house, now, Tyrone."

Told him, "Do you think you're ready for that?"

And then when Tyrone shook his head no, and while the rest of us, I'm sure, were thinking, *Roger, give it a rest, leave the kid alone,* Roger gave him a bit of a shake and told him, "I think you are.

"I think you're stronger than you think.

"I think you're stronger than all of us.

"But that doesn't mean you can't cry, that doesn't mean you can't be sad.

"Only really strong guys like you and me know it's okay to be sad and it's okay to cry, but that we still have to be strong, right?"

And Tyrone started to snuffle and started to nod, and Roger said, "Right?"

And Tyrone's lips moved, but maybe it was a quiver and maybe it was him saying, "Right."

And Roger said, softly now, "Right?" and then pulled Tyrone into a bear hug, which set Tyrone into a sloppy hiccuping mess of sobs and snot, at which point I looked around with a do-we-have-time-for-this-sort-of-thing? look on my face, only to find everyone else mooning over the scene, Mary with her hand pressed up against her chest and the security guard wiping his eyes in that way men sometimes do when they find themselves crying unexpectedly at the end of a movie.

⸙

I want to hate him, in other words, maybe because he's everything that I'm not, or maybe because he's the type of person who wants me to believe that he's everything I'm not, but then there's some strong and growing part of me that wants to admire him, too, can't help but admire him, and that just makes me want to hate him even more.

The news has spread that we're making our way out through the ceiling. I wonder what this means for the one among us who is infected.

Because he's the biggest of us, the security guard is hoisted up first. Roger and me and two other guys, whose names I don't know or don't remember, heave him up there, and I watch him scramble and pull himself the rest of the way up, wondering why it is that I can't remember or don't know his name, either.

Then Roger turns to me and says, "Okay, Cowboy, you next."

I'm not sure why he has decided all of a sudden to call me Cowboy, but, against my better judgment, I decide I kind of like it.

The plan is for the security guard, who is also the strongest (or so we've all assumed) to lower himself down enough to help lift up the rest of us. He tries it first with me, but the two of us together are too much weight for the flimsy ceiling tiles and supports. The whole thing starts to crack and collapse before he simply lets go of me and I crash down on top of Roger.

"That won't work," the security guard says, and it's hard for me to believe, but I think that's the first time I've heard him speak, and the sound of his voice, nasal and off-pitched, makes me for a moment reconsider his story. No longer a tough guy or a former addict trying to atone, he now strikes me as that kid, pale and a role-player, weak and trembling through high school, who discovered that the kind of devotion he heaped onto twenty-sided dice and gamemasters could be more beneficially applied to a gym membership. And while he might now be a much bigger geeky, trembly, insecure nerd, he's still a nerd all the same, and I wonder why he hasn't died yet.

"Good call," Roger says, as he picks himself up. "Gonna have to figure something else out."

Then he looks at me, and I don't know what he's about to propose, but I know I don't much like the look in his eyes or the attention he's giving me.

"All right, Cowboy, time for you to shine," he says to me, and now I realize how stupid the name he's given me really sounds. "This is taking way too long. I'm going to need you to scout ahead for us, find us the way out, so that once we get everyone up there, we're not just a bunch of ants scrambling around in our ant pile." Then he slaps me hard on the shoulder with his good hand, and then he looks up and calls out, "Okay, Francis, scooch on back, and we're going to help Cowboy here the way we did you."

Is Francis the security guard's name? I wonder. Or is Francis a nickname?

And then, before I can think about it too long, I'm lifted and heaved and shoved upward, and I panic for a moment because there's nothing for me to grab hold of or on to that hasn't been bent or cracked or crumbled by Francis, the security guard. Then I see a rail within reach and lunge for it, or try to lunge for it, unleveraged as I am, and I hear one of the guys below squeal as I accidentally kick him in the face while lunging. I grab hold and pull myself into the ceiling, and I wonder what the hell I'm supposed to do next.

I also wonder why Francis couldn't have gone in search of a way out.

"Maybe that way?" he whispers, though I don't know that, if we spoke in our normal voices, the creatures in the mall could hear us or do anything about us either way. "I think, depending on which supply closet we ran into, your best bet is either going to be that way, or back over there," he says, pointing to my right and then over my shoulder. It's not a lot to go on, but I go right, anyway, because I hate going backward.

◇

About ten minutes and twenty yards into my search for a way out, I begin to wonder if it all isn't some elaborate ruse. If sending me on this search for a way out wasn't part of Roger's plan to begin with; if, in fact, I'm the one they all suspect of being the one among us who is infected. And then I wonder, *Am I?*

But, no, I'm not.

But am I, maybe?

No.

But, maybe?

Then, to put the argument to rest, which is a dumb argument to have with myself in the first place, I perform a quick body check—head, hands, legs, arms, feet—and find myself completely free of scratches, bites, or wounds of any kind, and finally I move on.

◈

At one point, my foot punches through a ceiling tile and I hear a commotion below, a sound of moaning and scrambling and yelping. I don't know what to expect when I look through the hole left by my foot. An undulating mass of undead bodies, I guess, but even imagining that, the picture doesn't linger for long before being replaced by the kind of shot you'd see in a movie, a medium-long shot that pulls you out of the mall and into the parking lot, which you can see is surrounded by them, and then farther still, to a long and wide shot of the city—cars abandoned, streets overrun—and then maybe a series of close-up shots in quick succession:

—A woman, screaming, clutching her baby as she runs from a gang of them, so racked with fear she doesn't realize her baby is already dead, and, worse still, changed or changing into one of them;

—A man on a rooftop, cornered and with no other choice but to jump, to kill himself rather than be eaten and transformed, only to be caught and saved by the very thing he feared;

—At least one hopeful image of a little kid or a couple of little kids with bats or sticks or some strange build-a-better-mousetrap contraption taking out at least one of these monsters;

—And then back to me, gazing in astonished horror at the sight below.

That's how I imagine it will be.

How it is, looking at the undulating mass of undead bodies below me without the benefit of edits and quick cuts and pans and long shots and fades, is a different kind of unsettling thing altogether.

For one thing, they're looking right up at me.

For another, they are, each one of them, smiling.

It's not a pretty sight, the sight of them smiling up at me. Their teeth have a wormy, gray quality to them. A rotted and soft yet somehow still dangerous quality to them.

There is something, let's say liquid, there is something liquid about their smiles or their teeth or the pulse of them watching me. Something liquid and alive and mesmerizing, and I begin to feel myself pitch forward. And only at the last moment, I grab hold again of the ceiling braces, and everything comes back into focus, and for a second, it looks to me as if they are laughing at me.

I move away from the hole, and I push on, and I shove my foot or sometimes my hand through the ceiling tiles a few more times, and then I come to a wall, a dead end, and I stop.

I wait.

I breathe and listen and breathe some more.

Hearing nothing but the sound of me, I remove a tile and lower my head down through the ceiling, and I want to close my eyes, just in case, but I don't, and I see the exit, and I see the coast is clear, and I let out my breath.

On my way back, I find Mary.

I hear her before I see her. Or rather, what I hear is the sound of a tile break in half followed by a sharp gasp.

When I find her, her left leg has gone completely through, and she's sobbing, and I think, *She's a goner, for sure, she's a goner.* But I get to her and cover my hand over her mouth before she can really start to wail, which would lead them right to us, no doubt, and then that much closer to our way out. But she feels my hand on her mouth before she sees it's me and that makes her bite my hand—though, give her credit, as I don't know that I'd be desperate enough to bite one of these things if it snuck up on me—and that makes me want to hit her hard in the back of the head, but I don't. "It's just me," I say through gritted teeth, my hand still over her mouth, or in her mouth, however you want to look at it. "It's me, it's me, I've found the way out," I say.

It is a way out, I know that for sure. It's a run, twenty, thirty, forty yards, but straight and with a little coverage, too, so that if you run a little hunched, no one can see you.

What surprises me most about this isn't that I found a way out, though that is a bit of a shock, but that I found it and tried it, dropping down from the ceiling, landing loudly but safely and without drawing attention to myself, and then, hunching, ran to the glass doors, and pushed them open and then stepped outside into the bright midday sun. The parking lot was full of cars, though I don't know why I expected it to be empty. I didn't see anyone—neither people nor monsters—and I shaded my eyes and looked at the long expanse of cars and then over the concrete just past the cars and then down that road farther still, and I thought to myself, *Now's my chance. I could start running and not look back and no one will know, and I'll be free, or I'll have a better shot at being free and alive than if I go back inside, than if I go back for those fools still stumbling around the ceiling.* But I didn't run. I could have left, but I didn't, and here I am, struggling to lift Mary, who doesn't even know my name, back into the ceiling so I can help her escape, but not just her. Her and Tyrone and Roger and the security guard and those two other guys, or at least one of those two other guys because I've decided that the other one has got to be the one among us who is infected, and in the end, that is what surprises me most. I found my way out and didn't take it.

What happens next seems almost too easy. I point Mary in the right direction and then immediately stumble across those two other guys, and then point them in the right direction. And then I'm back where I started, and it's unreal that I found my way back at all, let alone this quickly, and I wonder, *Is this how your life starts to change?* I wonder, *Is this how Roger feels about every day? About every decision?*

"Francis," I say.

He turns, startled, and then smiles. "Cowboy," he says.

"I found the way out. You ready to go home?"

"Hell yeah," he says. "Just waiting on Roger and the kid."

And I surprise myself again when I tell him, "Go on. I can handle Tyrone."

He hesitates, but then I give him a look. It's a look I've

never given anyone before. It's a look that says *I got this.* Says *I'm in charge of some things, and I got this, so go take care of the rest of them,* okay? Or says something like that, anyway.

Whatever the look says, Francis buys it and starts off, and then Roger, straining with the weight of Tyrone, calls out, "What's the holdup?"

I lean down and grab for Tyrone, and he's not as heavy as I expected him to be, and I lift him up, and the ceiling doesn't collapse, and his arms don't slip through my grasp, and I don't pitch forward under the weight of him, and nothing bad happens, and I let the thought that maybe this is how things will be from now on filter softly into my head. When he's finally up, I smile at him and pat him gently on the head and tell him something about how brave he's been, how we're proud of him, how I'm proud of him, and he smiles back and gives me a "Yeah, me, too," or a "Thanks, Cowboy," before I send him on his way.

And right about then is when I realize that something funny just happened.

⚙

I lean my head over the opening in the ceiling after Tyrone scrambles past me, and I look down at Roger, who's looking up at me. I'm about to ask Roger why the hell he sent them all up and who the hell is the one who's infected, but before I can say anything, two things happen.

The first thing that happens is this: The door bursts open and a roiling mass of them fills the closet, a clawing, moaning, death-gray crowd of arms and legs and bloodied heads, and I think, *Oh my God, they've got Roger.*

The second thing that happens is that Roger, still looking up at me, bares his rotted, wormy teeth at me.

And then he leaps.

I pull my head back in time, but only just. I see Roger's dead hands grab blindly through the opening in the ceiling at whatever part of me he can catch hold of. Then he jumps again, and then again, and then I hear the crash of shelves and boxes on the floor, and while I'm not sure if zombie-like creatures can construct things like stacks of boxes to climb up on so they can follow after us, I'm pretty sure I don't want to find out, so I leave.

⊚

From that point forward, things go from bad to worse.

I stumble across a hole in the ceiling and look down only long enough to catch sight of one of the men whose name I do not know, or parts of him, anyway, as they seem to have rendered him into his smallest components, such that I don't know for sure which one he is, or was.

For a moment, I wonder by what criteria they determine who is all-consumed and who is infected, but I don't have much time to dwell on this, as I see Francis the security guard ahead of me, struggling to pull himself back into the ceiling. Suddenly we seem to be surrounded by weak or weakened ceiling tiles. I think I should help Francis, my security guard friend, but I have no desire to go down with that big ship. I slip past him. I feel bad for it, but that's what I do. I slip by and then I hear and then come up on Tyrone.

He's looking down at his feet and then back up to his hands, which barely grip the thin metal support. He doesn't see me. His eyes are crazed with fear, or blank with it, or blinded by it, I don't know. A huddle of them are jumping at him, grazing the tips of his sneakers. Any concerted effort on their part gets them their prize.

But he's not so heavy. And he's a kid.

I grab his arm and he squeals at my touch, jerks and tries to break free, and I almost let him drop. I shake him instead and repeat his name again and again and again, but I never find out if I get through to him. The ceiling drops out from under me, and I fall.

I take them by surprise and knock two, maybe three to the floor by landing on them. I see Tyrone's white shoe slip back into the blackness above us and take some pride in the fact that, while cooked myself, I pulled Tyrone out of the fire.

Then they're on me, grabbing at whatever's in reach, and I choke on their smell, and I gag on the strips of their now rotted clothing flung into my mouth and nose and eyes. But there are too many of them and they are too eager to have at me, and for a moment I find myself in a kind of cocoon. A pocket made up of flailing arms and teeth and feet. Then one of them swipes at my face, so close I hear the soft *whisht* of air and feel its knuckle graze my nose, and that swipe lands in some hidden recess of their bodies and dislodges a packet of cigarettes from some torn pocket, and after the cigarettes falls a lighter.

The ones nearest the one I light go up like dry kindling.

◈

And then I'm running, exhilarated by what I have just done, by what this might mean for me—not just escape from the mall, but a kind of escape from life, from my old life, from that tired old existence.

I think to myself, *This was for the best. All of this.*

And maybe I should feel worse for Roger and the security guard and the rest of the human race, but I can't help but wonder that maybe we need these kinds of moments. Not moments of quiet, but moments when our lives are upended by violent tragedy, monsters, zombies, because without them, how would we meet the men and women of our dreams, how would we make up for the sins of our pasts, how would we show our true natures—brave, caring, strong, intelligent?

I wonder, How would we?

And then it happens: I slip. I'm looking one way and moving the other, and maybe there's a wet spot, or a blood spot, or a stray piece of gray matter, some viscous thing that grabs just enough of a hold over the toe of my boot, and I fall forward. Falling like this, so unprepared, so forcefully, hurts more than I could have imagined it would, and the wind is knocked out of me.

As I land, out of the corner of my eye, I catch sight of

them coming for me. But I'm not done yet. I can pull myself up. I can pull myself to my feet and run and run harder and faster than I've ever run before. I can make it to those doors and burst through them and into the parking lot and find my car. I can outrun those bastards and start this all over. I will watch less television. I will spend more time outside. I will foster stray animals and donate to charity walk-a-thons and look both ways at intersections. I will call my sister and apologize for what I said to her on her wedding day. I will let love into my heart. I can survive this. I can run and my life will be different and I will not look back. I will gun the engine and peel out of the parking lot and merge onto the traffic-less freeway and speed down newly empty streets, and not look back, not once look back.

ACKNOWLEDGMENTS

Thanks to the many people who have helped me pull this collection together, most notably Dinaw Mengestu, who nudged me forward just when I needed nudging, and PJ Mark and Megan Lynch who, when I was nudged in their directions, saw my work and liked it and took it upon themselves to help me make it better.

To Jennifer and Kit at the Paris Bakery, who not only opened their doors to me but gave me a key and license to drink as much day-old coffee as I could stomach, I'm very much in your debt. I'm grateful to Ryan Bartelmay, Mark Binelli, Bryan Dunn, Julia Holmes, Hillery Hugg, E. Tyler Lindvall, Meredith Phillips, Liza Powell, Jessica Lamb-Shapiro, and Marcela Valdes for suffering through early first drafts of these stories and remaining my friend afterwards. Thanks also goes out to Judy Budnitz, Maureen Howard, Heidi Julavits, Paul LaFarge, Ben Marcus, and Victoria Redel

ACKNOWLEDGMENTS

for helping me find a good way to write the stories I wanted to write when I first decided I wanted to write them. And to everyone who's ever given me a job and didn't mind that I wrote while on the job or didn't notice that I wrote while on the job, thanks.

Nothing I've done would have been possible, of course, without the love and support of my parents, Juan & Juanita Gonzales, and my sister, Cecilia Gonzales. And no one means more to me or to this work of mine than you, Sharon.

Manuel Gonzales is a graduate of the Columbia University creative writing program. He has published fiction and nonfiction in *Open City, Fence, One Story, Esquire, McSweeney's Quarterly,* and *The Believer.* He is the executive director of Austin Bat Cave, a nonprofit creative writing center for students aged six to eighteen. He lives with his wife and two children in Austin, Texas.

Printed in the United States
by Baker & Taylor Publisher Services